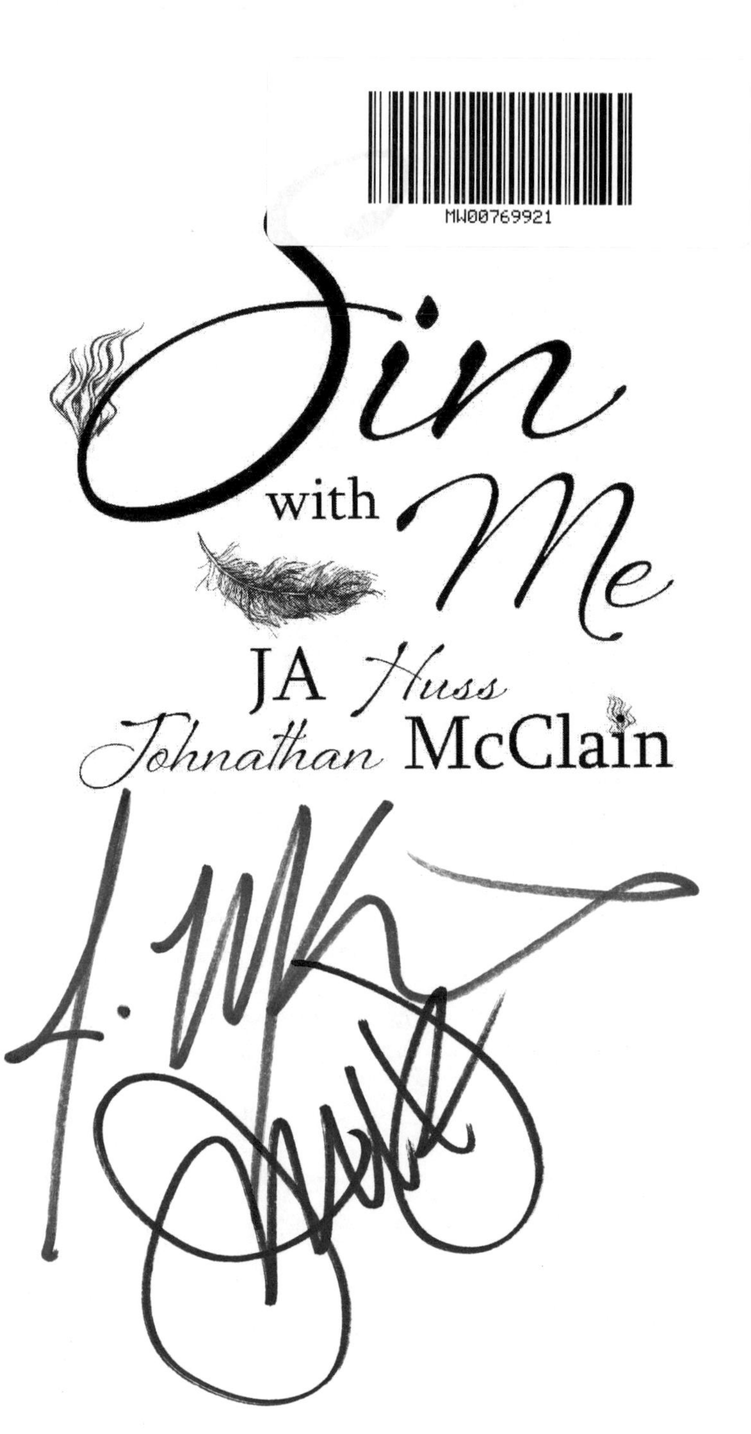
MW00769921
Sin
with
Me
JA Huss
Johnathan McClain

Julie & Johnathan

HussMcClain.com

ISBN: 978-1-944475-37-6

Edited by RJ Locksley
Cover Design by JA Huss

For anyone who has ever slipped and kept climbing.

J.H. J.M.

CHAPTER ONE

I never dreamed Heaven would look like this.

To be fair, for a long time, I never really dreamed at all. I trained myself not to. Because the dreams I hoped for would never come and nightmares would fill the void. So maybe what I mean to say is that I never *imagined* Heaven would look like this. I dunno.

Semantics.

Point is that had I dreamed, or imagined, or fucking *speculated* on an idea of Heaven, I doubt very much that it would look the way it does spread out before me now. Which is kind of like an Apple Store, but without a bunch of goddamn computers and watches and shit. Just clean white desks against clean white walls—that aren't actually walls, because there seems to be no terminus to the sprawl—and lots and lots of people asking stupid questions.

Oh. And it smells like frankincense. I know because I got used to the smell when I was stationed in Somalia. I like it. It grows on you.

The angels (I'm assuming that's what they are) are overly friendly. Not to some, I suppose, but I don't trust anyone who's too nice. Never have. And just because they're angels doesn't mean they get a pass. Fuckin' angels.

And besides, OK, sure it's Heaven and all, but that means I'm dead. And I don't need some cocksucking angel trying to make me feel OK about it. I wonder if they get paid. Probably not. Not in money at least. In eternal salvation or whatever. Whoopie.

Oh, and they're wingless. No wings? Yeah, I really don't trust these fuckers. One of them did get me a cup of tea, though. She was pretty hot. The blue shirts they wear on earth tend to make them look kind of shapeless, but this angel chick has tits that defy the laws of physics. And they're real. I kind of brushed up against them when she brought me the tea. Mostly by accident. So yeah, she's definitely some kind of angel. I've never fucked an angel before. I wonder what that would be like.

The tea is rooibos, I think. I also like rooibos. Developed a taste for it in Saudi Arabia. Even though rooibos is from South Africa. Not that these things matter.

Details.

So. Here I sit, in clean, white, frankincense-infused Heaven, being tended to by blue-shirted, perfect-titted, wingless angels, drinking a cup of what I think is rooibos tea, waiting to talk with, I assume, God. Who—based on the current surroundings—will look like, I dunno, probably James Franco.

And I'm dreading it.

Because as soon as He checks the list on His GodBook Pro, He will realize that there has been a huge fucking mistake and my tea will be taken from me and I will be escorted out and sent promptly to a place that—I have to assume—will replicate approximately the back of the line at the DMV. Or the bathroom of a midtown Manhattan Starbucks. Or Afghanistan.

Shit. That sucks. I really like it here with this tea. And that angel with the heavenly tits. I start wondering how I can talk 'em into letting me stay.

And that's when the explosion happens.

An eruption of flame that consumes all the clean and white, and paints it in a bleeding orange and piercing blue, followed by a shrieking red. The screams are familiar. I've heard them before. They aren't screams of pain—that comes in a moment. For now they are screams of fear. Which is the worst, because fear implies hope. It means that they don't yet realize they're all already dead. People fighting against the inevitable always gives me the hardest time.

I look over at my angel and she is still there, only now she is wearing a hijab. Somehow the flames haven't touched her. All around her is a boiling cauldron of chaos, but she remains whole. I see her pretty green eyes framed by the dark headdress and try to let her know that while I can't save everyone, I can save her. I believe I can. So I start running through the flames, and the wailing, and the burning flesh.

I reach her and time slows. She smiles. It's unsettling. Because it's not a smile of relief or joy, it's a smile of… something else. Mournfulness. Accusation. She takes my face in her hands and that's when I realize that she hasn't escaped the same fate as the others. Her palms are being immolated as they reach my cheeks. But it doesn't hurt. It feels familiar somehow. She draws my ear close to her lips and she whispers:

"You brought this."

And that's when the rumbling, thunderous, final wave of flame engulfs us all.

And I wake up.

Wait. I wake up?

Are you shitting me?

Fuck.

An iPhone is vibrating next to my head on the bedside table.

On the other side, a cascade of black hair is spilled over my chest. And spread across the black hair is a wash of blonde hair. Oh, right. It's coming back to me. Blackjack table—no! Roulette. That's right. Then dancing at Tao. Then shots. Then Ecstasy. Then… well, then everything gets kind of muddy. It only pops into my head in flashes, but I do have a clear recollection of someone shouting, "Never stop fucking me!" Whoever said it is clearly disappointed now that the fucking has, evidently, stopped.

Let me think… I assume the bodies attached to these heads of hair have names, but I have zero clue what those names might be. (For some reason I want to call them Kerosene and Glycerin, but I'm sure that can't be right.)

The phone is still vibrating. The screen says it's Evan. I have no reason to believe the phone is lying, so I answer, "Hey. Everything OK?"

I roll out from underneath Kerosene. (The dark-haired one. Obviously.) She reflexively grabs for my side. Glycerin (but I think I'll call her Glys) rolls the other way and falls off the bed. She moans but doesn't wake up. Maybe she knocked herself out. I dunno. Whatever.

Evan answers my concerned salutation. "Yeah. Everything's fine. Why?"

"Because it's—" I glance at my watch. "Oh. It's noon. Well, still. It's noon on a Saturday—it is Saturday, right?"

He laughs. "Yeah, dude. It's Saturday."

"Jesus. The week went fast. Anyway. There's no emergency?"

"No, man. I'm not at work. We're going car-shopping today, I thought."

Shit. That's right. I've been putting it off because I just don't care that much, but I should get one. I haven't really driven a car in damn near twelve years. I had a piece-of-shit Corolla in high school, but that fuckin' died as I was trying to get the hell away from home to make it to training. And then I got deployed to Iraq, so… Iraq? I think it was Iraq. Pretty sure that was my first deployment. Honestly, I can't remember anymore. But I had to drive in the Middle East a couple of times and I really learned to hate it. And after I mustered out, I just kind of went from train to plane to fucking… llama and shit for a long time, deciding what my next move was gonna be.

I've only been back in Vegas for a few months and because this ridiculous apartment is right in the middle of the Strip I haven't much needed a car here either, but then last week I was with this chick I picked up at the Cosmopolitan and she wanted to go fuck in the desert because that's like her thing or whatever—

(She said that when you're fucking and come into the earth you're replenishing the planet's life energy, or some kind of Burning Man bullshit. Didn't really care. Her ass was so perfect she looked like a cartoon character. If she had said she wanted to fuck in a feeding trough, I would have made it work.)

—and so we were in the middle of the desert and after we finished "replenishing the planet" she got pissed about the fact that I said, "Thanks." Which is just something I say. It's kind of a reflex. Not sure where I picked it up. But, I mean, if you have a problem with it, uh, go fuck yourself. I'm just trying to be polite. But she yelled, "I'm not a whore!" pulled her pants up over her bubble butt and jumped into her stupid Mini Cooper or whatever it was and left me there. (At that point I started to suspect she maybe has some issues.)

And, of course, there's no cell service in the middle of the fucking desert, so I had to hump it like ten miles in the goddamn cold-ass desert night before I could get enough bars to call Evan and wake him up to come find me, which is incredibly shitty because he had just come off working third watch for Vegas Fire and Rescue for three nights in a row because they were short-handed, so the poor guy should have been allowed to sleep. But he's the only person in town I still know well enough to call in the middle of the night to drive out and pick me up in the desert—we've known each other since we were two—so he did it, because he's a goddamn champ, but as we were driving back he did say, "Bro. You gotta get a car."

Am I rambling?

I feel like I'm rambling.

I do that. Sometimes out loud, but usually just to myself. I try not to let anyone see. But I can't shut my fucking brain off. I think I need coffee.

I head out of the bedroom and into the kitchen to make coffee. By which I mean drop a pod into a thing that looks like R2D2. And make toast. If I can. This toaster that came with the apartment is so fancy it took me like an hour to figure it out the first time. I'm still not sure I have it right.

"Yeah." I sigh. "Let's go fucking car shopping."

He laughs again. He's such a good dude. "That's the spirit! You ready to go now?"

"Uh…" I glance through the open bedroom door at Kerry and Glys. Glys is snoring pretty loudly. I take that as a sign that she didn't knock herself out.

"You're not alone?" he asks. It's a rhetorical question. Again, guy has known me for twenty-eight years.

"No. But I can be ready in an hour." I can probably be ready sooner, but I don't know how long it's gonna take to get… Jolie?… and… Witherspoon? (no, probably not) out of here.

As we continue talking, I wander over to the living room. I suppose? This is one of those apartments where every space just kind of blends into the next. I don't have much in the way of furniture so it's sort of hard to determine where one part ends and another begins. But I stand in what I'm calling the living room and stare out the window. Window. Ha. This whole fuckin' place is nothing but windows. Floor-to-ceiling. All the way around. Corner apartment. On the Strip. Overlooking everything from the fountain at the Bellagio to the faux Eiffel Tower at the Paris to the fake Statue of Liberty at New York-New York. Seems fitting. Because I'm not supposed to be here. I'm a fake king, in a fake castle, looking out over a fake kingdom.

In fairness, it's not like I didn't earn it. I did. I suppose. Depending on how one defines earning. Is it "earning" if it comes at other people's expense? I start wondering, can anyone ever really get anything in life without taking something from someone else in the process? Those steps we climb to get where we're going? More often than not, they're built on top of the discarded bodies of the less fortunate.

And suddenly I'm thinking about Nadir. And then I get fucking sad. Because all Nadir was trying to do when he came on as our platoon translator was to keep his family safe from being shot or blown the fuck up, and somehow I managed to fuck that up real bad and get him killed.

And then I remember that Nadir wasn't the first person I'm responsible for having managed to get killed.

And then I get fucking sadder.

Christ. My only job as an EOD Tech was to defuse and dispose of shit that can blow you up, and then me and Nadir and three other guys walk right into a fucking explosion that was created by a goddamn twelve-year-old. Killed Nadir and the others. But for whatever bitter joke of a reason, I lived. And by virtue of that bullshit we went through, I managed to wind up falling ass-backwards into all this damn money that I never asked for and don't even really want. But that's the way it goes, isn't it? Some people get shit on and die, some people get shit on and live, and some people get shit on and then get to wipe themselves off with more money than they can spend in five lifetimes.

I don't know why that last one is me. I've given up trying to figure it out.

But it is why, after kicking around for a few years trying to decide what to do with myself now that I'm all rich and fancy and everything, I moved back home. Because nobody but Evan knows me anymore and I don't have to explain myself to anyone. Because Vegas… well, Vegas is the kind of town where a terrible fucking tragedy can occur on Sunday and by Wednesday everybody's already gotten back to whatever fucked-up, selfish hedonism they're into.

The kind of place where I feel at home.

Because it is. Home. It made me. And now it has to own me.

So I bought this crazy corner penthouse that overlooks my city, so I can sit up here high above everyone and look down on them all with a big suck-my-dick expression plastered all over my face.

(That's probably something I should talk with my shrink about, but then I don't really think it's all that complicated.)

I must be rambling in my head again because the next thing I hear is, "OK? Tyler? Dude? OK?"

I actually forgot that I was holding the phone against my ear. That's disturbing.

"Yeah. No. Wait. What? Sorry?" I pretty well plead.

"I said I'll meet you at the Land Rover dealership at two."

"Why do I have to get some fancy new car?"

"Because you can afford it and because I'm not picking you up in the fucking desert again. You feel me?"

"Yeah. I feel you…"

"Bro? Are you OK?" He sounds concerned. Shit. Is my inside-my-head voice creeping out to my mouth?

"Yeah, man. I'm OK. I just…" I pause to debate how much I feel like *sharing*.

"Yeah? You just what?"

"I… I was having a dream when you called."

"K. What kind of dream?"

Seems like a reasonably straightforward question.

"… I have no idea. Something about Heaven and tits."

I can feel Evan's brow furrow on the other end of the call.

"That's… specific. You want me to come pick you up?"

"No. No. I'm OK. I'll see you soon."

"OK, brother. See you in a bit. Peace."

Evan never says goodbye. He always says, "Peace." I have no idea if that's with everyone or something special he reserves for me.

As I'm pulling the phone away from my ear, I get, "Omigod, what the fuck happened to you?"

At least it sort of sounds like that, only way more slurred and with fewer definite consonants to distinguish the sounds as actual words. But I get the gist.

I turn around and Kerosene is standing in the doorway, naked, teetering a little bit. She's got a nice body. Fake tits, but they're good ones at least. She clearly spent somebody's money on a quality surgeon. She's pretty too. In a "please, please look at me" kind of a way. I think she told me she and Glys are from Virginia? The Virgin Islands? Fuck, man. I'm starting to get worried about my memory. Regardless, assuming I heard her question right, and assuming she's not talking about my cock for some reason (she's not—I have an amazing cock—I like to think it's my best quality) I imagine she must be referring to the scars.

"I got mauled by a gazelle on safari."

"Holy shit, really?" she maybe mumbles.

"No."

If I thought I might like her at all I'd keep fucking with her a little bit, but there's no chance of us grabbing breakfast and getting to know each other, so dragging out the joke feels like a waste of energy.

I just want to get her and her… friend? Sister? Fuck, I hope it's not her mother… out of here. I'm used to women having reactions when they see the scarring on my chest and back and sides for the first time. Hell, when I saw it for the first time I almost cried. Not because I'm vain or because I was worried about how people would view me or whatever, but because it looked so… painful. I don't remember being in pain. I was in a coma for like two weeks after the explosion, so it felt false to get all bent out of shape about it, because I was still alive and I had no real memory of being in pain or shock or anything like that. But when I saw it for the first time, I felt like I had an *obligation* to feel something. So I got all misty so that the nurses and doctors could pat me on the shoulder and tell me everything was gonna be OK. Seemed like they needed it.

I wonder how she didn't notice it last night. Nah. Not really. She was high, it was dark, and after we got naked I was behind her for most of the festivities. In fact, she and the other one were so high that I debated whether bringing them home was the right thing to do. But then I remembered… I don't really give a fuck. And now I need them to go. But I should be thoughtful about it.

"Hey, can you grab your friend and get the fuck out?" Eh, eh, eh… thoughtful. "Please?"

She says something that may be "You asshole," or "Go fuck yourself," or less probably, "You got it! Sorry to be a bother!" But whatever it is, it has motivated her to scramble back into the bedroom where I hear her rousing… Rapunzel?… from the floor. I turn back to the window. The street below is teeming. Like always. People rushing to… whatever. Do whatever fucked-up thing it is they came here to do. I spread my arms out and press my dick against the glass.

"You. My royal subjects! I piss on you all!" (I don't say it aloud. I just think it. I may be crazy but I'm not insane.)

Goddammit! I need to slow my brain down. That dream was… What the fuck *was* it? And when did I start dreaming again? Have I been dreaming for a while and didn't know? Shit, am I dreaming right now? Who's to say this whole fucking reality I've been living isn't just some dream that I will wake up from just like I woke up from the last one? No. Fuck that. I'm not in the mood for an existential crisis today.

I hear, "Yawafuggindickgofugyerseeeefff" from behind me. And the door slams shut. I better go get in the shower. I—

Just then… the fire alarm goes off. Loud. Fuck. What the fuck? I sniff. I smell smoke. What the hell is—Maybe I am still dreaming. I must be. Am I? Or did Kerosene and Glycerin betray me and set the sheets aflame? Would they? Did they? Fuck! Those fucking—! How could they?

I cough. I can feel my chest tightening. Oh, shit. Oh, shit. Where's it coming from? Where the fuck—?

I run into the bedroom. Nope. The sheets are white and crumpled and there are some errant black and blonde hairs, but that's it. But the smoke is definitely filling the space. Shit! Where is it coming from?

The alarm is blaring. I would say it's deafening, but it's not. It's jarring, shaking, screaming.

I run back into the living area and look to my right and that's when I see the toaster. Smoking. Flames shooting up from the inside. Like the whole silly apartment, the exterior of the toaster is made of glass, so I can see the bread burning and shriveling to a crisp through the clear pane. It suddenly occurs to me that if the apartment were on fire that's what I would look like to all the people on the street watching me burn.

And for some reason, that gives me an incredible sense of relief.

I need to slow down my brain. It feels like it's on fire. It always feels like it's on fire these days. Maybe it always has.

Maybe a shower will help. Maybe it'll wash off the smell of smoke. And booze. And sex with strange women whose names I don't know.

Maybe I'll turn the heat on the water up as high as I can and see if I can scald the rest of my skin off.

Maybe I'll open my mouth and swallow it all in. Maybe I'll drown. Maybe I'll punch a hole in the sky and sneak back into Heaven to find my angel.

Or shit, maybe I'll just get dressed and go buy a fucking car.

It's all the same to me.

CHAPTER TWO

There is a right way to do everything. A right way to make toast, for example. Or the right way to get to work. Or take your clothes off once you get there.

Toast is easy. You pop the bread in, make sure the setting is halfway between three and four, and push down that little lever. Up pops perfect toast.

Getting to work can be trickier. Sometimes I have to make snap decisions because of traffic. I work just off the Strip here in Vegas, so traffic is something I can't really avoid. But I can plan for it by learning all the secret access roads around the casinos.

Taking off your clothes on stage is definitely a process and if you do it right, it's just like toast and nothing at all like getting to work. You gotta do that tease first, right? Shake the money-makers a little. One strap here, another there. Make those guys work for the big reveal. You gotta do that little ass wiggle as you drop one bra strap, then the next, and then… ta-da!

Easy.

Money, that is.

Which is why I do it. Why else would I? It's not my first choice. It's not even my thirtieth choice. But it's the one that I've got in front of me. And I need it. Money. To, y'know, live and everything. Hell, quick, easy money is why everyone does it. Pretty much the only girl I know who actually thinks of stripping in Vegas as a career is—

"You're late, Scarlett."

Her.

Raven. Bitchy boss extraordinaire and the oldest stripper down here at Pete's. She's thirty-seven, so not really *old.* But…whatever. If I'm still getting naked for money at thirty-seven… well, I just won't be. That's all.

Which is why doing things the right way is such a good idea and why I'm sticking to my plan, no matter how much money I go home with each night. There's no way I'll end up managing a strip bar in Vegas ten years from now. Of course, if you had asked me when I was eighteen what I'd be doing when I was twenty-five, I might've said a lot of things, but pretty sure none of them would be this. So best not to get overconfident.

"That's the third time this month."

I glance at the clock as I walk towards the dressing room. Five minutes is technically late, so I don't argue. Just drop my bag on the chair next to Raquel and get busy.

"Hey, sweetie," Raquel says as she glues her eyelashes on. "Big crowd tonight."

"Good," I say, rummaging through my bag to find my outfit. It took me a while to get used to being called *sweetie* and *honey* and *baby* by other women, but I'm a go-with-the-flow kinda girl, so I caught on quick enough.

"You got any regulars coming in tonight?" Raquel asks. She's just trying to make conversation, but I'm not really here for conversation.

"I don't believe in regulars," I say. It's my standard answer.

"I just don't understand that," Jasmine says, catching up on the conversation as she comes in from the stage clutching her bra and panties. "They pay good. It's almost like a regular paycheck if you work them right."

I don't want to work them right. And I won't be here long enough to care about a regular paycheck.

"Plus…" Raquel says in her sing-song voice. "Sometimes they take you home and…" She does a wink-wink with the one eye that already has the fake lashes glued on.

"I don't believe in that, either," I say, finding my outfit and stripping bare. I adjust my girls in the cups and then get busy on my garter and stockings. Three minutes later I'm slipping on the stilettos.

"Why do you wear that?" Jasmine says. "It's not what they want, honey."

I shrug. "I think it's sweet. Very girl-next-door, ya know?"

Jasmine makes a face. "The girl who lived next door to me growing up was a crack whore. Not a good comparison."

"Fair," I say. "Well, I lived next to—" But I stop. Because I realize I'm about to divulge something personal about myself. That's not part of my process. "To a church," I say, recovering. "And this is probably something they'd wear."

"Ha." Raquel laughs. "Baby, no church girl is climbing into bed with her boring church boy wearing *that*."

True. But I'm done with this conversation, so I let it drop. My typical outfit is what you'd call… virgin wedding night. It's usually white, or pink, or sometimes pale blue.

But it's always made of cotton, has a little ruffle somewhere, and a little satin bow between my tits.

"I like it," Otis says from the door. He's the dressing room guard. More like a peeping Tom, but whatever. "Makes you look… wholesome."

"Thank you, Otis. That's exactly what I'm going for."

Because I'm trying to hold on to some part of the life I used to have. Even here.

I wrap my long, auburn hair up into a bun, pin it high on my head, and slip the blonde wig on.

It comes with pig tails.

"You look like jailbait," Raven says, pulling up her black stockings. "Not girl-next-door."

"Maybe," I say, unwrapping a pink sucker and giving it a lick. It's my only stage prop. "But don't knock the power of youth. I'm pretty sure that's why I take home four figures on a good Saturday night and you take home three."

Bitch.

The rest of the girls erupt in laughter, but I'm already leaving, so I don't catch whatever comeback Raven throws at me. She's sensitive about her age.

I'm not only good at devising the perfect process for every possible scenario, I know how to find a person's weakness and use it against them. I developed it as a way to deflect. To protect myself. And eventually it just became a part of me.

It's kind of what I do out on stage. I analyze. I critique. I process shit and make predictions. I'm here to make money. I have very specific reasons for taking my clothes off in front of strangers and none of them include finding regulars or letting one of these people take me home for a night of extracurricular sexual favors.

As soon as the stage lights hit me in the eyes I morph into someone else.

This girl.

As opposed to *that* girl.

This girl is carefree and innocent. Blind to the cruel ways of the world. Sheltered and pure. At least that's what I want these men to think.

They want that, right? The pure ones.

As long as that virtue doesn't prohibit them from sucking a cock, that is.

I stifle a laugh as my hand automatically grabs the pole in the middle of the stage. I swing lazily around it as I enjoy the bubblegum sucker in my mouth. I don't do gymnastics upside down with my thighs wrapped so tight around the brass pole, they make squeaking sounds. I just saunter around. Lick my candy seductively, flash my eyes at them all innocent and shy.

I tease them. And I don't even have to do much either. Just let them look at me. Take off my top, wiggle around, and pretend I'm having the time of my life. That these men are my secret fantasy. That they might be the one to take that innocence away tonight…

Blah, blah, blah.

My point is—I don't really give them much out here. I don't want these guys to think, *Hey, this bitch has talent. She was born to fuck that pole.* I don't want them thinking about anything except how many bills they need to stuff into the strings of my panties in order to get my attention for a few more seconds.

I don't need them to think. I just need them to forget who they are, why they're here, and what happens when they leave. I need them to see the character I'm portraying, not the woman I am.

And it works.

They always make a few lewd comments when I come out dressed up like—as Raven put it—jailbait. There's the usual jabs about looking like someone's little sister—mostly to get the older brother in the group riled up. And of course, they have to go one step further. "I'll be your daddy, little girl."

Gross.

But very predictable. And I like predictable, so I don't even mind it. Because in my experience, surprises are very rarely a good thing. Predictable is safe. Predictable has rules. It makes sense.

For instance… I'm predicting that this room is filled with about three hundred men with money in their pockets. Pete's isn't the classiest strip joint, but it's not a dive, either. And there's a cover charge to get in. These guys aren't here to wallow in self-pity at the bar over some bad week at work. They're here to get a hard-on, maybe a lap dance so they can come in their jeans, and then go back satisfied to whatever girl they're avoiding at home in bed.

Or maybe they don't even have a girl. Maybe this is just the way they like it. Romance from afar, paid for in single bills, one stage act at a time. No commitment, no expectations, no reality.

That's how I like it, so there's those guys here too.

I bend low, opening my legs to give the group of guys in front of me a nice panty shot. They beckon me with dollars. One holds up a twenty so I ignore his cheap friends and stare him straight in the eyes as I wiggle, licking my sucker, twirling my pigtail between my fingertips, my ass so close to the floor I start to worry about getting the little t-back ruffle dirty.

So three hundred men, give or take a dozen or two. Once my act is over I'll go out on the floor to see if anyone wants some special attention. I'll do a dozen or so private lap dances—hands off only, I follow the rules and make no exceptions—and then I'll do one final act towards the end of the night for people who came in late and missed the first one.

Then… voilà. Night over. Scarlett counts her money, changes her clothes, turns back into Maddie, and goes home.

Money Bags gives me a wink, so I stick to him for a little longer. Getting close and bending over so he can tuck that twenty into the back of my panties. I can't afford to give him all my attention. That would piss the other guys off. But he pulls back the string near my hip and tucks twenty bucks worth of attention next to my skin, so I turn, slip a strap over my shoulder, and give him first look at one of my girls.

He smiles. Coyly. He's kinda cute, I realize. But then I let that thought wander away as quick as it appeared. I would never—*ever*—date a guy who came here and saw me dance. Ever.

"Logan," he yells over the music. Like I care what his name is. But then he takes a fifty out of the wad of bills he's holding in his hand and waves it in front of me, capturing my attention with a come-closer gesture with his finger.

I look at his friends, at a few other guys sitting up in the front, and give them a little attention too. They tuck bills into the panty strings at my hips. Raven will chew me out if I pick a favorite while on stage. "That shit is for later," she'll snap.

But eventually, because I want that fucking fifty—and only after I've taken off the babydoll nightie and thrown it off to the side of the stage where I exit (just to make it easy to collect when I'm done)—I go back to him.

I bend down, legs open, ass wiggling close to the floor. And smile. "Scarlett," I say over the music.

"Ah," he says. And then he leans forward and says, just loud enough for me to hear and no one else, "You don't look like a Scarlett."

I recoil a little. But just a little. Patrons don't get to rattle me. "What does a Scarlett look like?" I ask, my tone teasing.

"Like you," he says. "But without that stupid wig covering your blazing red hair."

This time I more than recoil. I stand up, thinking way too hard about that little offhanded comment. Because that's what it was, right? I mean, all these dumb men have to know I'm wearing a wig. It's what strippers do.

"Good guess," I say, lowering back down in front of him, shaking my tits a little more. Getting my Scarlett on. "But wrong. I'm blonde under the wig as well."

His eyes dart down between my legs and he nods his head. "Prove it."

I laugh as I coo, "Pay me."

He holds the fifty out, but not very far. Not far enough so he can reach me to tuck it into my t-back. "Crawl over here and take it with your teeth," he says.

I smile and stand back up. Move on to another group of men across the stage.

Fuck him.

I repeat my staged seduction with them, but they only offer up singles. I move on to another group and get the same. My act is almost over, so I gotta make a better impression. Mr. Money Bags might've just ruined my take-home by showering me with bad luck.

So I work harder. I stand up, begin to ease my panties down over my hips. Turn, stick my ass out, and wiggle them down the curve of my ass before pulling them back up and letting the elastic snap against my skin.

That gets them all going and the bills start flowing again. I glance down, see a few fives tucked in with the ones, but that's it.

My gaze involuntarily wanders back to Money Bags. He's casually holding the fifty between his index and middle finger, like he's waiting for me.

I take my attention back to the men I'm dancing for now, mentally telling him to fuck off.

My song begins to wind down, just a few more moments to collect. So I strut back over to the asshole with the fifty, sucking on my sucker in a way that makes every man in the room think their cocks are my candy, and drop right in front of him—legs open. I debate with myself, hard, for less than a second, then I decide to hell with it and pull my panties aside quickly to give him what he wanted.

"No fair." He laughs. "You're bare."

I shrug, then snatch the fifty from his fingers and say, "I gave you exactly what you paid for."

But he grabs my wrist as I try to pull away. He leans in, close, and then he growls, "Carlos didn't get what he paid for. And he's out of patience, *Madison*."

He lets go before I can even properly freak out. Stands up, turns his back, and walks off. My song ends and the lights go out, leaving me in the dark to grab my nightie as I make my exit and remind myself why I'm here.

"Good set," Raquel says as she brushes past me to make her way out on stage.

"Thanks," I hear myself mumble, almost stumbling into the dressing room. I stuff my money in my backpack and take a seat in front of the mirrored vanity Raquel just vacated.

And look at myself. Take a good, long look at myself.

I pull off the wig, still staring at the reflection.

There's not one thing I like in that mirror. Not my green eyes. Not my high cheekbones. Not my small nose or even the deep cupid's bow of my lips.

I hate all of it.

"Hey," Raven says behind me.

My eyes meet hers in the mirror.

"Cleo called in sick, so one of us will have to do an extra act tonight."

"Not me," I say.

"I wouldn't waste the opportunity on you." She snorts. "I'm giving it to Jasmine."

"Really?" Jasmine says next to me. She pauses her application of red lipstick. "Thanks, Rave. I appreciate it. My kid's daycare bill went up this month and I'm strapped. I need all the attention I can get."

"Well, if Cleo calls in again," Raven says, "she's out of here. And you can pick up all her acts until I find someone new." Raven smirks at me as she says it. She knows a girl like me—single, no kids, college-educated—would not be here if I had any other options. So she thinks she's getting even with me for making that crack about her age.

I do need the money. And after Cleo, Jasmine makes more money than all of us. She goes for the slutty look, which, as she pointed out earlier when she turned her nose up at my outfit, these men like a lot more than the girl-next-door look.

I have a few moments of regret for not following her lead.

My phone buzzes in my backpack.

"And turn that fucking phone off when you come into work, Scarlett," Raven says. "It's been vibrating since you went out on stage."

My heart skips a beat. This cannot be good. First that asshole who works for Carlos shows up out there in the club, now someone's been calling me the whole time?

I suck in a breath of air as I reach for it. But the anxiety eases as I see the name on the screen.

"Hey," I say, after tabbing accept. "What's up?"

"Jesus fucking Christ," Annie says. "My night just went from bad to fucking bad in the span of twenty minutes."

"What happened?" My heart is beating fast again. Did Carlos get to *her*? Is he going after my friends now?

"My fucking date!" Annie wails. "He left me at the motel!"

"Motel?" I ask, confused. But she sounds like she might start crying. So I go into crisis-management mode. "Shit, can't you grab a cab?"

"He took my fucking purse! I got no money! He got my cards too!"

"Jesus," I say, trying to picture all that shit happening so early in the night.

"I'm stuck here, Maddie. Can you come get me?"

"Where's *here*?" I ask, getting a very bad feeling about this. Because I'm totally confused. Annie isn't a stripper, she's a call girl. A very high-class one. She's the one who suggested I take this job, against my better judgment, to make some quick cash. She usually works out of five-star hotels. The Aria, or the Bellagio, or the Four Seasons.

"Some cheap-ass fucking place out on the north end of town. Just standing on this disgusting carpet is making me itch!"

"What the fuck are you doing out there?" I ask. Seriously. Nothing she's saying makes sense right now.

"I have no clue. I met him at Planet Hollywood and then he said, 'Come with me.' And we ended up out here. My gun was in my purse too!" she says, on the verge of hysterics.

"Shit," I say.

"Shit is right," she says. "I'm so fucking tired of this shit!"

"I'll come get you. Just stay put."

"You're not leaving," Raven says, listening in on my convo. "I'm already short tonight."

"Fuck," I mumble into my phone. "Can you call Diane? Or Caroline?"

"No," she says. "They're working the whole night. Their phones are off. My calls didn't even ring through."

The four of us share a house out in the desert. They're all call girls. I actually went to college with them, then lost track, but ran into Annie about three months back—just when this Carlos shit was starting to go sideways. They had an empty room in their house, so I signed on to be roommate number four. I didn't know they were call girls at the time. I found that out after. Four girls went to college together, three of them became hookers and one is a stripper. Probably not a great ad campaign for UNLV.

But I figured it couldn't hurt to disappear from my usual surroundings for a little bit while I decided what to do about this Carlos business, right?

Good while it lasted, I guess. Because obviously Carlos has found me again.

But back to Annie. "Can you hold tight until after my shift?" I ask.

Annie gulps on the other end of the connection. "Oh, my God. I just want to go home, Maddie."

"I get it," I say, cutting her off. Raven is still standing behind me, tapping her fucking stiletto on the floor with her arms crossed across her tits. Like I'm on her last nerve. I don't want this job—but I do *need* this job. "Text me the address and I'll be there as soon as I can."

I quickly change outfits and head back to the floor, constantly scanning for the henchman sent to warn me of my outstanding obligations. But he's gone. Or he's hiding in some corner, waiting to spring on me. Snatch me away, take me out to the desert and kill me.

I have to laugh at that. I mean, this is a serious situation. But I didn't do anything wrong. It's not my fault I owe Carlos Castillo a hundred and eighty-five thousand dollars. It's his stupid daughter's fault.

I decide I'm overreacting. Carlos sent the guy to rattle me into delivering what I owe him. Even though I don't owe him. I was planning his daughter's wedding. He gave me two hundred grand for the event. What did he expect me to do with that money? I spent it on wedding shit. Catering, and the church, and the reception hall. All but fifteen grand, which was all I was able to return to him after his daughter called off the wedding and Carlos decided he deserved a refund.

You don't get a refund on a wedding because your stupid daughter was pregnant with another man's child and her fiancé called it off. It's not even reasonable.

But Carlos Castillo isn't exactly a reasonable man. He's some Mexican tequila mogul, but I'm pretty sure that's mostly a front for his drug-running empire.

How was I supposed to know he was some kingpin? I mean, really? I don't run in those circles. And what kind of drug lord books a wedding planner online without even meeting her?

Well… maybe that should've been my first clue.

I just can't win. I really thought I could make a go at the whole wedding planner gig. I mean, I fucking majored in business at UNLV. I'm capable. I'm smart. I have ideas. Good ideas. No. *Great* ideas. It should've worked.

But then again… I did have that pet bakery business, and the whole multi-level marketing make-up business, and the information research business. Not to mention the cleaning business.

All of which failed. Miserably.

And now I'm in debt up to my fucking eyeballs. Every credit card I have is maxed out. And my parents have already loaned me more than twenty thousand dollars for the first two businesses. I owe them too. They're too nice to ask for it back, thank God. Because I don't have it. I don't have shit.

My newest venture—aside from stripping to pay back Carlos money I don't owe him so he doesn't start imagining me better off dead than alive—is an aerial photography business. I already have ten realtors on my books looking for video of their multi-million-dollar property listings.

This one is a winner. I can feel it. I know it. I've tried and lost too many times not to catch a lucky break soon. I even have a cool drone to take the photos and shit. It set me back almost two months of stripper pay… money I should've been paying Carlos. But it was worth it.

And fate seems to agree. Because tonight I make more than three thousand dollars in lap dances before closing time. I have so many customers, I don't pick Annie up from the dumpy motel on the north edge of town until well past three AM.

She's too tired to complain, so she slips wordlessly into the passenger seat of my car and doesn't speak again until forty-five minutes later when we enter the living room of our modest four-bedroom ranch house.

"I quit," she says, flopping down on the couch and kicking her shoes off so hard, they go flying into the wall.

"What?" I ask, sinking into the cushions next to her.

"I've had it, Maddie. What the fuck are we doing?" She looks up at me with sad brown eyes. "We're educated women. Why the hell do we have to sell ourselves just to make a living?"

I start to say, "I don't sell myself, we're not the same," but then I decide that right now isn't about me and try to be a good friend instead. I shrug. "Bad luck," I say. "That's all."

"It's not bad luck," she says. "It's… it's something else. It's bad planning, or bad decisions, or bad whatever. I don't know. But it feels like fate."

"Fate?" I laugh. No. That's not what this is. It can't be. I can't believe that this is what fate has planned. "We're not fated to be losers, Annie. We're just stuck, that's all."

"Men," she says, growling out the word. "You don't owe Carlos shit. And no matter how much I make, I can't seem to get ahead. Fucking student loans, and credit cards, and that damn car. I want to burn it. And Kimberly. Why the fuck do I give her fifty percent of my take when she only fixes me up with guys like this all the time?"

"All the time?" I ask, completely confused. Annie's clients are high-end. Aren't they? "Since when?"

Annie looks away. Sighs. "We… we might've… embellished our status a little."

"Embellished how?" And then I get it. "You don't get guys like this all the time, do you? Assholes who leave you stranded in shady neighborhoods? Low-class jerks in town for what… a convention? Trying out the old 'what happens in Vegas, stays in Vegas' thing?"

Her guilty, embarrassed silence is the only answer I need.

Wow. She's not raking in the money. She's not some high-class call girl. She's nothing but a fucking prostitute.

Not that I'm judging. I mean, come on. I'm a stripper. I have no room for self-righteous judgment.

But it makes me sad. For her and for me. I don't know why I didn't see it earlier. Why live out here, in the goddamned desert, sharing a house with two other women in the same profession and a damn stripper, if you didn't have to?

"I want to go home," Annie says, sniffling. "I want to go back to Iowa, find my high-school boyfriend, and pretend I didn't fuck up my whole life with one bad decision after another starting when I got out here for school. I just wanna be eighteen again and start over."

I just stare at her for a second. Imagining this other life she lived before she knew me. And then thinking about the other life I lived before I knew her. And how she made bad decisions starting at eighteen and how at eighteen bad things, one after another, just kept delivering themselves to me, and now, seven years later, here we both sit. It makes me want to cry. Or scream. Or run away. Or all three. But I can't. It's not who I am. I can't quit, I can't lose it and give in to weakness. I have to just knuckle down and keep going. Sometimes… sometimes I wish I was a quitter. It would be easier.

"I'm tired, Maddie." She curls her legs up onto the couch, placing her head in my lap. "I don't want to do this anymore. I don't want to fuck strangers for money. I don't want to drive that car. I don't want to live in Vegas. I want this to be over. I want to go home right now."

I play with her long, dark hair as she gives in to sleep. Silent. And introspective. And wishing I had such an easy way out.

It's not the money I owe Carlos, either.

It's everything else.

This *is* home. This is all I have.

There's no going back to something else. Something easier. Some more innocent time when things were good.

Those days are gone. Forever.

All I can do is pull myself back up to ground zero.

CHAPTER THREE

There she is again. My angel. I see her coming towards me with my tea like the last time, her red hair in sharp contrast to all the clean and white that surrounds her. And in its fiery redness, it feels like a portent of things to come.

I feel like I know her. Do I? Have we met before? Nah. Probably just seems that way because she's an angel and she's trained to make you feel comfortable and loved. I bet they have whole seminars on that shit in angel school. Because I don't know her and she doesn't love me. We're just tacitly agreeing to this whole interaction because… I dunno. Because we're both dead, I guess? We have that in common.

She's smiling. I'm not. Because I know what she doesn't. That in about two minutes this whole place will be soaked in fire. Maybe it's because I touched her tits the last time. Yeah. Know what? That's probably it. I sullied up this whole joint with my craven, feral desire. So I'm careful not to press up against her now. I keep my distance. I say, "Thank you," super polite, and—

Fuck.

Flames, screaming, agony, the whole nine.

And I wake up.

OK. What the hell is going on? Not only am I dreaming, but I'm now having recurring dreams? I don't like this shit. Not one little bit.

I look over and there's no one in the bed next to me. It's probably not a great sign that I have to *look* to know whether or not I brought someone home last night. I'm not even sure what day it is. I barely know what century it is. I should get out of here. I should see people. Dr. Eldridge says I'm spending too much time alone. Maybe she's right. Being alone allows my mind to drift to places it shouldn't. Never a good thing.

"Of course it's not a good thing, genius. Just figuring that out?"

And now I'm talking to myself out loud. Dynamite. Insanity is wooing me hard.

I stumble out of bed, walk past the massive windows, making sure to give the street below a nice long look at my cock (although I doubt anyone's looking up here—everyone's so focused on their own bullshit), plod into the kitchen past the burnt charcoal brick that used to be toast still sitting in the toaster, past the fridge, straight to the liquor cabinet. There's an impressive selection from which to choose. Did I buy all this? I must have. I don't remember buying all this. Oh, well. Johnny Walker Blue to start the day. Which, I mean, it's the smoothest of the bunch, so duh.

My phone is sitting on the counter. There's a text from Evan. "*Lunch at the station?*"

Phone says it's ten-thirty AM. Still morning. Nice. Earliest I've been up in a while.

I pick up and text back. "*Dunno. Pretty busy.*"

I take a sip of Blue and wait while little thought bubbles appear on the screen. They disappear. They reappear. He must be composing an essay. Finally, his text comes through.

"No, you're not."

Christ.

I take another pull from the bottle. Sigh. Then…

"*S-U-R-E,*" I type. *"Be there in a bit."*

I can't say no to Evan. I really can't. I don't know why. Most everyone else on the planet I can take or leave, but Evan… I dunno. I actually kind of know. History. Shared experience. But it's more than that. It's what most people would call chemistry. That thing one person has with another person that they can't explain. When people call it chemistry, they're wrong, of course. Chemistry is science and finding someone you can stand being around, that's alchemy. Some people just get you. Others, not so much. But whatever you call it, Evan and I have always had it since we were kids. I don't remember us ever even having a fight. Is that true? Man, that's crazy. Anyway.

I take a couple more hard swigs, give the city one last good cock shot (you're welcome, world), and pull back on the jeans, boots, and t-shirt I left sitting on the living room floor last night.

I smelled them. They're fine.

OK. I'll admit it. This car is pretty awesome. I really don't love to drive, but this thing might make me change my tune. It just got delivered last night. (Turns out it's

Friday. Don't ask me where Sunday through Thursday went.)

When Evan and I got to the swanky Land Rover dealership last week, I saw a poster of this one on the wall. I don't get hard over cars. I've never been a gearhead. But this one looked badass so I told the showroom guy, "I want that one."

He was all, "Oh. Well, that one's not actually for sale."

I was like, "Fuck you mean it's not for sale? You sell cars, right? That's what you do?"

Evan laughed. He got a kick outta that.

Car dude goes, "Well, yes. But *that* is a photo of a limited-edition Land Rover Defender that was made specially for one of the James Bond films. It is quite something. Black-on-black wheels, thirty-seven-inch tires bolted directly onto the wheel rim, suspension upgrades, a full roll cage running both externally and internally. It has a hundred and eighty-five brake horsepower and five hundred newton meters of torque!"

He looked at us like we should know what any of that means or give a damn. You know, like a toddler who just took his first big-boy shit and wants you to think it's amazing.

"Wow. Neat. How much?" This seemed to me like it should be a simple transaction.

"No, no, no. Again…" Fuck. Again? "Only ten of these were manufactured. Eight are in the hands of private collectors, one is in our museum, and the other one is owned by our CEO, so—"

"Great. Get him on the horn. Find out how much he wants for it."

Car guy stared at me like he's never sold a car before. I didn't understand why this was hard. He looked at Evan, who shrugged. Because of course he did, because JUST SELL ME A FUCKING CAR.

— By the way, that? There? That whole thing that I just described? THAT'S why I don't like to talk to people. Jesus. —

Anyway. The CEO was much more business-savvy and, yadda, yadda, boom ching, I now have a car. And it only cost me five hundred K. Which, yes, is a lot of money. Unless it's not. So. Whatever.

I glance at myself in the rearview as I'm pulling up to the station house. I look like shit. My eyes are bloodshot and my dark hair is all over the place. I try to keep it pushed back, but lately it's so gotten so unruly that this one wavy tress (lock? Ringlet? I dunno) keeps falling right in front of my damn eyes. I should probably get a haircut. I should also probably think about shaving again someday. I haven't shaved since I moved back to Vegas. I'm starting to look like a lumberjack. Or homeless. Or like a hipster douchebag who's trying to cultivate the appearance of being a homeless lumberjack. But it doesn't seem to have affected my social (aka sex) life so really, who gives a shit? (In fact, this one chick told me I look like Brad Pitt in *Legends of the* Fall, and even though she said it's her least favorite Brad Pitt movie, I'm taking it as a compliment.) And besides, getting a haircut would mean finding a barber, and shaving would mean buying a razor and shaving soap and… yeah.

Effort.

Evan strolls out to meet me as I'm parking. There's another guy with him that I've met a couple of times. Young guy. Baby-faced. Evan is kind of like his mentor at the station. Jim, I think his name is. Evan whistles as he approaches the car.

"Ho-ly shit. It came."

"Yup," I say, drawing myself out of the cab.

"Is it all you dreamed it would be?"

"I don't dream about cars, dude." That's for damn sure.

Evan gestures to Jim. "You remember Jeff, right?"

OK. Jeff. Fine.

I reach out for his hand. "Yeah. Of course. Jeff. What's good, man?"

We shake. He's definitely young. Guy has weirdly soft hands for a firefighter. Just one of those things I notice. "Nice ride," he says. Which is unoriginal, but one hundred percent right.

"Thanks. It's got a roll cage with sixteen hundred kilowatts of flux capacity."

Evan laughs. I do too. I'm super fucking witty. Everybody says so.

Jeff sort of smiles. He's either too young or too stupid to get that I'm making a joke. Probably too young. I can usually spot stupid from a ways off, and Evan would never mentor some fucknut. But I do the worst thing you can do to a joke. I try to explain.

"See, the guy at the dealership, he—Um. I saw this poster and—" I sigh. "What are you guys having for lunch?"

Evan and Baby-Face Jeff lead me into the station house and, just like every time I walk into one, a swell of memory washes over me.

Evan, our best friend Scotty, and I were six. First grade. Our very first field trip ever was to check out the inside of a real firehouse. It was the coolest thing any of us had ever seen. The firefighter leading the tour started a fire in a trash can and then put it out by dropping a newspaper over the top of it! Yeah, sure, now we know about oxygen and physics and shit, but at six? We thought firemen were fucking magicians.

After that, we became little goddamn pyromaniacs. But only so we could figure out the best and most effective way to put the fires out. We burned some shit up though.

Kids.

As time went on, I became more and more interested in blowing shit up. And then in trying to keep shit from blowing up. Especially after my mom died. Once it was just me and Dad, keeping shit from exploding all over the place seemed like a really fucking important job.

Evan, good guy that he is, genuinely just wanted to help people. There was a time where he thought he might try to be a doctor, but then he realized that doctors don't get to run into burning buildings and ride in bigass trucks and climb ladders and shit. They *can*, I suppose. Nobody's stopping them. But it ain't part of the job description.

And Scotty…

Yeah. No. Not right now. I'm having an OK day. I don't feel like I wanna get swept away in those memories right this second.

Besides Evan and Jeff, there's five other guys on the crew at the moment.

Bear (I have no idea what Bear's real name is. Could be Bear for all I know), who's over in the gym, currently bench-pressing the equivalent of a Fiat, is the company officer. He supervises the crew and deals with any shit that rolls downhill from battalion or the district. He's well-suited for it. In my brief encounters with him, he's the kind of guy who, if he said, "We're all gonna put our nuts on this anvil and then smash 'em with a mallet!" would somehow inspire you to be like, "YEAH! LET'S DO IT!" Occasionally you find natural leaders in the world.

He's being spotted by Rod, who is half a foot shorter than Bear, probably half his weight, and scrappy as hell. Honest-to-gospel third-generation Irish firefighter from Boston who sounds like a comic book version of a Southie come to life and wound up in Vegas because he fell in love with a showgirl. You can't make this shit up. He's encouraging Bear to push out his last reps. "Come on, ya fuckin' pussy! Push that fuckin' shit out, ya sorry fuck!" You know. Encouraging.

I clock Dean sitting over by the engine, hanging out with Gladys, his French Bulldog. Gladys is cute as all fuck and represents an evolutionary leap in the traditional perception of firehouse dog stereotypes.

"'Sup, Dean?" I nod his way.

"How you living, playboy?" he says as he keeps petting Gladys. Dean's the coolest guy I've ever met. Evan told me they once had to rescue some people from a motel fire. Dean personally carried seven of them to safety, and then when they checked his vitals to make sure he hadn't inhaled too much smoke or anything, his *accelerated* heart rate was sixty BPM. Good-looking cat too. A young Denzel Washington with the temperament of Snoop Dogg, if instead of acting or rapping, Denzel and Snoop saved people from burning buildings. Fuck, man. Some people get all the gifts.

Alex is in the kitchen, making lunch. Been on the job for twenty-eight years. Pushing fifty and can still outrun and outlast any five guys you meet on the street. Normally, the newbie, Baby-Face Jeff, would be the one making lunch, but Alex loves it and nobody's gonna argue. Guy can cook his ass off. I don't shout hello to him because the last time I did I got reprimanded. "You wouldn't talk to Picasso while he's painting, would you?" That's what Alex said to me. I laughed. He didn't. Fine by me. It smells goddamn delicious. There's curry in whatever he's making. I didn't realize I was so hungry. I'm running on Johnny Blue and no toast.

The last guy, I don't recognize. Because they've been shorthanded due to some shakeups, some guys have been shifted around from different engine companies. But he's over by himself, headphones on, ignoring everyone in the room.

"Who's that?" I ask Evan.

"Brandon. On loan from Heavy 44."

Wow. The Heavy Rescue guys are no joke. The SEAL Team of Vegas Fire and Rescue. They're essentially the ones who rescue the rescuers.

"Good guy?" I ask.

Evan shrugs in that way he does. "No idea, man. Dude's barely spoken a word to any of us."

I lift my left eyebrow. (I can't lift my right. Don't know why.) "How's that working out for crew cohesion?"

Evan shares a look with Jeff. Jeff answers. "Guess it doesn't really matter as long as he's there when we need him to be."

I smile at Evan. He smiles back.

I love that. In my work with the military I was forward-deployed as the bomb tech for a couple of different SEAL Teams, and working with elite soldiers taught me something. There's a perception in the world that people who work in teams, especially in life-or-death situations, succumb to kind of a hive mind. That's true and then again, it isn't. You can train people and prepare them and unify them to a degree, but at the end of the day, they are who they are. There was this one dude on one of the teams I was with in… shit, I have no idea, doesn't matter… who was a total prick. Absolute fucking narcissistic asshole. One of these clowns who never missed a chance to tell you how awesome he was. One time I asked the team leader if having a dude like that around was hard on morale. He said, "Man, I don't give a shit what kinda fucking dipshit somebody is as long as they do their job and have my six when we're in the suck."

The motto for Vegas Heavy 44 is "So that brothers and others may live." Be whoever you are, just be there for me when I need you. That's all there is to loyalty.

"Hey," says Evan, shifting gears, "Tomorrow's this little fucker's birthday." He tousles Jeff's hair.

"Stop, man. Jesus." Jeff pushes Evan's hand away and smooths his hair back. "I'm not a kid."

"How old you gonna be?" I ask.

"Twenty-one."

"You're a kid," I say. "Embrace it. Life doesn't get any better." I'm a truth-teller.

"We're taking him out," says Evan. "You should come."

"Where you going?" I ask.

"Strip club," says Jeff with about ten percent more enthusiasm than is appropriate.

I scrunch my eyes closed. "No fucking way."

Jeff asks, "Why not?"

"You can't touch the girls, most of the assholes in there are sad losers, they overcharge for drinks, and you can't touch the girls."

Evan starts, "Man, come on, it'll be—

"If I wanted to sit around with a hard-on in my pants pretending that some chick was into me, I'd just stay home and jerk it to Stacy Patono's Facebook page," I interrupt.

Jeff asks the obvious question. "Who?"

Evan responds. "Girl we went to high school with. Broke his heart."

"She didn't break my heart. She gave me blue balls like five different times. THAT is what broke my heart. I value my balls highly."

Evan continues, "Anyway. You should come out. You can't keep just picking up girls, bringing them up to your ivory tower, fucking them, and then starting over again the next night."

"I disagree," I say. "I really, really believe I can."

"You need to develop a healthy social life."

"I'm super-social."

"You're super-slutty. It's not the same thing." Evan bends his head toward me with a knowing look like he's my fucking basketball coach or some shit.

"Is Robert coming?"

"Dude, have you met my husband? I can't get the guy to go to see *Magic Mike* with me. No fucking way I'm getting him to spend the evening in a dark room filled with fake titties and sad erections."

"Y'know, you're not really selling this as a good time," I note.

Evan ignores me and continues half-complaining about his husband. "I imagine Robert will just sit around, drinking Merlot, polishing his watch collection, listening to *Tosca*, waiting for me to come home and blow him."

Relationships.

Jeff kind of looks down at the floor. Which is adorable.

"Come on, man..." Evan steps in close. Jeff steps back, pretending to look at a piece of paper on the wall. "Bro, I love you. I'm worried about you. You're spending all this time alone, you're fucking a different girl every night—"

"I didn't fuck one last night. Pretty sure."

"You need to find an anchor, man."

"And you think I'll find that in a strip club?"

"Dude, I just think you'll have a chance to hang out with some friends, tell some of your dumb jokes—"

"Fuck you."

"—and just like, have some *fun*. Come on. I've known you a long time. Come out with us. We understand, bro. We get it."

He takes me by the shoulders and gives me a deep, meaningful look square in my blue eyes that are rimmed with bloodshot red and are now starting to fill with tears. Which is monumentally unexpected.

"Did you want me to come here to trick me into an intervention?" I joke.

He grips my shoulders tighter, stares into me harder, and doubles down. "We get it," he says, gravity dragging down the earnestness of his tone.

Goddamn it, I don't wanna cry. Not here. Not in the middle of the fucking firehouse. Not with Jeff, and Bear, and Rod, and Dean, and Alex, and new guy Brandon all here. I choke it down, swallow it back, and nod my head almost imperceptibly. Evan slaps my shoulder.

"Good deal," he says. "Let's eat something."

I hang back for a second, trying to not cry, pretending to respond to a text, as Evan moves toward the dining table. Just as Alex starts to bring out what looks like Indian food (I knew I smelled curry), a call comes in. The alarm rings, everyone's phones start blowing up, and all seven of them jump to get into their gear.

The whole process is lightning fast and before you know it, they're onto the engine and pulling out. As he darts past me to jump into the cab, Dean says, "Yo, brother, watch Gladys for me 'til we get back? Thanks, man."

And then… they're gone.

It's shockingly quiet after the sudden mayhem, except for the fact that I can still hear the alarm. Even though it's stopped. I approach Gladys. She backs away. Cowering. I don't blame her. I sit down in front of steaming plates of food abandoned at the table. I'm hungry. Alex made it. I should try. I take up a fork and attempt to eat a bite.

My hand is shaking.

I work to steady it.

I can't.

I put the fork back down and sit alone in the eerie quiet of the empty firehouse, with the faint, tinny squeal of a phantom alarm still vibrating inside my brain.

I take two deep, shaky breaths.

And then I go ahead and give up, allowing the tears to fall while Gladys cocks her head and eyes me with a mix of suspicion, curiosity, and what feels like pity.

CHAPTER FOUR

MADDIE

The card throws me right off my game when I come home from meeting with real-estate agents. Of the six I met with today, only one of them had any interest. Most of them already have this service with someone else. Someone more experienced. Someone they trust and probably go out and have drinks with every now and again.

But I decide to see the positive side of things. I have ten—possibly eleven—people lined up, and that means this aerial photography business might just be the one. In fact, I know it is! I can feel it!

But that fucking card.

Annie, Caroline, and Diane are sitting under umbrellas by the pool. That's pretty much the only thing this house has going for it. It's got a nice pool. It's even painted that cool blue color. Tahoe blue, I think it's called. And it's got a stone deck and just a touch of custom rock with a trickle of a waterfall out near the deep end.

Ever since Annie copped to what her real job is, I've tried not to think too hard about it, because why should it matter? They were fucking men for money before I found out about the lie, and they're fucking men for money now too.

But it bothers me. Something about it bothers me. And the way she acted that night. Telling me about how she wants to leave Vegas.

It put ideas in my head. Like… maybe I'd want to leave Vegas too. If I had anywhere to go that wouldn't be a lateral move. If it wouldn't feel like giving up.

I grab a Corona from the fridge as I try to put the card out of my mind. I know what it is. A bad omen. A reminder that things might be bad now but they can always get worse. Like buzzards circling over a half-dead man at twilight. Something I do not want to think about right now.

So I cut a wedge of lime and force it through the bottle of my beer. Enjoy that little spritz of fizz, take a long draw… and yeah. That fucking card is still calling my name.

It's from my mother. There's an anniversary coming up. Not the happy kind. Hence the card.

Fuck it. I grab the envelope, rip it open, and read.

Thinking of you, it says on the outside. There's a pretty pastel picture of flowers and kittens. Kittens? Really? Surely it's not that bad, right?

Inside it says, *Come visit us soon! We love you, Mom and Dad.*

Which is sweet. They're in France. Monaco, to be exact. Like, pretty much the best place to be if you have to be in France. My dad used to work for a big casino here in Vegas but six years ago he got this offer and it was too good to pass up, so off they went.

I had just started my sophomore year in college by that time. And after I managed to make it through freshman year and how awful that all was, I wanted to try to see it through because I didn't think things could possibly get worse. I was wrong, of course, but at the time… And besides, I'm stubborn. I like to think stubbornness is my great superpower.

My parents wanted me to come. I think. For them, it was also a chance to get away. Make a fresh start. Put everything that happened behind. That's kind of who they are. Their way is to sweep the ugliness of life under the rug. But I just couldn't. It seemed to me like it would be… disrespectful somehow. So I don't necessarily blame them for going, but I don't think I took fully into account how hard it would be all on my own. Because, if I'm being truthful, I don't know that I realized I really would be ALL on my own. But it's OK. Because things are going well for me! I'm on the right track now. The perfect track. Aerial photography is practically my dream. Or so I tell myself.

This is Monday, the start of a brand-new week, and there's nothing I like more than a fresh start. So… I will not read between the lines with this card.

But then I see what else is inside the envelope. It's another card. Not the sympathy kind, but the business kind.

I read the name. God. I know her. Personally. The little note on the back in my mother's handwriting that says, *Just call her. Give it a few weeks. I'll even pay for it.*

I guzzle down the rest of my beer before throwing it, and the cards, into the trash.

Fuck Monday.

I change into my bikini, put the rest of the six-pack into a cooler, and go outside to bake in the sun with the girls.

Fresh Start Tuesday is my new motto. Mondays are for forgetting.

Tuesday, I'm cruisin' down Flamingo going to meet this guy who puts on a drone class for newbies. It's incredible how people make money in the twenty-first century. Meanwhile, me and my roomies are all engaged in some form of the world's oldest profession. I'm not sure if that makes us classic or obsolete.

I'm at a red light just minding my business when I get a message that the class has to be postponed. He got strep throat or something.

So I go buy shoes instead. Nice, high, break-your-ankle stripper shoes that set me back all of last weekend's stripper pay.

Wednesday I pull myself together, manage to stay away from both the mall and the Coronas, and make one more potential business contact. Which should make twelve, but three people have already left messages and canceled our appointments for a complimentary five-minute video, so now I'm down to nine.

One step forward, two steps back.

I start doing research for other business opportunities… just in case. I like a good back-up plan.

Thursday I hang out with the girls at the pool again, only this time I don't get drunk and ignore them. Annie is cool, but Diane and Caroline don't seem to like me. So I'm calling this Make-An-Effort Day.

I think I need friends. I don't have many friends. Not the real kind. Not the childhood kind. Which is weird, now that I think about it. Because I was born and raised in Vegas. Have never lived anywhere else, in fact. I—admittedly—drove most of them off after the… the tragedy that requires my mother to send me thinking-of-you cards every year.

"Who's making dinner?" Diane asks. She's got a buzz on, I can tell. Her face gets flushed all red when she's buzzing. "I'm starving."

"I am," I say, impulsively. "Burgers OK? I'll grill tonight."

I get a round of "hell yeahs" from the three of them, and then I excuse myself and go back inside, relieved to have a few moments to drop the fake smile I've plastered on my face all week.

But cooking is something I can do, so prep work is a mindless task that gives me time to think about things.

I don't have my rent money.

That's the first thing I think about. I fucking spent it on those hooker shoes. And I can't even take them back, because last night Caroline borrowed them without asking and they have scuff marks on the soles.

I have a twelve-thousand-dollar drone that I don't really know how to fly. I have gotten a few videos out of it, but it was dicey. And I'm afraid I'll crash the fucker and all that money will crash with it.

I'm also aware that these were all choices I made and that not having rent is my fault. But these aren't frivolous expenses. These are investments. Or so I tell myself.

I got a weird text this morning. I didn't recognize the number. I think it may be from Carlos. Or maybe that guy, Logan. His... henchman. It was a picture of a clown. That's it. Just a picture of a clown. Which is creepy, right? It is almost Halloween and it's kind of a running thing. Clowns jumping out at you. Scaring people, chasing them and shit. But clowns are still just objectively creepy. I'll know I've really hit rock bottom if I have to perform as a clown for like, kids' birthdays and shit. Creepy fucking clowns... But anyway, if I didn't have this Carlos thing hanging over my head, I probably wouldn't even think twice about it. But I do. So there it is.

Creepy clown text was definitely a threat.

"Hey," Annie says, coming inside through the slider. "Everything OK with you?"

"Me?" I laugh. "Fine. Why?"

"You've been kinda quiet all week. Just wanna make sure you're cool."

"I'm cool," I say, making the burger patties. "So fucking good right now. I got another contact today."

"That's great." Annie beams. "You're really gonna hit it out of the park with this business. You can probably even do videos for tourists and shit, right? Chronicle their time in Vegas. Follow them down the Strip, maybe?"

"Nah," I say. "The Vegas drone laws are pretty strict. Can't fly within five miles of the airport."

"Oh, that sucks," Annie says.

Yeah. It does. Wish I had looked up that little factoid before I spent twelve thousand dollars on a damn drone. Because real estate wasn't really my first choice. It's just the only one I have at the moment.

"So how's work?" she asks, making small talk.

I hate small talk. It's so fucking… forced, ya know? But this is Make-An-Effort Thursday. So I smile as I place all the patties on a platter. "Great!" I say. And that's not even a lie. In fact, the money from work is the one positive thing I'm holding on to right now.

I will make back that twelve grand. I will.

I must.

"So I found this in the trash the other day and I was meaning to ask you about it," Annie says, opening up the junk drawer and pulling out… "A card from your parents?" she says, opening to read the message inside.

Which she has clearly already read and that's why she tucked it in the drawer.

This might be an intervention.

"Yeah," I say, as casually as I can. "They're sweet, right? Always thinking of me."

But Annie's not paying attention, she's holding up the business card that came with it. "And this?" she asks.

I shrug. "Dunno." Lies. Lies. Lies.

Annie sighs and then places the business card down on the black countertop. The card is white, so it sits in stark contrast, practically screaming for attention. "She's worried about you," Annie says.

"Not really," I say.

"She sent that card, right?"

I look at the business card. Try not to think about it.

"Maybe you *should* see a therapist?"

"What?" I say, laughing it off. "This is just how my mother is. She's one of those crazy therapy people. She thinks talking about your problems helps, but it's all just bullshit."

"Hmm," is all Annie says.

"I'm fine," I say. My voice is slightly too insistent. But fuck it. I walk outside and leave her in the kitchen.

Make-An-Effort Thursday is over.

Friday night was a disaster and I can't help wondering if Annie showered some of her hate fate on me last weekend when she had her mini-breakdown. I don't believe in fate. Or anything supernatural or ethereal or…

well, anything. Except me, of course. Because I'm the only person in charge of my life.

There's a nice, solid period at the end of that sentence. Nice and solid.

I've learned a lot over the years and every single lesson has to do with self-determination and self-reliance.

There is no God, there is no spiritual world, there is no afterlife or grand purpose. There is only life. You get one, and only one—so you better make the most of it.

That's what I believe in.

Me.

But this job was going good, ya know? And Carlos doesn't even count. I'm still hanging on to the mindset that he's just pissed off that his daughter fucked up and he's taking it out on me. Pretty soon he's gonna come around, see my side of things, realize he's being a dick, and drop the whole you-owe-me-money thing.

Which is why I bought the drone last month instead of paying him. Paying him a shitload of money that I don't owe him—with no hope of recouping said money when all this is sorted out—is stupid.

I don't do stupid.

But… fuckin' Annie and her fuckin' confession that she's nothing but a whoring slut kinda threw me. I don't like to hang out with people on their way down, ya know what I mean? I like a winning team. Or, at the very least, a team with potential.

Run-of-the-mill Vegas prostitutes are practically what this town is made of. High-class call girls, on the other hand… a little more hard to come by. And yeah, I realize that being a Vegas stripper isn't anything close to winning, but I might've hitched my wagon to something that turned out to be bogus.

I'm annoyed with her.

And last night's take sucked. Pretty bad. I came out barely even after paying Raven for my stage time.

It's not fate, it's just bad luck.

I've been telling myself that all evening... but tonight isn't very busy either, so...

Tonight will be amazing, I chant in my head. This is my night. I can feel it.

But that card—that reminder from my mother, and her stupid hint that I should talk to someone—it's put a little cramp in my style.

Yeah. I might be more than annoyed with Annie by the time this night is over. Because I can trace all my negative feelings this week back to her. Why doesn't she just go back to Nebraska? Nebraska, right? Iowa? Idaho? Whatever. She should just go be a farmer's wife if that's her big missed opportunity.

"Why are you rolling your eyes?" Raquel asks. She's sitting next to me, fucking with her eyelashes. She's perpetually fucking with those damn eyelashes. Why wear them if they require more attention than toddlers?

"I'm annoyed," I say. "Last night sucked and tonight isn't shaping out to be much better. I only made seventy-five bucks on my first act. I can't even pay Raven with that."

And even though I'm talking myself into believing that Carlos isn't gonna be a problem, I sorta think that visit from his henchman last weekend might prove otherwise.

I have Otis on lookout for the guy. He put Drake on the job. Drake is the door bouncer. But I don't have a lot of confidence in either of them. They're big, but you know what they say about the big ones, right? I didn't have a picture of Logan and the security footage barely qualifies as footage, it's so grainy.

So yeah. I'm betting Logan shows up one night and neither of them even notices.

Jasmine comes in from off-stage. She's taking Cleo's time, since Cleo disappeared and Raven made good on her promise. So this is her second stage dance of the night and it's not even nine o'clock yet.

She's got so many dollars hanging off her, I start to regret my attitude with Raven last week. I could use more eyeballs on me tonight. For sure.

"You guys," Jasmine squeals. "This bunch of drunk guys came in while I was on stage and look!" She starts pulling the bills off her body, trying to count them. "A whole bunch of tens and twenties! I think I made like five hundred bucks off that last dance!"

Five hundred bucks. Jesus. I hate everyone tonight. Five hundred bucks would pay my rent, make up for last night's loss, and if I get a chance to work them like Jasmine just did, I might even come out ahead after paying Raven for tonight.

"You're not going to wear that, are you?" Jasmine asks me as she flops down into the seat on the other side of Raquel.

"What?" I ask, looking down at my outfit.

"I get it, Scarlett. You're smart," she says. "Too smart for us, right? You're a college girl who thinks she has all the answers. But let me give you a little bit of advice, *honey*. The men who come in here aren't looking for someone to save them. They're looking for sin, baby."

Raven walks past behind us and I catch her smirk in the mirror. "Don't miss your fucking cue, Scarlett. You've been pissing me off a lot lately. You're lucky you still have this job. Do you have an idea how many girls come in here every day looking for work?"

I think about that for a moment.

Raven doesn't wait. Apparently it was a rhetorical question. "And I don't care how much you *don't* make tonight. You owe me your stage fee, regardless. Now, go wow them with your wholesomeness and make sure they keep drinking, got it?"

I turn around to smirk back, but she's already gone and the only one who sees it is Otis.

"How many drunk guys?" I ask Jasmine, ignoring Otis's confused look. Like I said, not too bright.

"Enough," she sings.

"And they're dropping tens and twenties for stage time?" I ask.

She shoots me a look. "Well, for *me* they are, Scarlett. Don't expect to make what I do wearing *that*."

She tucks her money away, gets up, and walks back out onto the floor.

I look down at my outfit, internally second-guessing myself. "This outfit is kickass," I say, sounding a lot more confident than I feel.

"Don't listen to her," Raquel says. "It's not her slutty stockings that get the money."

"No?" I ask, hopeful that I can turn this night around.

"It's her smile, Scarlett."

I make a face at Raquel. Who is always smiling. Come to think of it, Jasmine is always smiling too.

"And she's nice."

I make another face. "I'm nice."

"No." Raquel laughs. "I don't mean that in a bad way. You're tough, Scarlett. And in the everyday world, people like that. But this isn't the everyday world you're working in. This is fantasy, baby. Which means no one likes a smartass and no one likes a girl who thinks she's too good." She nods to my outfit. It's pretty. I love it. "That outfit says 'I'm better than you. I'm better than this job. I'm above all of this.' And ain't no one out there looking for that, sweetie."

"You keep saying that the girl-next-door thing is played out, so…" I gesture to what I'm currently wearing. "So this is like a fresh take on that, right?"

Raquel eyeballs me, skeptically. "We'll see, I guess," she says.

"Look. I get it. I've been complacent. But I'm gonna work it hard tonight. Watch me."

Raquel just smiles as she bats her newly refreshed eyelashes in the mirror.

I hear the DJ telling everyone to thank Raven for her performance and realize I'm up next.

"Scarlett?" Raquel says as I grab the rest of my costume. "Just smile and be nice, OK?" And with that, she shoots me a big grin.

"Yeah," I say, pushing back from my dressing table and standing up. "Smile and be nice. I can do that. I'm gonna make a shitload of money tonight."

And with that thought, I slip on my angel wings, fit that glittery silver halo over my head, and strut out of that dressing room like a bitch in charge.

CHAPTER FIVE

"Thank you! Thank you, thank you, thank you! For your service!"

At present, my personal space is being invaded aggressively by a drunk, recently-turned-twenty-one-year-old firefighter in a strip club.

Jeff's shouting at me over the top of ZZ Top's "Legs," which is so hilariously cliché that it's almost quaint. This Raven chick (I think the DJ said Raven. Coulda been Condor or Hawkwind or something equally stupid) is giving it all she's got though. Bear and Rod are clearly in love with her. They've probably both already dropped half a week's pay on her and the dancer before her and we've been here like ten minutes. Dean's too cool for that shit, which has made her notice him even more than she naturally would and now she's got her titties all up in his face, which is causing Bear and Rod to spend even more dough to get her attention back. It's kind of incredible to watch in a stupid way.

New guy Brandon is just sitting by himself, off to the side, staring. I'm actually kind of surprised dude showed up. He's a for-sure-weird fucker, I've decided. Which is fine. Who isn't? But he definitely gives off a chop-'em-up-stick-'em-in-the-freezer vibe. But then again Evan said that at the emergency call they got yesterday, he kicked down the door of a makeshift meth lab that had caught fire, went tearing inside, and came back out carrying two tiny kittens like they were priceless jewels. Then I guess Brandon said he'd take 'em home himself and take care of them. Evan thinks he might have gotten a little choked up over it.

People, man. People.

Anyway, Jeff must have been drinking all afternoon before we came here because he is WASTED.

"YOU'RE the hero, man! You're the hero!" He's hugging me now.

Evan is smirking. He leans in so that I can hear. "He tried for Ranger Training School but washed out. He's got a soft spot for the military."

That's all well and good, but I hate this shit. I don't care that he's drunk. I pull him off me and square him up.

"Hey! I'm not a hero. And neither is Evan or any of you. You understand? They pay you to do a job and you do it. That's it. The moment you start believing in that hero bullshit, you will try to live up to it and you will fucking die. You get me?"

He blinks like he's trying to figure out what I'm saying and then his expression changes. I know that expression. It's the one of someone who realizes they're about to throw up.

"That way. Go." I turn him around and point him to the bathroom. He takes off running. Evan eyes me.

"Give the kid a break, man. It's his birthday," he says.

"Fuck. I know. I just… I can't stand that crap. From anyone. He's like your little mentee or whatever? You need to fucking educate him on that shit."

Evan steps back and looks at me hard. He's got dark, almost black, eyes, and sometimes it's impossible to tell what's going on behind them. If we're going with the metaphor that eyes are the windows to the soul, Evan's have blackout curtains over them. If he doesn't want you to know what he's thinking, you will not know. It's one of his superpowers.

"What?" I ask, with some annoyance.

"Is this about something else?

"Like what?"

I know exactly like what. We both know like what. It's why he's been so all over me this whole last week. It's the real reason he wanted me to come to the station house yesterday. It's why he's keeping tabs on me. It's why he's so insistent that I "hang out with the fellas." And as much as I appreciate the concern, I also resent the shit out of it.

"He reminds me of him too," says Evan.

I don't need this shit. I really don't. Not now.

I'm about to respond when one of the strippers (dancers? Do they call them strippers or dancers? Artisans of Pole Manipulation? I'm gonna call them that. Pole Artisan for short) approaches Evan.

"Feel like a private dance, sugar?" She's eye-fucking the shit out of him. Probably not because he looks like the more good-looking version of what would happen if Keanu Reeves and Johnny Depp's DNA got mixed in a lab and was artificially inseminated into Salma Hayek (although it likely doesn't hurt either—I'm saying, dude is offensively handsome), but because he looks like he has money.

Robert, his husband, is one of the hottest-shit land developers in Vegas and Evan is a self-proclaimed clotheshorse, so being married to a rich dude affords him the chance to indulge his textile addiction.

(First time I thought Evan might be gay: We were ten and a bunch of us were in Joey Butler's basement/his dad's home gym looking at a dirty website. This was like '97, so dial-up took forever—you'd get the slow reveal as the pixels loaded: part of a tit, then a belly button, finally the muff shot, and the room would explode with pre-teen boys going "Ooooooooooooohhhhhhhhhhhhh!"—and I looked around to share the moment of crotch-shot exultation with Evan to find him eyeballing a *Men's Fitness* magazine. Dunno if I grasped it at ten, but in retrospect… Pretty decent tell.)

Anyway, point is, Evan dresses really, really fucking slick when he's not at work. And this Pole Artisan can clearly smell the money. (Why I never upgraded my wardrobe when I got all my cash. Don't wanna send up any smoke signals to the gold-diggers. That and I just really could not give a fat baby's ass.)

"C'mon, sweetie," she coos, "you'll be real glad you did." She starts grinding on his hip with her pussy. I can see Evan getting stressed that his thousand-dollar pants might get pussy juice on them. He gently but firmly pushes her away.

"Uh, that sounds… super. But I'm OK. Thanks."

Some people can't take a hint.

"Awww, c'mon now, baby." She goes in to pitch him with her pussy again. Evan stares at her with those midnight eyes.

"I appreciate the offer, but unless you've found some secret place to hide a cock in there, I'm all set. Thanks."

You ever see a dog tilt its head at you trying to figure out what the fuck you're saying? That's what she offers back before she blinks twice and walks away. It's wonderful. Evan smiles and waves goodbye as she leaves. Then he turns to me.

"I'm gonna go check on Jeff. Don't go anywhere."

"I won't."

The hell I won't. As soon as he walks off to tend to Jeff I turn to the bartender to get my credit card back.

"Hey! Bro! Lemme get my card? Tyler Morgan. But, uh, go ahead and just run it for like two grand, and those two guys I was just with—and those guys over there…?" I point at the quartet of Brandon, Dean, Bear and Rod. Bear and Rod are looking desperate and sad as Raven or Parakeet or whatever her name is supposed to be leaves the stage and blows them a kiss. "Yeah, those idiots? Whatever those guys all want, just put it on the card? If there's any left over, add it to the tip. Cool?"

"You got it, chief."

Christ. I hate it when guys call me "chief." Not sure why. Feels condescending. But I don't wanna get into it with a fucking bartender at a strip club. I just wanna get the fuck outta here and go somewhere with actual women who will at least fuck me tonight for the money that I'll spend on them.

"All right, gentleman…" The DJ is as cheesy as I'd expect. You can hear the herpes in his voice. "Let's get ready to give a nice, big hand to the lovely, the seductive, the naughty girl next door whose parents are out of town…!"

Are you fucking kidding me?

"The innocent harlot! Magnificent Scarlett!"

Kill me. Just get the bartender to bring my card back so I can get the fuck out of here and—

And…

And…
And then…

Time.

Stops.

It's her.

She's ditched the blue shirt for a push-up bra and almost nonexistent panties, and she's covered her hair with an unnaturally blonde wig, but the eyes. The smile. The wings. The halo. It's her.

My angel.

What. Is. Happening. Right. Now?

It seems like they've plunged the rest of the room surrounding the stage into complete darkness because she's the only thing here anymore. All the light in the place is shining directly on her. Shit, all the light in the universe is shining directly on her.

I can't breathe. My chest is tightening. Just like it did when I smelled the smoke last week. And my hands are shaking, just like they did when I heard the alarm at the firehouse. But unlike those times, I feel… peaceful. I'm at ease.

I can't tell if I want to smile, cry, or just… breathe. So I don't do anything. I just stare at her. And then…

We lock eyes. She's looking directly at me. Only at me. She pounds forward to the edge of the stage, fierce, powerful, in control, but still soft and beautiful. There's no music, there's no sound at all. Just my breathing and my beating heart.

She walks over to the pole and she climbs up. She hooks her legs around the top, letting her head list toward the ground. Her halo and wings shimmer in the golden glow of light surrounding her.

She splits her other leg open wide, and she slides slowly towards the earth.

An angel falling from Heaven.

She arrives on the floor with a graceful release from the pole, resting on her ass, her torso lifted, head tilted forward, her beautiful, perfect stomach holding her aloft as, facing me alone, she spreads both legs open. Open as wide as the gates of heaven itself. Inviting me to enter inside.

And I know this is impossible, but… I can smell her. Even from as far away as I am, I have her scent. It's an odd mixture of fragrance that shouldn't be so intoxicatingly beautiful blended together, but it is. She smells like fresh cream, and sea salt, and cotton candy, and sunshine, and innocence.

And now I can feel the blood rushing to my cock. The inside of my jeans starts pulsing in time with my beating heart. I'm not wearing underwear so the tip throbbing against the rough denim is just making it even harder. It's like a divining rod leading me toward the oasis that is her perfect body.

I begin walking toward the stage. She's asking for me. This is what the dream has been about. It's not a dream. It's a premonition. This is why I have come home. I didn't understand before now what my true purpose has been in returning to this place. But it's so I can find her. Suddenly it's all so clear. I've heard of people's lives changing in an instant. In war, you hear that all the time. But until now, I didn't understand.

I push my way past the other men standing rudely between me and my angel and reach the edge of the stage.

My dick feels like it's going tear through the cloth. I want it to. I want to tear out of my own skin and into her. I want to take her in my arms and press myself deep inside her until we become indistinguishable from each other. Until she has taken all of me, deep, and I have filled her with my blackness and poison and together we have turned it into light.

She is now on all fours, crawling over to me. No, not crawling. She floats. Her wings ferry her to where I stand. The pulse that I feel in my shaft is quickening. I can feel the churning, urgent need inside me racing to get out. My breath catches as she is inches from my lips now. She smiles and I'm afraid I'm going to come right here. I open my mouth to receive hers, but she pushes her lips past mine and lands at my ear.

She whispers, "You feel like sliding any cash in here, baby, or you just gonna stare?"

She spins to the side and the silhouette of her perfect ass is next to me. She cocks her hip out and offers up the side of her G-string. I do as she says. I want to do what she asks of me. Anything she demands, I will provide. I reach into my pocket and pull out—

Shit.

I don't have any cash. I rarely carry cash anymore. I mean... everything's done electronically and on my phone, and... fuck! My angel requires cash and I have none! Goddamn it!

"I'll be back!" I shout. And I run to the ATM in the corner of the club.

As I'm putting my card into the machine and withdrawing the five-hundred-dollar maximum withdrawal, a small voice in the back of my head (I think it's in my head) calls out that I'm acting like a mentally ill person. I crush it before it can say more. This is the most rational, logical, sane moment of my life. I know it is.

When I turn back to the stage… she's gone. What the fuck? She's gone. The rest of the club has emerged from its blackness and all the sad, pathetic losers who think they're somehow going to get a stripper to fall in love with them are back in my eye line. The stage is no longer awash in its golden hue, but just in the lame glow of the gelled Klieg lights. And the sound of "Me So Horny" blares over the loudspeakers as the DJ announces the arrival of Honey Walls to the fucking stage. I run over to the bartender who walks toward me with my credit card.

"Here you go, boss. Sign here."

I grab the receipt and sign. I ask, "Where's the girl? The one who was just up there? The angel?"

"Scarlett?" he says. "She'll be out in a second, probably. For lap dances." He hands me back my card and says, "Thanks a lot, pal." (I have a brief moment where I consider that I am neither this guy's chief, boss, nor pal, but again, I let it go.)

I see a kind of fat guy in a dark, rumpled, stained suit, sitting by what I imagine to be the dressing room door. He'll presumably know where my angel is. I head over.

"Hey," I say, as I approach. "'Scuse me? That girl, um, Scarlett. She back there?"

Big guy eyes me like he's sizing me up. I know exactly what that looks like. I've seen that look more times than can be remembered.

"Who's asking?" big guy wants to know.

"Nobody. She's… She just… She back there, bro?"

Big guy seems unsatisfied with this response. He rises from his stool in the way that almost always happens after the sizing up part is concluded.

"Dude…" I begin. Because here's the thing: I don't wanna have to take this guy down. Well, that's not exactly true. I kinda do. Because he's fucking underestimating me. I can tell. And that drives me crazy. But just like with the bartender, I'll let it slide because I've got other fish to fry. Also, if shit jumps off now, then Evan and his brothers will step in and have my back. That's just a fact. And those guys have to work in this town and it'd be terrible PR for LVFRescue if the *Review-Journal* ran a story about how one of its engine companies got into a fucking melee at a strip club. So I'm trying real, real hard to be the shepherd. (That's a line from *Pulp Fiction*. Samuel L. Jackson says it. Every time I take the high road in a situation like this I think of that line. I love that movie. So many good lines. People say the phrase, "I'm gonna get medieval…" all the time now and forget that it came from THAT movie. So rad. I haven't seen it in a while. I'm gonna watch it later when I get home. I think I'm rambling in my head again…)

And just as it looks like shit's about to go to a place it can't be rolled back from…

… she walks out from behind the curtain.

It's weird. She's still just as beautiful and magnificent as she was a moment ago—perfect lips; taut, toned stomach; incredible, *real* tits; emerald-green eyes—but she seems less… angelic… somehow. More of this earth and less like she was in my dreams. More, I dunno, human. I decide not to think about it too much.

"Hey, Scarlett," says big guy. "This him?"

"Him?" She eyes me for half a second. "Oh. Oh, no. No. No. S'not him. Thanks, Otis." She gives big guy a pat on the arm, eyes me with more than a little suspicion, and crosses into the room where she plasters a big smile on her face (not sure why it looks painful) and starts talking to the losers.

I give old Otis a look that says "you're lucky, buddy" (totally unnecessary, but fuck it, he is), and follow Scarlett. Whose real name simply cannot be Scarlett. I'll bet it's Persephone or, like, Ephigenia or something. Something real elegant and biblical.

I come up behind her just as she's reaching this douchebag wearing a gold chain.

"Hey," I say as I lightly touch her shoulder. She feels like baby powder. "Can I—?"

She turns around and interrupts me before I can finish. "You. The guy who took up my attention for almost half my song only to have no money. Whattayou want now? I'm all outta free lap dances. Go ask her." She points at a girl who's currently shoving her comically oversized fake breasts in some poor schmuck's face. "Name's Charity. Maybe she'll give you some."

"I'm sorry," I say in return. I really do not feel like myself all of a sudden. I feel nervous and awkward. Which has simply never been me. The weirdest part? I don't hate it. "I wasn't actually planning on staying, but… Whatever. I went to the ATM and got out some cash. I feel bad. Here. Please take this."

I pull out the wad of cash. (I never carry a wallet. I wind up losing money in the street all the time.) She eyes it with some skepticism. Then she eyes me up and down with the same skepticism.

"What kind of work do you do?"

"I'm, uh…" Fuck it. "I'm a lumberjack."

I hand her a hundred bucks. She takes it. Stuffs it inside her bra. I get a glance at her nipple and remember that I'm still rocking a savage hard-on.

"Lumberjack, huh?" she says. She glances down at my stiff cock. "I buy that. Looks like you're packing some serious wood."

I simply can't be anything be proud of her observation.

I come back with, "I'd love to take you to the forest sometime." Jesus. That was pretty fucking weak.

She rolls her eyes. "So," she says. "Looks like you have a couple more dollars there. You want a dance?"

(No. I want to fuck that halo off your head and die in your arms.)

"Sure. Is there a, whattayoucallit? A champagne room? Like, y'know, someplace more… private?"

"We call it a VIP lounge. But it's very expensive."

"OK."

"It's three hundred dollars for the hour."

"OK."

"Plus the cost of drinks."

"Sure."

"Bottle service only."

"Fair deal."

She continues to eye me with uncertainty.

"Yeah. OK, lumberjack. Let's go."

She takes me by the hand and my dick freaks the fuck out. As she's leading me to the back, I see Evan emerge from the bathroom carrying a spent-looking Jeff. He sees me heading back with Scarlett and a smile threatens to completely overtake his face. Until… Jeff heaves and throws up on Evan's fifteen-hundred-dollar Tom Ford shoes.

This night is not turning out like anybody planned.

CHAPTER SIX

MADDIE

I've still got one of his hands. It's kinda hot. Not… making me hot. And not sweaty. Just kinda… hot. Which, to my surprise, is perfectly OK. For the moment.

"OK, soldier," I say, then stop when I notice the pained look on his face, recover, and continue with, "Let's have the credit card. You wanna start with one hour?"

He stares at me for a second. Like maybe he's changing his mind about this. For a second I think I went too far and maybe I should've lowered my opening bid to thirty minutes.

But I shut up. I need this hour. I mean, that hundred bucks was a good start, but it's not enough. I need more just to break even and if I want to come out ahead after last night, I'm gonna need at least two hours from this beard and a few more like him when he's done with me.

So I squeeze his hand and he relaxes.

"OK," he says, handing me the credit card.

I hand it over to the waitress as we pass her, saying, "Bring us fresh drinks every fifteen minutes. Top-shelf Scotch," and take him through the curtain and into the room.

I look over my shoulder to see what he'll say about that, but he's just staring at me.

Kinda creepily, actually.

You got this, Maddie.

I lead him over to the couch, turn, making him turn with me, and then flatten my palm against his chest and push. He sits, his head tilted up, his eyes looking a little more dangerous than they did out on the floor.

Shit. I might regret this.

"Listen," I say, stepping forward so I can straddle his legs and look down at him from my position of authority. "I'm very strict about the rules, OK? No. Touching. I mean it. If you touch me, I'm gone, got it?"

My heart beats fast as he considers my conditions. But then he nods his affirmation and I relax.

I don't care how much money I need to make tonight, I don't compromise on the rules.

I smile, because that's what Raquel told me to do. And throw him a bone. Because that's how you be nice, right? "You can touch my hands though. That's it. You touch my tits, I'm done. You grab my ass, and I get the bouncers to throw you out."

"Hands," he says, blinking. "Got it."

He reaches for both of them at the same time. I exhale, annoyed. But I did give him permission, so I try to let it go and just start dancing.

TYLER

I don't remember the last time I held a woman's hands. Which is, of course, not true. I held some chick's hand just the other day as I was sticking her in a cab. But that's not really holding. That's "taking," or just "touching." Holding implies care. Holding implies consideration. And that's what I find myself doing now. Considering her hands.

They feel warm. But that may just be me. They also feel small. Which is surprising. Just because she's tall. Which, I realize, makes no sense. I guess I don't know what I expected. Because I didn't expect any of this. Ten minutes ago I was ready to walk out of here, and now here I am, in the VIP room of a strip club with an angel who I certainly didn't expect to see here grinding on my dick.

And she's amazing at it. She's an OK *dancer*, but she's amazing at *grinding against my cock*. She's not slamming herself into it in some awkward way, she's… I dunno… caring for it. It's so easy for girls to forget that a guy's cock is attached to a, y'know, guy, but she seems aware of me.

This is so fucking wild.

"Tell me your name." I say. I was not expecting to speak. I certainly wasn't expecting to say that. But it's what happened, so I must really want to know.

"Scarlett," she purrs. Goddamn fuck me, her voice is sexy.

"Yeah, uh-huh, but no, seriously… What's your *name*?"

She slows her grind for an almost imperceptible moment, then she says, "What's yours?"

OK. That's how we're proceeding? That's fair. She doesn't know me and I have caused her to be burned alive in two separate dreams now, so she's being cautious. But like her, I'm not sure I'm ready to part with that information just yet. Until I'm certain she won't bail once she recognizes me as the guy who destroys Heaven, I should be careful.

I dunno if it's because I just went car-shopping or if there's some other reason this pops into my head, but I pull the first name I can think of out of the air. "Ford. I'm Ford."

"Ford what?" she asks.

I stumble for a second. "Uh…" Then I just decide to go with the car theme and pick out the first car company that comes to me. Aston Martin. "Um, Aston. I'm Ford Aston."

Ford Aston? Seriously? Jesus Christ. She's gotta know that's fake. It's like the most made-up-sounding name anybody's ever thought of. Why didn't I go with Ford Martin? Or Martin Ford? Or… Fuck. What an asshole. I need to pull it together. I should stop talking.

But she doesn't call me on it or make a thing out of it. She just keeps grinding her perfect, pretty pussy against me and I shut up and keep holding her gorgeous hands.

MADDIE

I'm not the greatest dancer here… but I'm fuckin' motivated tonight. So I put some extra effort into it. Get my hips moving, just barely skimming his dick. It's hard. Which distracts me a little.

The waitress comes in, sets our drinks down on a nearby side table, and then leaves without comment.

I wrangle one of my hands from his grip—he puts up a small fight about that, but I win—and then pick up one glass and hand it to him. "Here," I say. "Relax a little. You seem a little tense."

He takes the glass, downs the drink in one gulp, and then sets the glass back down so he can grab my hand again.

"Jesus." I laugh. "You really need some attention tonight, huh?"

He says nothing. Which is kind of disturbing, since he was pretty forward out there on the floor. Maybe even desperate. Fumbling over his words and acting all awkward like a strip-club virgin.

Now he's… different. More in control. Definitely not a virgin.

"So are you really a lumberjack?" I ask.

He looks at me for a long second. And then his thumbs start caressing little circles against my palms. It tickles a little. Sends a shudder up my spine. I want to pull my hands away and shake it off, but his fingers are wrapped around my wrists. Giving me the impression that there's no way in hell he's gonna let me go.

I'm just about to put an end to this when he says, "Yeah. I cut shit down for a living."

His voice is low and throaty, his dick still hard.

"OK," I say, looking over his shoulder with a sigh. I stare at the wall for a moment and wonder just how the fuck I got here—in a dark room, alone with a guy who might've just hinted his job is killing things. People, not trees. I'm pretty sure he's not talking about trees.

But he lets go of one of my hands to reach for the other drink on the table and downs it. I breathe a little easier. Maybe he'll just get drunk and sit here quietly? Hell, maybe he'll fall asleep and wake up in five or six hours?

I almost snicker at that thought.

But then I stop. Not the snicker, but like… *stop.*

Because he's caressing my shoe.

"What are you doing?" I ask. And there's nothing nice about my question.

"You said not to touch you."

"Right. So why are you playing with my shoe?"

"You said hands only," he continues, ignoring my question.

"Yeah."

"So what about feet?" And with that, he slips my shoe off. It drops to the floor with an audible clunk.

TYLER

I cut shit down for a living? Good Christ, I really am a fucking tool. I take her foot up just to see if I can distract her from my unforgivable display of toolboxery.

And this is it. I'm fucking this whole thing up. She told me only hands, and I broke that rule, and in about two seconds she's going to scream for someone to come save her. I hope it's that Otis dude. If I can't fuck an angel tonight, at least maybe I can get out some frustration by busting open his fat melon.

I'm sorry, angel. I'm sorry. I won't blame you if you hate me. Fuck.

MADDIE

I'm about to scream for the room monitor when his thumb does that little circle caress on my bare sole.

The shiver is back and it shoots right up my spine, leaving the hair on the nape of my neck tingling.

There's a few places on the human body that rarely get attention. So when these places do get that attention, everything about it is heightened.

The calf, for instance. When a man touches my calf it drives me wild.

The back of the knee. Kiss me on the back of the knee and I practically come.

And the foot.

I sit down on his lap as he continues. Placing my hands on his shoulders, feeling the hard, taut muscles underneath his shirt. My thighs brush against his jeans, which are soft. Like he's owned them for years and they've been washed a million times.

I close my eyes a little, so they're half-mast, and enjoy the heat of his body as it mingles with mine.

His cock is pressing against the thin fabric of my panties, reminding me that I've got a job to do. So I start moving again. Slowly. Just enough to keep him entertained and not so much that this turns into something more than I usually give.

I gaze down into his eyes as he stares up into mine. And I want to say… *What? Why are you looking at me that way?*

But I can't find any words. We just stare at each other. Finding something in this moment. In each other. Something we recognize. Like… a dream you forgot and then remember. Or a stranger who feels like an old friend.

He lets go of my other hand and slides his fingers over my other shoe. A moment later it too drops to the floor. And then I've got thumbs dancing on the soles of both feet.

This time my eyes don't stop at half-mast. I close them and enjoy the unexpected tingle of… *attraction.*

TYLER

Holy. Fucking. Shit.

This is not how I expected this to go.

I'm starting to get the sense that my angel needs something. That's why she's been so kind to me in my dream. That's why she came back with me here even though she seemed like she didn't want to at first. (*That, and the money,* the little voice in the back of my head tells me. *I know,* I respond to it silently. *I'm crazy, not fucking stupid.*)

But she's hurting. Somehow. She is. I can see it. I've seen plenty of suffering. Enough to know when someone is in pain. And she's in pain. And it hurts me to see her hurt. And I do know this is insane. I know that she's not really my angel, and that we're in the back of a filthy fucking strip club, and that everything in me right now that feels hopeful and warm is a fucking lie. I know that.

But I don't give a shit.

Because there is something here. Alchemy. You know it when you feel it. And I can feel it the same way I can feel her pain. And I decide that I'm going to help her. I haven't been able to save her in my DREAM, but maybe that's the point. Maybe THE DREAM is just a notification that I'm supposed to save her in the real world. Save her from what, I don't know. But I think I have to try to find out. I know this is nuts, but I can *feel* it. Just like I can feel the end of my erection pounding against her creamy thigh.

I take a breath to keep from coming right now, and I keep rubbing her foot. Because she's letting me. My angel.

MADDIE

"It feel OK?" he asks.

I take another moment before I answer. *Get it together, Maddie.* "Not really," I lie. And it's such a fucking lie.

He knows it too, because he lets out a small laugh. "I can follow the rules, *Scarlett*." He makes a point of emphasizing my name to let me know that he knows it's fake. But something about the way he says it makes me open my eyes all the way again and really look at him.

He's… scraggly. His hair is a shaggy mess of unruly darkness. And his beard looks like he just can't be bothered to shave. Not the trendy kind of beard that some guys like to wear.

"But, y'know, I like to bend them backwards as far as I can when I get the chance."

"Is that so?" I ask. My voice is low and throaty, just like his.

"If you don't like it, tell me to stop. I will."

I stare down at him and consider my options. He doesn't seem to be concerned about getting his money's worth. And that's a good sign. But he also seems interested in… me.

Every guy who comes in here with me comes for me, right? I don't know why I think this is different. But there's something about this guy. Something more in the look of him, in his quiet assertiveness that makes me reconsider everything about what's happening.

"Do you want me to stop?" he asks.

I'm not in control at the moment. And this is very unusual. At least while I'm working here at Pete's. Lately, Pete's is the only place I have any control over my life. I get to call the shots. I get to lay the ground rules. I get to say yes or no.

"Scarlett? Angel? Give me a road map. Or I won't know where the limits are."

"Do you have a problem with limits?" I ask, snapping back to the moment.

"Yeah. Sometimes."

I decide he is, at the very least, being honest. So I'm gonna give it a little longer before I make up my mind about whether or not to cut this short. Besides. It really does feel fuckin' amazing. "No," I whisper. "Don't stop."

He offers up a small smile. But it's kind of a sad smile.

And I don't know how I know this, but I do. Because I recognize it. And I think I'm smiling back at him in the very same way. We are two people filled with the same world of hurt and for some reason, it makes me feel better and worse all at once and I need to know more about him. Because… because I don't want to see myself in this stranger. I don't want to see the pain and sadness. Whatever's bothering him… I want to fix it.

"Did you have a bad week?" I ask, letting my fingertips slide up underneath his hair. It's soft. Softer than I would've imagined. If I imagined those kinds of things.

"No worse than the thousands of bad weeks that came before."

Now we frown together. Understanding each other. My hands are fully engaged in feeling the texture of his hair. My fingertips brushing lightly across the little bit of bare skin above his shoulders.

On an impulse, I reach down and tug his shirt up. He raises his arms and lets me take it off. It brushes past my thigh as it falls to the ground.

TYLER

Here we go. And not in a good way. Well… that's fucking life. Shit.

MADDIE

And that's when I see the scars.

"Jesus," I say.

When I look at him, he's just… looking back at me. Expressionless.

"What happened?" I ask. It's a stupid question because there's only one way to get scars like that. Fire.

He shrugs and squeezes both of my feet. Like he needs to hold on to me. "You don't wanna know."

OK, soldier.

My words when we first came in here echo in my head. The pained look on his face.

I decide he's right. This isn't something I need to know. It's too close to my own pain. Way too close. So I do something else instead. Something I never do. I take his face in both my hands and I kiss him.

He doesn't respond at first, but I don't give up. I brush my lips against his. Softly at first. Then harder and more persistent. For some reason I know he needs this kiss. And I'm the one who needs to give it to him.

I take it a step further. Just add one more thing I never do to the growing list of things I'm already doing, because I need to forget and how can I forget if he remembers? So I touch his chest. Feel him. Feel the jagged edges of his scars.

And that's when he kisses me back.

His mouth opens and his tongue slips inside me. I breathe heavy, my heart beginning to gallop as his hands leave my feet and land on my hips.

"Sorry," he says into my mouth. But when he withdraws them, I clamp my hands down on the back of his and keep them there.

"Don't be," I whisper back, still kissing him. My body feels limp and soft and he feels like a goddamned rock. Hard. Stable. Secure.

I start to grind on him. Moving seductively.

The waitress appears with fresh drinks, but neither of us cares.

He's mumbling something as I take my kisses to his neck. Something about Heaven or…

I don't care what he's mumbling. My mind is spinning with what he's been through and what I've been through. And what it means that this guy—someone who seems just as lost and vulnerable as I do—might be just what I was looking for tonight.

It's dumb. And I feel a little naïve for buying into the bullshit. Like the customers must feel at the end of a lap dance. Taken for a ride, but unable to step off because… because they *need* it.

I unbuckle his pants, slip my hand inside. Find him very hard.

His hands are wandering too. Slipping between my legs, his fingers pushing inside me.

I grind my hips even more forcefully, even as I try my best to hold back.

"Hey," he says, breaking the moment. "You don't need to do this. You don't have to."

I'm conflicted. Because I'd forgotten where I was for a moment. At work. With a customer who is paying me money to be here with him.

So I pull away and reach for the fresh drinks. I hand him his, then take mine. I don't ever drink at work, either. But what the fuck? I guess I'm just throwing out every rule I have for this guy.

He takes a sip of his Scotch. It's watered down so much, he doesn't even wince at the burn. And then he sets it down and places both hands on the back of my calves.

I close my eyes and bite my lip to stifle a moan.

It's like he knows me. All my deepest secrets. All my desires. All the pleasure spots on my body. *How the fuck does he know me?*

"Should we go back to the ground rules?" he asks.

But I just shake my head. "No," I say. "We've gone long past ground rules tonight."

We talk for a little bit after that. Turns out, he's kinda funny. I find myself laughing more than I have in… hell, years, I think.

He tells me about his car. Which is pretty typical of men, right? But I don't even know what kind of car he's describing. He calls it some kind of Land Rover. But when I say, "Yeah, I can totally picture it," he insists that no, there's no fucking way I can picture it.

And I believe him. I don't know why. He's just some random stranger and his word means nothing to me at all. But I do. I believe him.

I let him describe it to me in every detail. The wheels and suspension. And a whole bunch of other shit that's lost on me. But he's smiling the whole time, so I don't care. And I don't even know why I don't care. I just… want to listen to him. Hear his voice and see his smile. I want to feel his bare chest under my fingertips and know that we're in this night together. Whatever pain we have. Whatever regrets and bullshit are haunting us. We're in this night together.

TYLER

I have no fucking clue why I'm talking to her about my stupid car. I feel dopey. High, almost. It's not like I'm trying to show off or brag to her. I could give a fuck if she thinks I'm awesome because I have a fancy car. In fact, if she DID think I was awesome because I have a fancy car, I'd be fucking out of here.

But I know she wouldn't think that. Because that's not who she is.

No, I'm telling her all this shit I guess because… I like her. I don't know her, but I feel like I do. We have something in common, but I'm not sure what. I only know that I feel immediately comfortable with her. And I'm positive that it's not just because I'm paying her. Something inside me tells me that she's not good enough at her job to fool me that much. No, there's something else between us. I promise myself I'm not wrong. And, shit, I don't really like anybody, but I like her.

I laugh and shake my head at that, and that's when I glance down at my watch.

It's four-fucking-thirty in the morning.

What happened to the night? It's almost gone. How did that happen? Haven't we just been here a few minutes? How has all this time flown by and it feels like I've only just arrived here with her? What have we even been saying? Not much. Stupid stuff. Nothing even really that personal. Just talking about cars and… drones… and "Tahoe Blue" being a color… and…

I haven't spent all night talking to a woman without trying to fuck her since I was fifteen years old.

I start thinking maybe we should get out of here. Continue talking at breakfast. I can bring her to my place. I have burnt toast and whiskey. Or maybe we can just head out and watch the sun rise. Or maybe…

Maybe I should just tell her my name.

And, in an instant, I remember that happiness and good times are things that are generally reserved for other people. Because I stop my fucking fantasy thrill ride into the future when I look down at her hands. And I see that she's touching my history again.

MADDIE

I trace the edges of his scar, this time paying more attention to them. And when I look up at his face again, he's frowning.

He says, "Seriously. You don't wanna know," like he's reading my mind.

And he's right. I don't. But I picture it anyway, because I don't really need the details in order to take a good guess.

"Stop," he says, again with the mind-reading.

And then his hands remember what we started earlier. Fingertips slip between my legs and I realize I've been sitting in his lap for hours. The waitress has come and gone so many times, we've got dozens of drinks covering the table—most of which are even more watered down with the melting ice than they were when they arrived.

"Don't try to figure me out. It's bad in here." He points at his head.

I place my palm on his face. Look at him. And feel so much sadness I get a lump in my throat.

He grabs my hand and pulls it down onto his cock. "But it's excellent down here."

TYLER

I'm like a goddamn vampire. I know the morning is just about here and soon they're going to kick me out and I can't risk this being the only chance with my angel that I'll get. I also can't fucking wait anymore and I can't pretend to be somebody I'm not.

So I take her hand and force her to take my dick and hold it. Tight. It is, by far, the best thing about me and if I'm going to leave her with anything, any memory of this night, it's not going to be about me stumbling to get words out, or dumb shit about cars, or the fucking scars all over my body—which, until this very moment right now, I have never given a shit about, but suddenly I hate them and wish they were just not there. But they are. And so I want her to remember something else about me.

Please, angel, remember what happens next instead.

MADDIE

My hand wraps around his shaft and begins to pump. He lets his head roll back into the couch as his fingers play with my clit.

I can't stop. And I don't want him to stop either. We can't even think about stopping. So I grind on him, the wetness almost pouring out of me as he continues to stroke me.

And then… before I can get a hold of myself…

I come all over his fingers.

He grabs my hair and pulls me forward. His mouth on mine, his tongue inside me again. His hands are on my tits, pulling them out of my angel outfit. The wetness from my release smears across my nipple.

"You're my angel," he says, lowering his head so he can take my breast in his mouth.

"Yes," I say, knowing everything about this night is wrong and I'm going to regret all these sweet, perfect moments the second I lead him out of this room…

But I don't care.

"Yes," I say again, his teeth nipping me until I throw my head back and wince. "I'm your angel."

TYLER

I can't wait. I can't hold out for another second longer. She can see that I'm about to release all that's inside me all over the inside of her thighs, so before I can, she stops pumping with her hand, drops to her knees, takes me in her mouth and slides the warmth of her tongue down the length of my shaft.

She's barely gotten her lips all the way around me before I explode onto her tongue. I can feel hot come throbbing out of me and sliding down into the back of her throat.

She takes it all in. She drinks it all down. She keeps bobbing her head back and forth, making sure that she has drawn every last drop of me dry.

My stomach clenches and releases as I moan, "Angel."

She finishes taking it all in, draws her lips back, slowly, kissing the tip of my softening cock as she goes, then draws herself up to my waist and kisses me on the belly button.

Then up to my chest and kisses me over my heart.

Then finally to my chin, where she lurches forward and kisses me on the mouth so that I can taste the salty residue of myself on her lips.

She places both hands on my knees and pushes herself to a standing position, her breasts and stomach passing my face as she lifts up until her pussy is directly before my mouth.

And I start to get hard all over again.

I rise up so that I'm standing with her. Once again, I take her hands in mine. I lift them, studying the soft curves where her fingers crook and bend. I go in for another kiss when the curtain swings open.

It's the waitress. The one who's been bringing us drinks all night. She surveys the two of us without judgment, but she does twist her head to the side.

"Hey, Scarlett," she says. "Uh… you missed your last stage dance and uh, Raven's heading this way. Just, y'know, in case you guys wanna put any dicks back inside any pants or anything." She closes the curtain.

"Um, I—" I start, before my angel interrupts me.

"Shit. Raven's gonna have my ass. We gotta get it together."

I nod. I push my dick back in my pants.

She adjusts her tits into her bra.

I put my shirt back on.

She straightens her halo back upright and reattaches her wings.

I try to smooth my beard down as much as I can.

And we stare at each other.

For what feels like a very long time.

CHAPTER SEVEN

MADDIE

It's dark in here. They do that on purpose so customers can't tell how late it is. But it's not late anymore. It's early. So the only reason I care if it's dark or not is because I want to see his eyes. Like… really see his eyes. And I can't. Because it's too fucking dark.

"Uh," I say. Because even though he was really chatty all night—told me stupid jokes and funny stories—he's quiet now. Like he's wondering what the fuck just happened.

I'm wondering that too. "Thanks?" I say.

It comes out like a question and I roll my eyes at myself.

I have never—ever—given a customer a blow job. Shit. I don't let these jerks touch my tits, let alone sit in their laps and get giddy like a stupid fucking schoolgirl. *And* get off, I remind myself. *And* swallow their fucking come.

I glance at the table of drinks. You know, the ones that are still full. So I can't even play this off like I was drunk.

I sucked his dick and swallowed his…

I shake my head and turn away as the waitress comes up with the bill. "Sign here," she says, handing him a pen.

There's a shuffle of paper—the credit card slip, I guess—so I glance over my shoulder to look at him one last time before he walks out, and catch him pocketing his card. He's looking at me like…

"No," he says. "Thank you."

And then he turns away, rubbing his hand over his beard. I'm not sure if he's feeling as lame as I am due to the lackluster final conversation taking place, but I don't want to leave it this way.

So I open my mouth and I'm about to say something… maybe explain myself. Tell him I'm not that kind of a girl, I never do this sort of thing, he's the only one… but that's when fucking Raven bursts in.

"Time to go home, big spender." She shoots him a wink that's sexy, but only in a sad stripper sort of way. And then she glances down at the bill and laughs. "Jesus, Scarlett! What'd ya do? Suck his fucking dick all night?" Raven. Real class act.

"He's a fucking customer, Raven," I snap, a little louder than I should. Pissed and trying to play it off at the same time. We're not allowed to fuck the customers. I mean, girls *bend* the rules all the time. Mostly we get them all excited and they come in their pants. But we don't *fuck* the customers in the club. And we certainly don't get on our knees and let them shove their cocks down our throats. If we wanna do that shit, we gotta take it someplace else.

Raven squints at me.

Shit. She knows. She must. I glance at the waitress, who is playing monitor for this room, and she gives me an almost imperceptible shake of her head. Meaning—*I didn't say nothin'*.

So I go all in with my defense. Because I cannot lose this job. This guy right here might've saved my ass tonight, but one night does not change a girl's situation. I gotta think of myself. "You know I would never suck a customer's cock. Especially this guy," I whisper, loudly, thumbing over my shoulder at him. "Come on, Raven."

I glance behind me, just to see if he's gonna play along or decide to out me, but his face is almost blank.

Almost.

There's a slight frown if I'm reading him correctly. It's hard to tell with that beard.

Did I hurt his feelings?

And now I feel like shit. I feel confused and stuck between two worlds. Maddie and Scarlett. The person I am and the person I *have* to be. I want to say more, tell him that's not what I meant, goddammit. But he's already heading for the door.

"Hey, chief," the bartender calls from the other side of the room. "Thanks for the tip!"

My guy says nothing. Just huffs and keeps walking until he passes through the doors, and out into the early-morning light.

"Did you—" Raven starts.

"No," I snap. "Don't be a bitch, Raven. I don't appreciate you accusing me of inappropriate behavior, OK? Keep that shit to yourself."

"Well." Raven laughs. "You're certainly taking this personally. But OK," she says, holding up her hands in surrender. "Whatever. You didn't suck his cock. Congrats on getting him to spend more than two thousand dollars on you tonight. Plus the liquor and room tab. Guess you won't have a problem paying me now, will you?"

"Yeah." The bartender laughs as he approaches us. "And that fuckin' hobo spent almost two grand on drinks at the bar too!"

"He tipped us good too," the waitress says. "Almost eight hundred bucks."

Jesus. That's like… seven grand, all in. On one night with *me*.

I saw his credit card. It was one of those green American Express ones. Not even the gold one.

Who the fuck was that guy?

And then I realize… I never got his real name. Ford Aston. What a crock of shit. No one is called Ford Aston.

I head for the door and for a second I feel like chasing him out to the parking lot. Making him tell me who he is. Getting his fucking number, or writing down his license plate, or… something.

"Hey," Raven calls, stopping me in my tracks.

"What?" I snap again, so sick of her shit.

"You better watch yourself."

"What's that supposed to mean?"

"I saw you flash a customer last weekend."

"What customer?"

"Sitting in the front row during your dance? Waved that fifty at you? And then you spread your legs and pulled your panties aside. Gave him a peek and took his money."

Shit.

"Guys like that, they—"

"Guys like that, they what?" I ask.

"I'm just saying, watch yourself, *Scarlett*." She sneers my name. Of course she knows it's fake—Raven is fake too—but it's a hard-and-fast rule that we don't call each other by our real names in here. Too easy to slip up in front of customers. "Because rules are rules. And I don't even like you, so if you think you're gonna break the rules and still have a job… think again, sweetie."

She pats my cheek—two quick slap-like taps to make her point—and walks out.

I am torn between chasing down the beard guy and just wanting to grab my shit and get the fuck out of here.

I go for option two.

Fuck this place and fuck that guy.

He's just some stranger I met at work. Just another sad dude who needs to watch girls get naked to make himself feel better. He's nobody, and the quicker I put this night behind me, the better off I'll be.

The next day—or night really, since I slept all day—I am ashamed of what I did. I just stare at that money he paid me and feel… dirty. Sinful. And I'm not even religious. Like at all. But this is Sin City, right? I mean, I grew up in the Devil's playground and last night I broke every rule I have in place that lets me pretend I have values. But the truth is, my job is a ticket straight to Hell if it turns out there is a God standing guard at some pearly gates checking everyone's moral compass before he lets them pass through.

I'm totally fucked after last night. I mean, before that I could play it off. Pretend I'm nothing but an entertainer. But the longer I work at Pete's, the looser I get. I did pull my panties aside for that Logan guy. Raven saw. And he works for Carlos, and now I can only imagine what they're all saying about me.

Not that I care what some kingpin's henchmen think of me, but… I sorta care.

I spend the rest of the week beating myself up for what I did. Promising myself I'll never do it again. Maybe it's because I wore the angel garb or maybe I'm just starting to lose it a little bit, but I find that I now seem to have an angel of my own sitting on my shoulder that I'm begging to forgive me and a little devil sitting on the other side—who really likes having extra money for once—that I'm telling to fuck off.

But the devil is winning. He's got a much better argument. I like having extra money. And I do need it. Because two more real-estate agents turned me down. I even made them each a free video. It's like they were just taking advantage of my freebie offer and wanted nothing to do with my services.

Fucking freeloaders.

Plus I think about that guy.

A lot.

All week.

Almost every minute of it.

And that makes me stare at that money and wonder if I should give it back.

My angel is saying, *Yes, Scarlett.* The angel is calling me Scarlett. Jesus. *Give it back. You'll feel better and your soul will be cleansed.*

But the devil is the one I listen to. Because he says, *Fuck that! You earned it. And after everything you've fucking been through? Everything you've dealt with, all on your own? Fuck it. You take that shit, Maddie.*

But why does he call me Maddie when the angel calls me Scarlett? Before I can reflect on that too heavily, he speaks up and interrupts. *And you're never gonna see that guy again. You can't give it back. You* need *it. And you don't even know his name. So this guilt is a pointless moral exercise.*

Like I said, he makes a lot more sense.

So I listen.

But here's the part I don't expect: To my horror, when Friday night rolls around, I discover myself hoping that my guy will come back and give me more.

Not money, though.

Just… *more.*

CHAPTER EIGHT

When I get home, I try to process what just happened.

Let me go through this for a tick.

I show up at a strip club.

I see an angel I've been having dreams about riding the pole.

I go into a private room with her.

She tells me not to touch her.

Hours go by, she sucks my cock until I blow in her mouth, I pay out like seven large, and then she kind of talks shit about me and sends me on my way.

It is entirely possible that my life is a little out of balance.

The rest of the week is kinda hazy.

Every time I close my eyes, flashes of her skin against mine, her hands touching me, the feel of her pussy against my fingertips, all come charging in. Which is kind of fucking me up. Because I don't usually do that—have what are basically *fantasies* about something that's already happened. But this, with her—I dunno. I can't shake it.

So I start taking a Klonopin and chasing it with a shot (or five) of whiskey. (Dr. Eldridge, my shrink, gave me the Klonopin. She said I should take it for anxiety. She didn't say I should take it with the whiskey, but in my experience mixing any two drugs is usually a pretty good method for relaxation.) And that cocktail helps me sleep. But when I fall asleep, I have THE DREAM. And so then I wake up, sweating. Shaking. And I have to take another Klonopin with a whiskey chaser to calm the fuck down.

The whole thing is super sexy.

I order food. I watch TV. I fuck around on the internet. I find myself Googling random shit like, "Scarlett Pete's Strip Club Vegas." You know. Random.

And days go by.

At some point it looks like I punched the wall? I think? Someone did. Because there's a hole. I wander over to it and place my fist inside. Yep. Musta been me. Perfect fit. Besides, no one else has been here. Have they?

I wander around my place to see if I can find evidence of anyone else having been here. I stare out the window. I think about leaving. I don't. I ignore the phone. I take anti-anxiety medication. I sleep. I DREAM. I wake up. It starts again.

And days go by.

I should leave. Go out. Fuck some chick. Or two. I don't wanna. Is that weird? That seems weird. Somehow I know though that if I leave I'll just drive to that strip club and see if she's there. And I don't wanna do that. Or I do, but I'm not gonna. And…

Fuck! What was that? Did someone fire a gun somewhere? No? Sounded like someone fired a gun. Fuck. OK. It wasn't? Shit. My heart is fucking beating again. Goddamn.

I take a Klonopin. I'm not sure how many I'm supposed to take, but they seem to be helping. Maybe? A little? I dunno. I take a second Klonopin. I chase it with whiskey. I order more food. I think about going to the strip club. I don't go to the strip club.

I try to sleep. I DREAM. I wake up. And…

Ha!

It is entirely possible that my life is a little out of balance.

But fuck it. I take a K-pin (I don't know if people call 'em that, but I do) and a chaser.

I sleep.

Maybe I'll get lucky.

And I won't wake up.

And I won't wake up.

And I don't wake up.

And I don't wake up.

And I…

Holy shit.

I sleep.

"OH, MY GOD, WHAT THE FUCK, DUDE?"

I wake up. Fuck me.

I have woken up with strangers in my bed a thousand times, but very rarely are they fully dressed men eating a Pop Tart.

"Hey," says Evan. He's sitting on the foot of my mattress. (The Pop Tart is Brown Sugar Cinnamon. They're our favorite. Since we were kids.)

"What the fuck are you doing in my apartment? What's happening? What time is it? Is everything OK? What the…? Who…? What the fuck, dude?"

At least I'm pretty sure those are the questions I ask. I'm not entirely certain what I say, if I'm being honest. It's possible I'm having another weird fucking dream. Goddamn Klonopin. Anti-anxiety, my ass.

"Y'know," he says, standing up, "it takes a lot of balls to ignore my calls and texts for a fuckin' week and then ask me 'what the fuck.' Also, you're out of Pop Tarts. See ya."

He throws the foil wrapper on the bed and crumbs spill everywhere. He starts walking out of my bedroom and towards the front door.

"What?" I ask, jumping out of bed to follow. "What are you saying? How did you get in? Where are you going?"

I come up behind him and put my hand on his shoulder to turn him around. Those eyes. I have no idea what his expression is. My guess would be… No. I got nothing.

He counts off his answers to my questions by holding up a finger as he responds to each. "I'm saying, fuck you for making me worry all week. I got in with the key card you gave me, and fuck you for making me worry all week. And I'm going to work because you're clearly OK and apparently just being a cunt, so fuck you for making me worry all week."

He starts off again. I stop him again.

"Wait. Wait. I'm… really fucking confused. What day is it?"

He steps back, closes his eyes slowly. Opens them again. Breathes in. Sighs out.

"It's Friday, but…" He looks me up and down. "But man, I can't talk to you until you put some clothes on."

Oh, right. I'm naked. It's possible I've been naked for a few days. The whole thing feels very *Apocalypse Now* all of a sudden. "OK," I say, "just hold on. All right? Just hang here for a sec."

He acquiesces. Nods. As I'm going to put on some pants and a shirt he calls out, "Nice dick, by the way!"

The coffee tastes extra bitter as we sit around my kitchen island and I try to explain what I've been doing all week. "… and then somebody punched a hole in my wall, I guess. It's possible it was me." I sip the coffee. Evan looks through me, his eyes blacker than the liquid in my cup.

"So this girl. This dancer…"

"Scarlett."

"Sure… So you and Johansson got freaky, you fell in love, and then when you remembered it was just a business transaction, you… lost your fucking mind? Is that more or less what I'm hearing?" He arches an eyebrow. He can arch both. This time it's the right one.

"I dunno what you're hearing, bro. I barely know what the fuck I'm saying."

There's a long pause. I sip my coffee. It's not very good. Then…

"What are you going to do?" That's Evan.

"About what?" That's me.

"With the rest of your life, man?"

I take a beat. Then I answer as honestly as I can: "Dunno. If I'm lucky, I may not have to worry about it much longer."

Evan closes his eyes. He kind of laughs a little. Which I appreciate. I'm funny as fuck. Everybody says so.

"Why did you come home?" It's weird that he's never asked me in all these months.

"Where else am I gonna go?"

"You never have to worry about money again. You could go anywhere. You could travel the world—"

"Seen it." I cut him off. He bows his head and raises his hands.

"Fair enough. But, just, I dunno, man. I love you and I'm glad you're here—if for no other reason than so that I can keep a fuckin' eye on you, but…" He smiles. I smile a little too. Son of a bitch actually means it.

I take a breath. "I dunno, dude. I mean, I kind of do. I've tried to, y'know, do good. Y'know? With my life. I really have. But everything and everyone I try to help or get close to just gets blown the fuck to smithereens. No pun intended."

Evan smiles. I did intend it a little.

I go on, "So whatever. It seems like I just wind up fucking up everything I come near, so rather than go someplace new and leave a smoldering heap of wreckage in my wake, I thought, 'Well, it's Vegas, I know it, it's already a churning cesspool of sin anyway, what's the worst I can do?' I mean… this is where I'm from. This place made me. So I feel like it's the one place that might actually be able to stand up to the battering ram of catastrophe that is Tyler Morgan."

It feels a little weird to use my inside-my-head voice on the outside in such a vocal way, but shit, it's Evan.

After a moment he says, "I'm still here."

"Dude—" I start.

"No, no. You say you're this amazing force of nature. You blow up *everything* and *everyone* you come near. Well… You haven't blown me up. I'm still here."

"Whatever. You're sturdy." I pause now, debating whether or not I want to say the next thing we both know is coming. "Scotty wasn't." (I decide I do want to say it.)

And then Evan stares at me for what feels like five minutes even though it's probably five seconds.

And finally he says, "Scotty wasn't your fault."

And that's it. That's all he says. Which is both annoying and perfect. Just like Evan. He stands to leave. This time I let him go.

"OK. I gotta get to work. I'll call later. Pick up. Or don't. Do you, bro."

He pats me on the shoulder. Crosses to the door.

"Hey," he says, "I know you're done helping people and are just here to set the town on fire and watch it burn or whatever, but we're doing the Haunted Firehouse fundraiser thing for Halloween. If you feel like coming by, that'd be cool. There'll be kids and stuff. You can teach 'em how to… I dunno… be an asshole."

"Halloween?" I ask.

"I know," he says. "I know. It's his Yahrzeit. That's why you should come."

"Fuck's a Yahrzeit?"

"It's Hebrew. Just means the anniversary of someone's passing."

"The Jews have a word for everything."

"We're chosen for a reason," he says. "You'll come?"

"I'll think about it," I say. And then, "Hey. Ev…?" I start.

"Yeah?" He turns around.

There's a lot I want to say. I want to say, 'Thank you.' I want to say 'I love you, bro.' I want to say, 'Dude, I'm fucking scared.' But instead what comes out is, "Do you really think I have a nice dick?"

He drops his head and smiles. Then, "See you later. If you come next week, you should bring the stripper with you. There's a big pole in the middle of the room. She'll feel right at home. Peace."

He winks at me, closes the door, and I take another sip of bitter coffee.

CHAPTER NINE

MADDIE

I'm just minding my own business, walking past the living room to the laundry room on the other side of the house to grab a clean t-shirt so I can jet out of here and be early for work instead of late—for once—when I see Annie pacing outside in the front yard.

Well… front yard is a stretch. You don't have grass in Nevada unless it's fake or you're super-rich because it's the fucking desert and trying to grow grass in the desert is just stupid.

But it's a yard. And Annie is walking back and forth, talking on her phone. Then she starts screaming. You know, the kind of phone screaming that involves holding it at arm's length you so can blast the person on the other end with your anger.

What the hell is going on?

Then she does that poke thing to end the call—hanging up on people was so much more satisfying in the old movies, right? You get to slam that handset down with a bang. But now it's just a poke. She looks up at the sky, hands balled into fists, and screams at it.

God, maybe. She's probably screaming at God.

She comes inside and since I'm still standing in front of the window, she quickly realizes her little temper tantrum didn't go unnoticed.

"What's up?" I ask, trying to sound casual.

"Fuck you, fuck him, fuck her, fuck the world, fuck Caroline, fuck Diane, and most all fuck…" She stops. "Whoever's left."

She stomps past me and is about to reach for the handle on her bedroom door when she whirls. "You know what I don't understand?"

Annie doesn't lose her shit often. But this is the second time in as many weeks that I've seen her falling down. And even though I'm not really interested in her personal life, I've fallen down myself. Plenty of times. And I know where it can lead if you don't pull yourself back up real fucking fast. So I say, "What?" and actually mean it.

"What's the point?"

"Of…?" I'm confused.

"Life, Maddie. What. Is. The fucking point?"

"Ummm…" I have to stop and consider this for a moment. Because I think we all know, there is no point, right? You're just here. You do shit. And then you're not here. "Get rich?" I say.

She frowns, then busts into a laugh I didn't expect. "Get rich," she repeats. "It's as good a goal as any, right?"

I shrug. "Why not? I mean, at least when you're rich you can stop worrying about stupid things like rent."

"And new tires for your car," Annie adds.

"And food."

"And how to pay back your pimp." She sighs.

I walk over to her and take her hand. "Is that what this is about? You owe Kimberly money?"

Annie swallows hard and shakes her head. "No. Not Kimberly."

"You have another pimp?" I ask.

"It was supposed to be a step up, right? This guy, he runs some really high-class girls in all the best hotels. I just figured… at least I wouldn't end up at the edge of town calling you to come pick me up, right? It would be safer. And swankier. And sweeter."

I make a face at that last part.

"Kimberly set me up with him."

"What? How's that work? I mean, do pimps lend out their girls like that?" I'm not really up on hooker etiquette.

"These two do. That's the whole reason I took the job with Kimberly in the first place. It was as a stepping stone. I didn't really lie when I told you I was a high-class call girl. I just… fast-forwarded my life a little."

I'm so out of my league right now. There are stepping stones in the prostitute business. Who knew? "So what happened?"

"I have to pay him rent, right?"

"Oh, like me and the stage fee. Sure, I get it."

"Well, I walked out on a customer a few nights ago, so they docked me that night and gave me a penalty."

"Penalty? Is that legal?"

"Who gives a fuck if it's legal? I owe them two grand and I don't have it."

She sighs heavily and then disappears into her room. Not with the slam she surely intended before her little impromptu confession. Just a small, sad *click*.

My angel pops up on my shoulder.

I know right where this is headed.

You should give her that money, Scarlett. She needs it.

"*I* need it," I say back. "And stop fucking calling me Scarlett."

You need it more than she does, Maddie, my little devil says. *You earned it, chick. You sucked—*

"Yeah," I say, brushing them both away and walking towards the laundry room to get my t-shirt. "I did earn it. And I do need it. So both of you can just shut the fuck up."

But the whole time I'm getting ready for work I'm thinking about that money. Like… it's far from the worst thing that's ever happened to me, but it has consumed my thoughts. Taken over my week. And made me think about that guy—a fucking customer, for Christ's sake—to the point of distraction.

And at the same time, it did save my ass. I paid my rent to Raven and my rent to Annie. I don't even have two grand left, ya know? I bought groceries, and gas, and—

And now you have what you need, my angel says. *So give the rest to Annie. Because she needs it or bad things might happen to her.*

Bad things? My devil laughs. *She's a fucking whore. Of course bad things are gonna happen to her. And it's not like she can't get another job. She's an engineer, right? If she doesn't want to have sex for money, she doesn't have to. Just go be an engineer.*

The angel and the devil are now arguing past me. Like I'm not even here. Little bastards.

She barely graduated, says the angel.

So we're supposed to give a fuck, just because she's stupid? the devil says.

I interrupt, "She's not stupid, she—" The angel ignores me and continues.

She has the degree, but not the skills, or the contacts, or the résumé.

Yeah, the devil says, *and whose fucking fault is that? Dumbass Annie's. Maddie here was the goddamn salutatorian of her high-school class! Probably coulda come outta college* summa cum laude—*or at least* magna! *But life fucked her right in the ass! And not in the good way! None of the shit that's happened is her fault! So why should she have to pay for someone else's fuckup?*

"Guys," I try to interrupt.

You're cruel, says the angel.

Yeah, no fucking shit, you ignorant twat, I'm a devil. Christ. You're as stupid as that cunt, Annie.

"Hey—" I try again. But they're on a roll.

Have you no compassion? Annie has had to prostitute herself to survive, sings the angel.

Oh, boo fucking hoo, the devil chimes in. *Life's been so hard for poor fucking Annie the Whore. She's stupid and her pussy hurts. Wah, wah, wah. Fuck her. If that's the worst thing she ever has to deal with—*

It's not a competition! the angel shouts.

It better not be! screams the devil. *'Cause if it was, chick standing right here would smoke that bitch! Ain't nobody more tragic than poor, sad, lonely fucking Maddie!*

"Shut up!" I shout.

Then I open up my sock drawer and fish around for my cash. I find it, pull it out, count it up. Eleven hundred and seventy-two dollars.

I stare at it.

I did shameful things for this money. Things I never thought I'd do. Things that make me feel bad about myself. Things that would make my parents wonder where they went wrong and how it's all their fault I have failed at everything.

It's not their fault. Everything that has happened to me is because I fell down. Fell hard. Hit my head on the way down that dark rabbit hole of grief and despair and fucked my brain up. And then I just… turned into this. It's not. It's not their fault. It's nobody's fault but mine.

I sigh, feeling sad, and lonely, and really, really wishing I had it in me to give up.

But I don't. I'm just one of those fighters. One of those people who loves to punish themselves and keep going. The kind of person who makes it to the top of Mount Everest on tenacity alone, but loses all ten fingers to frostbite.

I take the money and walk across the house to Annie's room.

That's right, my angel says. *Good for you, Scarlett. Annie isn't like you. Annie is falling down and she won't get back up. She'll stay down in that dark hole forever. You're doing the right thing. I'm proud of you.*

"Go fuck yourself," I say.

I approach Annie's door and knock quietly. "Annie?"

"Go away," she says. I can tell she's crying. She's making those little hiccupy sounds.

I turn the handle, find it unlocked, and open the door. "I have some extra money," I say, holding out my handful of cash. "It's only eleven hundred, but you can have it."

She wipes the tears from her eyes and stares at me. Then she shakes her head and starts crying again. "I can't take it. I'd hate myself if I took your money, Maddie. I know you don't have any extra. You're lying. You need it and I did this and—"

I toss the cash onto her bed. "I don't want it," I say. "I did something I'm not proud of to get it and I can't keep it. Not if I want to live with myself. So please, just take it. Use it to pay back whoever this guy is. And then don't get in that situation again, OK? I worry about you,

Annie. I know we've never been that close. You and Diane and Caroline have been friends forever and I'm just some new girl who fills up a spare room in your house. But I like you. So take it."

Annie stares at me. Tears blurring her blue eyes. Filling them up over and over again as long streams run down her cheeks. "He's engaged," she finally says.

"Who?"

She waves her hand in the air, like she's trying to erase that last statement, and then cries harder.

"Who's engaged?" I ask again.

"My high-school boyfriend."

"Oh," I say. And suddenly the big picture comes into focus. "Back in Nebraska."

"Iowa." She sniffs.

"Right," I say. "Iowa. So that's why you're so down?" I ask.

She nods, wiping wildly at her tear-stained face. "He called to tell me. He wanted me to know because…" She draws in a deep breath. "Because we dated for four years. I was gonna marry him. But then I decided to go to UNLV for college and he wanted to stay in Iowa, so I left. And we tried to make it work that first semester, ya know? The long-distance thing. But I found another guy, so I broke it off. It wasn't even him who left me, Maddie. It was me who left him. Twice! What the fuck was I thinking?"

I don't know what to say. I mean, I do. I want to pat myself on the back. Congratulate myself for not fucking things up with love. But that won't be helpful to Annie. So I say, "I've never been in love. Not true love, at least."

"Really?" she asks, looking up at me all snotty and blotched, weird hope in her eyes. Misery loves company.

"Yeah. Really. I mean when I was younger I had this—" I sigh, because that's a long, sad story for another time. "Doesn't matter. But look, I know loss. Y'know? Like really know loss, so I get it, Annie. Maybe you should just go home one last time and tell him how you feel?"

"Don't you think I want to?" she says. "But then I'd be the horrible other woman out to ruin his marriage. I can't do it. I won't do it. So I'm just gonna stay here in Vegas and deal with the life I've made for myself. That's all we're doing, right? Me, you, Caroline, Diane. We're just a bunch of fuckups who have to deal with what we've done."

Her words echo in my head the whole way to Pete's. *We're just a bunch of fuckups who have to deal with what we've done.*

Truth.

I hate to admit it, but everything that's happening to me now is my own damn fault. I've never wanted to play the victim and blame anyone else for my problems, but on some insidious level, that's exactly what I've been doing.

I pass by a billboard for a show tonight and wince as I see the date.

Why do I constantly have to be reminded of what the date is? Does the universe think I'm oblivious? Do my parents think I'm oblivious? I know what the fucking date is. I know what's coming up. It's burned into my brain like a goddamned brand.

I think I was drunk for eleven days straight, but it might've been twelve, or fourteen, or quite possibly an entire month.

All I know is that the world I lived in—the *reality* I lived in—stopped. Just ceased to exist. Then a new world emerged. The one where my parents moved to France. The one where I was left here in Vegas to half-stumble my way through college, determined to finish no matter what. The one that started this ball of bullshit rolling downhill.

And every year I relive it on the anniversary.

I typically get drunk. It's like… normal now. Just what I do to cope. But I have to work next weekend, so maybe that will take my mind off things?

Maybe? Hopefully?

I arrive at Pete's right on time, but that means I'm two minutes late by the time I walk past Raven's scowling face and enter the dressing room.

"You must really want me to fire you, huh, angel?"

I scowl at her new nickname. Bitch. But then I adjust—the way I always do—and smile. "Sorry, Raven. It won't happen again."

She squints her eyes at my retreat.

But what's the point? Why try to win this fight with Raven? She's no one, right? She's not in control of my future. Sure, I need this job. More than ever, actually. But it's not like there aren't a million other places in this world where I can take off my clothes for money. Hell, I'm not even close to the bottom of the barrel as far as adult entertainment goes. I'm practically a whore now. I did suck that guy's cock for money last weekend. I'm one baby step away from becoming Annie.

Maybe that's why I took up with her in the first place? It's a way to justify my fall from grace, right? She's setting an example of how much farther away the bottom is.

"It better not," Raven snaps. "I'm so sick of your shit. And I told Pete what you've been doing."

"What?" I say, a wave of panic rushing through my body. "What did you tell him?"

"Flashing your pussy *on stage*. He was pissed."

I gulp a breath of air. "What did he say?" I ask, serious.

"He said if you do that again, you're out. If it were me, I'd have shown you the door already. But he's sweet like that. And I'm not. And he's the boss, and I'm not. So you get one more chance. One, Scarlett. Got it?"

"Got it," I say. I should really tip that waitress who covered for me last weekend. If she tells them what I did with the beard guy, I'm fucked. And even though I hate this job, the thought of going out there to find another, equally degrading—possibly more degrading—job like this just makes me feel ill.

"And don't fuck around in here, either. Get changed and get your ass out on the floor."

I open my backpack and realize that my last-minute talk with Annie distracted me from my pre-work routine and the only outfit I have is the one from last week.

The fucking angel.

I sigh as I take it out and give it a sniff. It smells.

"Here," Raquel says, handing me a bottle of her perfume.

"Thanks," I say. "I'm so off my game right now." I spritz a little on the costume and change, hoping I don't smell like a whore, but knowing I do.

We're just a bunch of fuckups who have to deal with what we've done.

Still true.

I slip on my shoes, twist my ankle as I rush out of the dressing room, and limp past Raven as I enter the floor.

She shakes her head at me like I'm a total disgrace to this fine establishment.

That's a new low, I think.

But I ravel up all my loose ends and get to work.

It's busy, thank you Jesus, and that's great for me, because I gave all my extra cash away to a friend in need.

It was the right thing to do, Scarlett, my angel says.

"Please suck my dick," I murmur back.

There's one, the little devil says. *He looks desperate and loaded. Go get him, Maddie.*

So I'm heading over there, my focus one hundred percent on emptying that guy's wallet—because when the devil gives you a tip, you work it, right?—when a hand grabs my arm and pulls me aside.

"Scarlett," a familiar voice whispers in my ear.

My heart thumps wildly as I recognize who it is.

"Carlos is out of patience. Says you need to pay him tonight, bitch. Or you're leaving here with me so the two of you can have a little come-to-Jesus moment about what happens next."

Logan is back.

And he brought a friend as backup.

Where the fuck is Otis when you need him? Oh, there he is. Chatting with the bartender, oblivious.

Great.

"Hey, Logan," I say, shooting him with my finger. Then I realize that might come off as a threat and tuck my hand away. "How about we talk about this later, huh? When I'm off work. And I can pay you then."

He shakes his head. Slowly. "No can do, pumpkin. Time's up. Go get the money right now, or we're getting in my car, driving out to the desert, and you're gonna have that chat with Carlos."

I suddenly get the feeling I might've underestimated how invested Carlos is in my fake debt to him.

But it all becomes clear now. Because Logan is pressing a gun to my side.

So I do what all tenacious Mount Everest climbers do. I reach deep, find another handhold in the sheer, rock wall, and pull myself up another inch.

I yank my arm from Logan's grip and I run.

CHAPTER TEN

TYLER

The car door opens. The car door closes. The car door opens. The car door closes.

It's not doing this by itself. It's not magic. I'm doing it. Because I am, it turns out, a gigantic pussy.

I open the door again. This time I manage to actually step out into the parking lot. One boot. Two boots. Just like the start of a Dr. Seuss story. If Dr. Seuss wrote stories about dudes showing up at strip clubs to basically stalk chicks who've given them blow jobs. Maybe he did. Seuss coulda been a freak. We don't know.

What the hell am I doing? I've gotten my panties in a bunch over some Pole Artisan (I'm gonna keep using it until it catches on, I've decided) I met once. That's insane. Unless it's not. Unless the whole dream-to-reality thing is actually happening to me. Unless she is my destiny. Is that an overstatement? Who cares? Is she? I don't know. But here's what I do know: I'm gonna just go in and see if she's there. And then I'm gonna see if she remembers me. And then I'm gonna see if she wants to go to a Halloween party with me and maybe be my steady lady friend. Because that's how I feel right now and because that's all totally logical and will tell me whether or not we're supposed to be matched for eternity, in Heaven and beyond. Right? Right.

Fuck. I'm an idiot.

The car door opens. I step back inside. One boot, two boots, to hell with strippers in their birthday suits. (Damn, that Seuss shit is harder than it looks. Then again, dude was a doctor, so…)

FUCK!

I bang my head against the steering wheel. I think that if I hit it hard enough maybe it'll shake my brain back into some semblance of order. But that's a big ask from a steering wheel. Shit. I need to just go to a club or casino or something, pick up some skanky tourists, and pump some action into their coin slots. *Here you go, baby. I got a one-armed bandit you can pull on.* Ha. That's not terrible.

I throw the car into reverse and pull out of the parking lot. They're doing roadwork on Fremont (they're always doing roadwork somewhere in Vegas—I swear to God those roadwork guys must be mobbed up. There's no way there's that much damn roadwork that needs to be done) so I pull around to the alley behind Pete's so I can take side streets back to the Strip, and that's when—bursting through the backdoor of the club—she appears.

I slam on the brakes and she looks right at me. Time slows for a second. The headlights wash her in an unearthly glow, painting her wings, halo, and milky, perfect skin in an incandescent amber. I might hear a harp playing. It's probably just a synthesizer in the EDM I have playing on the car stereo, but I don't care. It makes for a very dramatic moment.

I throw the Defender into park and jump out.

"Scarlett?" I say. Stupidly. Of course it's her.

"Ford?" she replies. Oh, right. I'm still Ford fucking Aston to this chick. What was I thinking? Jesus. But she remembers me! That's encouraging.

I take a step toward her to ask what she's doing running out into the alley when, through the back door from which my angel emerged, two guys come charging. They're both a pretty decent size. The one in front is dressed a little better than the one behind him, by which I mean he wears a button-down and a pair of brown oxfords with broguing on the toe-box, and the other guy just has on a t-shirt and sneakers, but still, it's amazing how a collared shirt and nice shoes can dress up a pair of dark denim jeans.

For whatever reason, Evan's voice is suddenly in my head.

But only for the briefest of moments, because then I see the gun and forget immediately about who's wearing what as it becomes crystal-clear why she was running out into the alley.

"Scarlett. Come on, sugar. It's time to come with us," says the one with the collared shirt. The one who's holding the gun. The guy behind him steps toward her as button-down keeps the gun held on my angel's perfect tits. Which is a crazy fucking thing to be noticing right now, but it's what pops into my head. And I have a really, *really* negative reaction to the barrel of that gun pointed at any part of her.

"Hey," I say, stepping toward all three of them. "Um. What the fuck?"

Button-down snaps and turns the gun in my direction now. All four of us are standing frozen in the spotlight being cast by the Defender's headlamps, the stars of a surreal little movie that's unfolding very rapidly here in this alley. Man, I hate being the center of attention, but right now I don't have a lotta choice.

"Get back in your car and drive away, pal. This ain't got nothing to do with you." This from a guy holding a revolver directed at my chest. Yeah, at this point it's got at least a little something to do with me.

"I'm not your fuckin' pal, and given the rocky start we're off to, I doubt we're gonna get there anytime soon." Oh, shit! That was what I wanted to say to the bartender last week. I'm glad I held on to it. This is so much better.

Out of the corner of my eye I see Scarlett look at me with some astonishment. I think it's astonishment. It's hard to get a read on everything going on right now, and I need to keep my focus on the weapon in front of me.

"Man," button-down says, "I'm not gonna tell you again…" He tightens his grip on the pistol and extends his elbow slightly for emphasis.

"No? You're not gonna tell me again? So what are you gonna do?" I take another step toward him. Meanwhile, his t-shirted backup boy steps my way in return.

Run, Scarlett. Now is the time. Just fucking run.

"Bro, you don't know what you've wandered into," says button-down. "I'm giving you one last chance. You don't know who you're fucking with."

I decide in for a penny in for a pound, so I take another step and say, "I'm not your bro either. And you don't know who YOU'RE fucking with. Meanwhile you're wearing brown shoes with a navy belt. Dude, I know EVERYTHING about you."

The confusion on his face is goddamn priceless. I can't see my angel, but I can feel her kind of smiling. I can just feel it.

Button-down gestures to t-shirt, who's clearly supposed to be the muscle, and who starts toward me with some purpose in his stride.

Run, Scarlett. Run.

But she doesn't run, and t-shirt is almost in my face.

So…OK… Here's the thing about circumstances like these. The most powerful person in a conflict situation is one hundred percent, unquestionably, and without fail the one who is able to de-escalate the mounting crisis.

After that, the second most powerful person in a conflict situation is the one who's able to land the first strike and put a motherfucker on his back.

I don't wait for t-shirt to reach me. I have long legs so it takes less than two full steps before I'm on him. I'm ambidextrous, which I've learned is handy in lots of instances in life. Juggling. Playing basketball. Knocking bitches the fuck out.

I feint with my left, but I do it hard so it looks like that's the punch that's coming, which causes him to dodge to his left, which is incredibly helpful because that means his momentum is already carrying him in the direction of my right fist that lands square on his eye socket and the bridge of his nose. I've been using that shot for years, and I don't give a shit who you are, when I land it as perfectly as I just did on this asshat, you're going night night.

And so he does. He hits the ground so hard that I'm actually a little worried about him. But only for a second. Because button-down is still holding his goddamn pistol, and it's now against my temple. Fuck me. I've been out of the military for too long. My situational awareness is for shit.

He cocks the hammer. "Buddy, I don't know who the fuck you are, but you just walked into a world of hurt."

I think about what I told Jeff last week on his birthday. The stuff about being a hero. The moment you try to play hero, you get yourself killed. But it's also important to understand the predicament you're in. It's critical to be able to read the environment. And I didn't do four goddamn tours in some of the most hostile environments on earth by being the kind of person who scares easy. So I assess what I can about this circumstance, glance over at Scarlett, who looks pretty freaked out (which is appropriate—I'd be concerned if she didn't), turn to face the barrel of the gun, and look button-down dead in his weaselly eyes.

"Yeah… Man, I LIVE in a world of hurt, so anything you can do right now to help me find my way out of it will be a fucking improvement."

We stare at each other. I press my forehead into the barrel of his stupid gun. *Just do it, man. Just fucking do it. Come on. Just fucking make the sounds inside my head stop.*

"DO IT!" I almost surprise myself by how loud I scream. I know I surprise button-down, because he flinches. And when he does, I grab the gun out of his hand and punch him as hard as I can in the stomach. He doubles over and now I press the gun against HIS temple.

"Ford!" Scarlett yells. "Don't!"

I look at her with a look that says, *I'm not gonna. Relax.* And I wink. She doesn't know what to make of that. Which, again, is fucking awesome.

I lean down close to button-down so I can whisper in his ear.

"So, since Scarlett asked nicely, I'm gonna do what she wants. But I swear on my mother's soul, if you ever come near her again, I will beat you until you're begging me to finish you and then I will take you and leave your bleeding body in the desert for the snakes and vultures to take their fucking turns. Do. You. Hear. What I am saying?"

Button-down looks like he's about to choke on his own rage. Which I'm really grateful for because it means he's got some fight in him. There is nothing more inexcusable than taking down somebody you know you can take down. There's no honor in it. In fairness, I could've taken down both of these idiots with an arm tied behind my back while competing in a potato sack race, but it still helps to know he's got moxie. (I'm gonna bring back moxie too. Just like I'm gonna make Pole Artisan a thing.) But finally he nods, grudgingly.

"Great. Now get up, get your girlfriend, and get the fuck outta here."

I help him to his feet. T-shirt is out cold, still bathed in the lights from the Defender. I pick him up and hand him to button-down, who awkwardly takes him under the arms and tries to lumber with him down the alley and around into the parking lot. It takes forever. There's a moment where I almost think I should run up and help the guy. ("Here. Let me give you a hand. It was me who fucked you both up and all. Sheesh. So sorry.")

As they round the corner, out of sight, I turn around to see if Scarlett is still there. She is. Where she's standing the lights are bouncing off her wings, casting a massive shadow that looks like a butterfly on the wall of the building behind her. I don't know what to make of the look on her face. I really don't. I'm expecting her to ask any number of questions, starting with 'what are you doing here?' That's sure as hell what I would ask if someone showed up and pounded the crap out of two guys who were chasing me with a gun.

Wait. Two guys were chasing her with a gun. That actually seems like the more important issue to address. WHY were two guys chasing her with a gun? A gun that I am now holding. Great. I'm holding a gun. Which means I have to get rid of the gun. I suppose I could keep it, but who knows what awful shit has been done with this gun? Nothing, probably. That's the whole reason I felt like I could take it away from the guy. He threatened me like three times. I've been stabbed, blown up, and shot at more times than I can count and never once in any of those cases did anyone give me a heads-up. If your intention is to kill someone, you kill them. You don't give them a chance to walk away. Most people don't get that. In my experience, ninety-nine percent of all threats are hollow. Anyway… I think I'm rambling.

Scarlett (I have to find out her real name. I wonder if she'll tell me now that I've saved her life and all) steps toward me, carefully. I reach into the cab, stick the gun in the glove box, and move around the front of the car to meet her. She shakes her head just the slightest bit, like she can't understand what just happened. That's fair. I can't either.

I speak before she has a chance. "Are you OK?"

She nods and takes another step closer to me. She's close enough that I can smell her now. She smells amazing. Different than before, but still amazing. Like perfume, and sweat, and fear, and salvation.

I ask the obvious question. "Who were those—?"

Or I should say I start to ask the obvious question because before I get all the words out, she's on top of me, my back against the Defender, her tongue in my mouth, her hand down my pants, and the shadow of her wings flapping in time with the grinding of her body against mine.

MADDIE

It's almost an out-of-body experience. That's my theory. Because… because… it can't be real. It just can't be real. I can't be doing this. I'm not running from a kingpin's henchmen, Ford didn't save me, my tongue is not in his mouth desperately kissing him and wanting him, and my hand is not on his dick, squeezing as I push myself forward looking for… *more.*

But all that is happening. And all this is happening too, because now his hand is pulling my costume down and the night air hits my nipple, making it peak and bunch up as his fingers brush across it. And then we're walking—he's pushing me backwards. And I don't even feel the pain from my twisted ankle or wonder if I'm gonna trip or anything like that because… because he'll catch me. If I fall, this guy is gonna catch me. And it's such a relief to just let all the bullshit go and trust someone for once. I don't even have words. Or the time to think them up. Because he's got his hands under my thighs and he's lifting me up, and holding me close, and I can feel the ragged edges of the brick building cutting into my back and I *don't care.* I might be bleeding or fucking dying right now, and I just don't care.

I close my eyes when he pulls back, wishing he wouldn't do that, but then I forget about it and think about what he's doing next. Because his lips are on my neck and he's biting the skin behind my ear, and breathing into my hair, and he says, "I'm gonna fuck you now. So…"

And then he's done too. We're both just on some kind of collision course. We're crashing into each other in a way that's familiar, but new, and still dangerous. And then I see the gun again in my head, and the way he moved so fast and took people out. The way he hurt them and I know, I just feel, deep down in my filthy fucking soul, that he's gonna hurt me too, and I don't care. I just don't fucking care. Because that hurt is gonna be worth it, and I'm gonna live for once. Like really fucking live for once. And when we spin out of control later—next week, or next year, or next lifetime—I will look back and say, "I'd do it all again."

And it's stupid.

But I don't care.

So I say, "Do it."

TYLER

The way she says, "Do it," sends me into a frenzy. It's almost an order. And maybe it's my military training kicking into gear or more probably it's just that her rasping, anxious voice is the sexiest thing I've ever heard, but every single part of me is at full command and ready to follow orders.

I lift her higher and press her wings harder into the rough wall. I raise her so I can get my mouth around her gorgeous breasts. Wrapping my lips around the right one, I allow my tongue to skitter over her nipple. I draw my mouth back, sucking as I go, letting my teeth graze her skin just lightly enough so that she can feel the edges. Careful not to tickle, not to bite, just torture in the best way.

I can taste the sweat and the fear and the relief. I can taste it all. And I immediately wonder how the rest of her must taste. She's still pumping my dick, reaching, straining, almost like she's afraid to let go, and that has popped open the top button of my jeans so that my cock is throbbing in the night air, urging me to thrust myself inside her now. But I can't. Not just yet. I need to know what the rest of her tastes like first.

The pool of light from the Defender's headlamps is behind us, leaving us hidden in the shadows. Known only to each other. Cast in the faint, blue glow of an October desert moon.

I look up at her through my eyelids and she stares back down, swallowing, chest heaving, gulping for breath. I don't say anything, just begin to lower her slowly to the ground, allowing her long legs to land on the concrete.

With her shoes on she's almost as tall as I am. We stare at each other nearly eye to eye and she swallows one more time, her eyes closing as I bend my knees to lower myself down her stomach, kissing lightly as I go. I stop for a second and tickle her belly button with my tongue. She shudders as though a bolt of electricity has shot through her. I love that, so I stay there for a moment longer, letting my tongue make circles on her sweet and salty skin before I begin lowering her G-string from her hips and sliding it down her thighs, over her knees, down, down to her ankles, where she steps gingerly away from the fabric, first with her left foot, then her right, leaving herself exposed to me.

One high heel. Two high heels. I'm going to fuck an angel and know how that feels.

I lift my gaze to look up at her face one more time. Her head is back, her eyes are closed, and I hear a moan of yearning as I press my mouth forward and she feels my warm breath on the entrance of her beautiful, bare pussy.

The world has disappeared. We are not in an alley behind a strip club. We are on a cloud. High above everyone and everything. We are ascending. And I am intent on taking her higher and higher until the earth falls far away and we are both transported from the poison and pain of this small world.

At least for a moment.

I gently kiss the inside of her thighs. First the right, then the left. Then I nuzzle my nose against the soft, already wet space between her legs. I breathe in deep, taking in every bit of the way she smells. I can't get enough. I want to bury my face inside of her warmth and let her become my oxygen.

I can't get close enough down on my knees as I am, so I grab her around the waist, throw her legs over my shoulders, and rise up to my full height so that I can keep her placed directly above my greedy mouth.

I flick my tongue against the folds of her opening and her knees shudder. So I lick more slowly—I don't want her to come just yet—parting her wider with my fingers and letting my tongue slide inside. She tastes even better than she smells. Like the ocean on a perfect summer day.

I find her clit and wrap the whole of my mouth around it, building up pressure on her with my tongue and pulling back until I hear her say, "Oh, my God. Oh, my God, what are you doing to me?" And now I'm sucking and smiling at the same time.

I pull my mouth off long enough to look up and say, "Just getting started…"

MADDIE

He better just be getting started. Because I want more.

His hand slips around the curve of my ass, squeezing it so hard, I bite my lip to stifle a whimper. His fingers press into my skin, grabbing hold of me like he might never let go.

His tongue laps against my pussy, then flicks my clit. I fist his hair and let my head fall back—pressing against the brick wall. He does this little move with his tongue. Teasing me as he swirls it around, presses his mouth firmly against my clit, and moves it back and forth so quick, I drop a hand down to his shoulder and dig my nails in. Like I might never let go either.

It's been a while for me. Too long, really. And I can feel the climax building and building, and then—

"Not yet, angel," he murmurs.

"Yes," I say, insistent. "Now. We're in the alley and there's people—"

"There's no people," he counters. "And I want to be inside you when you come. I want you to be fucked as much as possible before I let you finish."

"Ford," I say. I really need this guy's real name. I can't keep calling him that. Especially during sex. "We gotta hurry. I'm at work and—"

"You're not at work. You're with me, Scarlett."

And I really need to tell him my name too. Because I feel like I'm morphing into Scarlett. This is the kind of thing she does, not me.

Isn't it?

He lifts my legs, still pushing me against the wall, repositions them so they drape over the crook in his arms. He's holding both ass cheeks, squeezing them hard and pressing against me with his hard cock. But we're eye level and I'm looking at him like… like we're *something*. Like maybe I am with him.

He grins. A devilish, mischievous grin. Says, "How do you like it?"

"Like it?" I say, my eyes darting around to make sure no one can see us.

"Scarlett," he says, demanding my attention. "Look at me. And tell me how you like to be fucked."

"Uhhh… good."

He laughs. "Roger that. Anything else?"

"Just…" I start. Because I'm not really into the dirty-talking shit. I'm not into alley sex, or wall sex, or giving blow jobs for money. But I've done all those things since I met him. *Last. Fucking. Weekend.*

So fuck it. I'm Scarlett now, I guess.

"Hard," I say. "I like it hard."

He smiles.

"And dirty."

"Filthy?" he asks. "Or just dirty?"

I take a moment to wonder how much difference there is between filthy and dirty.

"Scarlett," he says, pushing his stiff cock up to the entrance of my pussy. God, I'm wet. And the way he's teasing me has my whole body trembling. "Tell me how to fuck you. Because if you don't, you're just gonna have to get it the way I like to give it."

Jesus Christ.

But it leaves me an opening. So I take it and say, "Give it to me like that then."

A finger is suddenly pressing up against my asshole. I gasp in surprise. Surely he is not thinking about fucking me in the ass *here*?

He reads the panic on my face and shoots me that devilish grin again. "No. Not yet. Just exploring my options."

Oh, shit.

I swallow hard. His eyes track right to my throat and I know, I just *know*, he's thinking about what I did. How I took his cock in my mouth last weekend. How I took him deep and swallowed it all down when he came.

"Do you want me to stop?" he asks.

"Stop? Jesus, no. Fuck no."

"Then start telling me what to do. Because if someone does come through that door and I'm not done, we're still gonna have to finish. Bank on that shit."

OK, I get it. He likes to call the shots. And even though it might appear that he's asking me what I want so he can give it to me, what he's really doing is taking me out of my comfort zone so he can control me.

It's gonna piss me off later when I think this whole thing through. But now… fuck it.

I squirm until he drops one of my legs, and then I take his free hand, press it right up against my pussy, and begin to rub myself with the pad of his thumb.

"Now put your cock inside me," I say. "And don't stop rubbing until I scream. That's how I like it."

TYLER

Goddamn. Goddamn! GOD MOTHERFUCKING DAMN! Normally I'm the maestro of talking dirty and women just giggle or act all coy and shit. Scarlett (fuck, I GOTTA find out her name) is giving just as good as she gets. In every way. I'm not thinking anymore, I'm just reacting. And honestly, that's got me almost as hot as everything else that's happening. It feels so fucking good to be free of my thoughts and just… here. I want to do what she wants. Because it's also what I want. I want to make her scream.

"Done," I say.

But I don't want to scrape up her bare back any more than I already have on the rough brick wall, so I drop her other leg. Grab her by the shoulder. Spin her around. Pin her arms to the wall in front of her. Almost rip my pants in half getting them down below my knees and grab her by the hips as I pull her ass back hard and push myself forward, sliding my dick inside her wet, warm, perfect pussy.

"Oh, fuck, oh, fuck, oh, my fucking God, oh, fuck," she cries out.

It makes me smile.

I reach around in front of her so that I can keep rubbing her clit like I was ordered. Like a good soldier.

"Yes, yes, yes," she gasps as I rub in small, frantic circles with my index and middle finger.

I want to grab her hair. I want to pull on it hard, yanking her neck back and forcing her eyes up to the night sky. But she's still wearing that wig and I'm afraid I'll tug it off and fuck everything up and destroy the perfection that is this moment.

So instead, I slap her ass hard with the back of my left hand and she squeals. I love it. It makes me even harder, if that's possible. And now I take the thumb of my left hand and stick it in her ass again. I'm fingering her clit, playing with her asshole, and driving myself back and forth inside her at the same time.

"Oh, Jesus, stop, no, don't stop," she contradicts herself, and I smile.

I smile because she's moaning and panting and very nearly on the verge of coming all over my dick, but there's one thing she doesn't know, and that's that I'm not all the way inside her yet. I've been holding back just enough. Just far enough for her to feel almost all of me, but not quite. But now I'm ready to give her the whole thing.

I accelerate the rubbing on her sweet pussy and then in one hard thrust, I push myself inside her all the way, driving my thumb into her ass and manically rubbing on her clit…

… And she explodes.

She screams so loudly that for a moment I believe she'll pierce through the pounding bass that's thudding from inside the club, sending the whole place racing out the back door to see what's going on.

And I don't give. A. Fuck. Let them see. Let everyone see. Let the whole fucking world know that right now, for just this one moment, I'm happy.

I pause just for a second, long enough to ask, "So did you come?"

She turns her head over her left shoulder and sees me smiling. I slow everything down. I move my hand away from her clit. I take my other hand away from her ass. I stop thrusting inside her and am just… joined with her. She shakes her head the tiniest bit like she can't believe…

I'm not sure. I choose to think she shakes her head like she can't believe what a swell fucking guy I am. Then she just coughs out, "Fuck you."

"No. You," I respond.

I grab her hips and thighs with both hands and I start again. This time not with any extra tricks or subtlety, just pure, raw, unrestrained fucking. Pounding myself into her from behind again and again and again and again. Forcing my whole self into her whole self. The grunting whine she makes with each push just drives me to try to push harder.

"Oh, God. Oh, my God," she pants, "I'm going to come again."

"Do it," I say. "Do it. Come. Come all over me. Cover me with it. Fucking wash me in you."

I don't know if it's just because I'm so good at fucking or if it's because I said some shit that turned her on or if it's the thrill and danger of this whole insane night, or probably all of the above, but she does. She comes again. She orgasms like I've never felt a woman orgasm before. Her walls clench around me like a vise. She practically chokes my shaft with her pussy and her legs shudder so hard that I'm sure if she falls now, she'll drag me to the ground with her, cock first. So I pull back and hold her up, resting deep inside her until she stops shaking and quivering.

"Go. Fuck yourself," she whispers.

"No way. This is better."

She drops her chin to her shoulder so that I can see her profile grinning and I almost shoot myself inside her right there. She must feel me holding it back somehow, because she starts, "Will you…?"

She stops and bites her lip. Holy shit, she is going to be the end of me.

I prompt her. "What? I mean the answer is likely 'yes,' but what?"

"Will you… come on my ass? Please?"

Jesus Christ. The lip-biting was nothing. It's the 'please' that almost fucking kills me.

"That's what you want?" I summon the presence of mind to ask.

She nods her head in a way that conveys, *Yes. No. I'm not sure. But yes.*

And then I do something that I'm not expecting. Not even a little. I reach around her waist with both arms, wrapping her in a hug as I pull my chest down to the wings on her back and I kiss her on the shoulder, right by where she has her head turned to see me. I feel a small exhalation of breath whisper past my nose as my lips touch her skin.

And here, in this back alley behind a strip club, my pants around my ankles, her in heels, angel wings, and a ribbon of cloth now pushed below her breasts that constitutes what's left of her outfit, with the possibility that drunk, horny tourists or men with guns could walk up on us at any second… it feels like the sweetest, purest, kindest moment that I can remember having in my life maybe since I was a kid. And I have no idea why that's true. It just is.

So I savor it. I savor this brief tick of the clock like it's already a memory that I can call on when I want to think back to a time when I was happy.

And then I lift my chest up, draw my hips back, and begin pumping in and out of her again so that in a few seconds, I can shoot my load all over her pretty ass.

MADDIE

He's so fucking deep that I can feel him in my stomach. And I've stopped caring about what this says about me or what it means that I'm fucking a guy whose name I don't know in a back alley. All I know is that I feel good, and present, and *needed.* And I didn't even know I needed to feel needed, but I do. I am important to this person. Right now, for whatever it's worth, I am somebody to somebody else.

"Fuck," he grunts out, "I'm gonna come."

"Do it," I say. "Do it. Come on me. Let it all out. On me. Now." He pulls out and I order him once more, a little more forcefully, "Do it!"

And suddenly I feel warmth landing on my ass and hips and the backs of my legs. Jesus. It just keeps coming and coming, spilling over my skin.

I love it.

I take a peek and see him fisting his cock, the last bits of his sticky, hot come pulsing out of the thick tip of his dick and (I can't fucking believe this) I come one more time. Three times in like ten minutes. Holy shit. Who is this man who has forced his way into my life? And he has. Forced himself. Because he is. A force.

I moan again as my legs shiver and shake, and he moans as he drains himself dry. Then, both of us empty and shaking, he lets out a breath and says, "Thanks." Which I find kind of amazingly adorable and I'm not sure why.

So, "You're welcome," I say through a dumb smile I can't stop from spreading.

He laughs and slaps me right on my ass. And then he says, "Shit."

"What?" I ask. "What happened?"

"I got come all over my hand. Holy shit. Did I do all that?" I crane my head to see him staring at his handiwork and the look on his face is one of wonder and maybe pride.

Men.

"Yep. You sure must have," I say as I turn around, take his come-covered hand in mine, and place his fingers in my mouth.

"Jesus Christ," he says as I suck his salty semen from his strong fingers. "You're going to fucking kill me."

I just smile in return. Because who knows? Maybe I will. Maybe we'll kill each other.

And just then… the back door opens. Raven sticks her head out. He pushes me back, up against the wall, into the corner, lost in the shadows. She looks left, looks right. Please, oh, dear Lord, do not come out here to look around. "Scarlett?" she calls out.

He puts his head against mine and tries not to laugh. I want to punch him because I am definitely not laughing. Raven sees the abandoned Defender sitting in the middle of the alley, its lights still on. She walks over to it to look inside and we recess ourselves as deep into the dark as we can. I can feel the come sliding down the backs of my thighs and a thought occurs to me:

THIS. IS. FUCKING. INSANE.

"Scarlett?" Raven calls out into the night. *Just go back inside, Raven. Please. Just go back in.*

I close my eyes and pray to whoever might be listening to just have her turn around and head back in. Just please let me get away from this with my job intact.

That's what I'm praying for. Not to preserve my dignity or my modesty or my integrity or decency or anything that ends in 'y.' I just don't want to lose my J-O-

B. That's all I can think about and suddenly—I feel ashamed.

But whoever is out there listening to my plea decides to cut me a break, because Raven takes one last look around and heads back inside. It then occurs to me that she may have seen me run out back before (or someone may have) and that, coupled with an ominous-looking all-black Land Rover just idling in the alley, might just send up some alarm bells. So I need to get the hell back in there ASAP and make up some fucking excuse about where I've been. I put my hands on his chest and push him away.

"Um. I gotta go." I bend down, grab up my t-back, and start to step into it when I realize. "Shit. Do you have anything I can clean myself up with?"

"Uh," he says, looking around. "Uh, here." He pulls off his t-shirt and hands it to me. And I see the scars. Again. Oh, right. He said I don't want to know. OK. I do a quick inventory of all the information I currently have about this dude.

—He walks around looking like he's homeless but clearly has money to burn.

—He has scars all over his body that I don't want to know about.

—He fights men with guns like he doesn't care if he lives or dies.

—He may think I'm REALLY an angel. Which may make him A CRAZY PERSON.

—He probably has an actual name but I have no idea what it is.

—He fucks better than anyone I've ever met.

—I haven't been able to stop thinking about him.

Assessment: *This guy is bad news.*

I don't know what the hell I've been thinking or why I haven't been able to get him off my mind, but that shit stops right now. I grab the t-shirt from his hand and contort myself to try to wipe myself clean. Which, at present, feels like it's gonna take a lot of scrubbing and a long, long time.

"Do you want some help?" He reaches to give me a hand. I pull away.

"Nope. Got it. Thanks." I keep wiping. I just want to get the hell back inside. Back inside Pete's Strip Club. Where life makes sense.

I finish getting all of him off all of me to the best of my ability, wipe my hands, throw the shirt back at him, pull my panties up, fix my top back over my tits, adjust my filthy fucking angel wings, and look him square in his eyes. Which look confused. And maybe a little sad. Like a kid who's just dropped his ice cream cone on the sidewalk.

The way they did last weekend.

And that annoys me a little bit because… because I lost that night. And now it's happening again. This isn't me. It's not. I don't do this shit. And I know things have been hard, but that's not why I'm doing it. That's not why I'm all of a sudden losing my shit. It's… He's still looking at me like that. "What? I demand.

"I—Nothing," he mumbles.

"OK. Well, then, I gotta go. See ya." I pat him on the shoulder and head back in. Because this has to end. Now. I cannot lose myself to this fucking sadness again. I can't. Because if I do, no one's gonna pick me back up. Not this guy, for sure. He's not gonna catch me when I stumble. He's not gonna give me a hand up when I fall. He's just some random weirdo who stumbled into my life at just the wrong moment, but that's it. Random. There's no purpose to what we're doing other than survival.

And I can't go into survival mode again. I refuse to climb Everest again. I won't do it. Because if I have to scale that rock wall one more time I'll lose more than just my fingers. I'll lose every single part of me that's left.

"Hey," he calls out. Shit. *Don't. Whatever it is, just… don't. Just let me go.*

I sigh. Turn back. "Yeah?" I say, still annoyed.

"I don't… Do you have plans for Halloween?"

And at that, any feeling of anything good that I have left drains immediately from inside me. There are a lot of reasons for that, but the biggest one is that I am reminded, with startling clarity, that the most essential reason to stay away from this guy is that he knows NOTHING about me. And I can see no scenario now where changing that relationship would be a positive move. Because my life is being held together by the most fragile of adhesives, and that's sheer will. And this… situation… saps my strength. It tugs at my ability to hold it all together. And I am one hundred percent sure that if I take it even the smallest step further, my world is likely to be blown completely apart by this other human being. Blown to smithereens. I don't know how I know that. But I do. So I let any light in my eyes dim itself out and I stare straight through him and say…

"Thanks again for the help. Take care."

And then I open the door to the club, step inside, let the door close behind me, raise my chin up, and head off to give lap dances and make men think I'm in love with them.

CHAPTER ELEVEN

TYLER

"Thanks again for the help." *"Thanks AGAIN for the help."* Was she thanking me for the sex? Handling the guys chasing her? Both? Does it matter? She dismissed me. I can't blame her. I do that shit to women all the time. I wonder if it's because she knows that I'm gonna burn her Heaven down. She may sense that I'm bottled lightning. Of course she does. She's an angel. They're omnipotent. I think. Are they? They gotta be. They've got that great vantage point from up there in the clouds. I wonder if—

"Has the Klonopin helped at all?"

Oh. Right. That's Dr. Eldridge talking. It's... some day of the week. I'm just not certain which. Or what happened since the other night. Which is something I'm getting used to. I only know I haven't stopped thinking about the alley and Scarlett. But other than that? Shit. I mean, I literally couldn't say how I got here today.

But I am. Here. I'm sitting in front of the doc in her gorgeous office that somehow manages to always feel sunny. I've been to some other places—y'know, the ones where some dipshit shrink gets together with a bunch of other dipshit shrinks and they all buddy up to share a space, everyone with their own little room? Blech. Dr.

Eldridge don't play that shit. She bought a HOUSE. An entire house just to see patients like me. The fucked-up and rich kind. (I still can't wrap my head around the fact that I'm rich. But I am. So fuck it. I'll see a fancy shrink in a fancy shrink house.)

I do know that I've blown off my last couple appointments with her, but decided to keep this one because… I'm not sure. A bunch of reasons, I suppose. Because I can't stop thinking about Scarlett (even though I'm not gonna talk about Scarlett and what happened in the alley with the gun and the fight and the fucking). Because Halloween is this weekend, and Scotty died on Halloween (even though I'm not gonna talk about Scotty and how even though Evan says it isn't, it still feels like it's my fault). Because I'm really, really fucking lonely and feel like I'll always be that way (even though I'm definitely not gonna talk about that).

But I guess mostly I'm here now because Dr. Eldridge is nice and I feel like I owe it to her to show up every now and again so she'll feel like she's helping me. Kinda the same way I wanted to give the doctors in the hospital what I felt like they needed when they showed me my scars. I don't know what it is with me and wanting doctors to feel OK about themselves. Maybe it's because med school is expensive and they should all think the money they spent was worth something. Who knows?

But if I'm being honest with myself (and fuck it, why not be?) there's another reason I decided to come today. It's because Dr. Eldridge is what I imagine my mom would be like if she had lived. Well… lived longer. She did live for a while. Long enough to have me, after all. And on that level, I guess I'm kinda glad my mom isn't alive and I'm talking with Dr. Eldridge instead. Shit. That's not right.

That isn't what I mean to say. Fuck. I'm not glad my mom is dead. That's a fucking stupid thing to say. But I didn't. Say it. I'm just kind of thinking all this. So why am I apologizing? And to who? The universe? I dunno.

Point is simply that I'm grateful my mom doesn't have to see the fucking basket case her son has become. But then I suppose there's a real possibility I wouldn't be the way I am now and things wouldn't be like they are if she hadn't died when I was a kid. Hard to say. Nature/nurture and all that. Maybe I'd be this fucked-up weirdo no matter what. She used to call me her "favorite son." I was, of course, her only son, so we both knew she was making a joke. And I appreciated that. I appreciated that even as like a five-year-old, my mom didn't treat me all precious and shit. She just treated me like a regular person who just happened to be shorter than she was.

I know I got my sense of humor from my mom. She was also the smartest person I ever met. And even though I was thirteen when she died, thirteen years with somebody is enough to get to know whether or not they're smart. And cool. And irreplaceable.

God knows what the fuck she saw in my dad. I think it's possible that maybe he wasn't the way he is with everybody else when it was just the two of them. I think maybe she was the magic panacea that temporarily remedied his chronic asshole-i-ficatiousness. (Not a clinical term, but the right one.) And when she died, there was no counterweight anymore to keep him from turning into what he turned into.

Anyway.

What I'm trying to say is… I'm pretty sure I kept this appointment with Dr. Eldridge because I could really use a mom right now.

"Tyler?" Dr. Eldridge interrupts my mental ramble. Again.

"Sorry. What?" I'm sitting in my shrink's office thinking a bunch of stuff that I'm paying her to talk about, but then not actually talking about aloud. Maybe I should talk with someone about that.

"The Klonopin. Has it helped your anxiety at all?"

"I think so? I'm not sure. I took some with a bunch of booze last week and may have punched a hole in my wall. But on the flipside, if I did, I don't remember it so I don't feel anxious about having done it. So that's good, I suppose."

She does this half-smile, half-frown thing that is accompanied by a sigh. I get it. I exhaust me too.

"Have you been getting out more? Like we talked about? Seeing people at all?"

"I dunno. Kind of," I say. "I'm sort of seeing a girl, I think." What the fuck? I just told myself like two seconds ago that I wasn't gonna talk about Scarlett. Jesus.

"How'd you two meet?" she asks sweetly. Hell. I gotta lie. Right?

"Strip club. She's a stripper. At Pete's. That's where she strips. Pete's strip club. You know it? It's just off the Strip." OK, that was an absurd sentence, but it seems I have no control over my mouth, so to hell with it. Let's see where this goes…

She smiles and laughs a little. "No, I don't know it. So you met her there? At the strip club? Where she strips?" She smiles wider. (Goddamn, she reminds me of my mom.)

"Yeah," I say, unable to keep from smiling myself.

"OK. Well, that's terrific," she says.

And that's it. That's all she says. No prying. No cajoling. No judgment. She just lets it sit there. I've been made to see a few therapists over the years and Dr. Eldridge is, no question, the fucking tits at this job.

"So what else?" she asks. Which is genius. Because now she knows I know she's not gonna try to manipulate me and shit, which means that she's created a safe space for me to say more, and figures that I'm ready to open up. Sometimes I'm too smart for my own good, I'm afraid. Because since I know that's what she's doing, there's no fucking way I'm gonna fall for it.

"The anniversary of my best friend Scotty's death is this weekend."

Oh, come on, Tyler!

"OK. You wanna talk about that at all?" Her brow is furrowed almost imperceptibly.

"Shit. I dunno." No. I do know. Hell with it. Dam's open. So I say, "I guess. Sure. Ok."

She nods and waits politely while I decide how to begin.

"Fuck. I don't… Me and Evan—you know Evan." She nods. "Me and Evan and Scotty were best friends since like kindergarten. And you know how kids will become close and then, y'know, like get fickle or whatever and stop being friends?" She nods again. "We didn't. We just stayed best friends. All through elementary school, middle school, high school. We were brothers. None of us had brothers, and we wanted them, I guess, so we became them for each other."

I pause to consider what parts of the story are important. We only have fifty minutes together and some of that time is gone. So I decide just to cut to the chase.

"But so, after high school, Evan joined the fire department because that's what he had always wanted to do since we were kids. And by the way, Evan had like a 4.0 GPA. Could've gone to Stanford or an Ivy or something, but the guy just really, really wanted to be a firefighter."

(That part isn't actually important to the story, but it is important to distinguish Evan's trajectory from my own. I barely finished high school and it would be easy to think that Evan's a fucking wash-out like me and had limited options. But he isn't and he didn't. He's just an honestly noble motherfucker. Or father-fucker, as is a more accurate designation. No disrespect intended. That'd be one lucky father. Anyway.)

"But I needed to get the hell away from here, so I joined the Navy, right?" I pause to make sure the doc is still with me.

"Right. Yes." She is.

"Yeah, right, so, Scotty. See, Scotty always, well, he always kinda looked up to me and Evan, I guess. I dunno. I mean we were the same age, but he was always a little smaller and a little more… boyish… and just like super-eager to, whatever, to *prove* himself, y'know?"

She nods again. And I suddenly realize that I haven't talked about Scotty in kind of a long time. It feels good and terrible all at once.

"And like I said, we were best friends, and I think he saw Evan becoming a fireman and me becoming a bomb tech and whatever, and… look. Scotty never really wanted to do that kind of thing. Like, he was fascinated by it—fire and explosives and stuff, I mean—but I think he really kind of wanted to figure out WHY things burned. Or WHY things blew up. Or WHY this chemical interacted with that chemical or whatever. Like the dude shoulda been a scientist or physicist or something, but…" Holy shit. I realize that I haven't, in fact, talked about this next part to anyone. Ever.

"Yes? But what?" She has this warmth in her eyes that just fucking sucks me in.

"But… I gave him shit about it. Like all the time. I just like constantly gave him a hard time about the fact that he was gonna spend his life in a lab or a classroom or wherever instead of out there DOING shit. Like I was going to. Like Evan was going to. And I told him shit like…"

I take a long breath, thinking about what an unconscionable cocksucker I can be. Dr. Eldridge waits patiently.

"Just shit like, not everyone can be a hero. Some people have to carry the hero's jock. Blah, blah, blah. Whatever. Just dumbass fraternity talk and shit like that."

"OK," she says. Still no judgment. Which is making this harder. Because I don't even have the choice to be defensive.

"And Evan used to tell me to ease up on him. But I thought that I was just doing what brothers do to each other. Giving each other a hard time."

"I'm sure you were," she says.

"Yeah, but… Fuck. But I wasn't. Or, shit, I was. I mean that's what I was trying to do. Trying to be. But like, I didn't know how. If that makes sense. So basically I think I was just channeling my fucking dad. Just saying the kind of mean-spirited, putting-somebody-else-down bullshit that he does. Y'know. Being a fucking prick."

Dr. Eldridge nods her head, takes a calming breath and then asks, "So how did Scotty die?"

"Fuck. Um, yeah, right. So… so I'm in the middle of my second deployment, or… I think it may have been my second… My third? Shit. I dunno anymore. Doesn't matter. I was gone. And I get an email from Scotty that he's moving to Colorado for firefighter training. 'What? Firefighter training? Colorado? What the fuck? And why Colorado?' I ask him. He tells me… Do you know what hotshots are?"

"Hotshots? Like…?"

"They're firefighters," I interrupt. "Specially trained firefighters who work in what's called 'wildfire suppression tactics.' In other words, when there's a fire raging out of control because some fucknut forgot to put out their campfire or dropped a cigarette in the forest, these dudes are the crews trained to put that shit out."

"And so Scotty was going to Colorado to become a hotshot?"

"You got it."

I think she expects me to say more. But I don't. I'm starting to feel like maybe I'm all talked out.

But then I get a second wind.

"So yeah. So he's moving to fucking Colorado to become a fucking hotshot. Oh, and by the way, don't think the fact that they're called 'hotshots' is lost on me. Only thing that would be more on the nose is if they were called Big-Dick Badasses Who'll Show Fucking Tyler Morgan Who's The Man. I think they actually tried that for a while but it didn't fit on the back of the jackets." I pause for a beat to give the good doctor a moment to take in just how goddamn clever I am. She grins, tightly. It makes her eyes squint.

"So anyway. So, you know. You know me. I can't just let anything be without being a smartass or making some fucking joke, because then I might risk actually having a genuine emotion and that doesn't sound fun. So know what I did? No, seriously. Know what I did? Guess."

She continues to just eyeball me with compassion and lack of judgment and it's tearing me completely in half.

"No? OK. I'll tell you. I gave him shit about it. I gave him shit about were they only gonna let him put out fires in flower gardens and would the helmet fit his tiny head and shit. And his head wasn't even that tiny! He had a totally normal-sized head! It was a stupid joke! Fuck!"

I'm starting to get a little emotional now. I'm worried it's going to freak her out.

"And what happened?" she asks calmly.

"Whaddayou mean?" I say. "He told me to go fuck myself."

"Sure," she says, "but I mean what happened that caused him to die? You don't have to talk about it if you don't want."

"No, no. I do. I mean I DON'T, but..." I take a deep breath. Sigh it out. "So he's up in Colo-fucking-rado, and it's Halloween, and... and look, I don't know all the details. Obviously, I wasn't there. But as I understand it some goddamn kids—they think—are out in the woods getting high and shit and they start a fire somehow, and it gets out of control real fucking fast because it was like a weirdly dry October or whatever and Scotty's crew is the first deployed to try to contain it, and..."

It's very clear I don't need to say more. But I've come this far.

"And one of the other hotshots was standing in the way of some falling timber or something and Scotty pushed him out of the way and the tree fell on him instead and he fucking died and it was Halloween and Evan says it's not my fault but it is pretty much my fault because he was trying to be a hero and I know for a fact that he was trying to be a fucking goddamn motherfucking hero because of all the fucking years that I gave him shit so fuck me and fuck Halloween and fuck God and fuck everybody and Scotty's dead the end."

Silence. Can. Have. Weight.

And the silence in the small room after my big outburst is intensely heavy.

"I swear too much, don't I?" I ask after a few thick moments pass.

"As compared to who?" she responds. Bless her heart. Then she commences again. "Do you mind if I say a couple of things or do you have more?"

I shake my head no. I don't want to say more. If possible, I'd like to un-say everything I just said.

"So you don't need me to tell you this, but Evan is right. Your friend's death is not your fault. That's the first thing." She bends her head down to seek my eyes because my gaze is now pointed directly at the floor.

"Also," she continues, "I know you've been diagnosed with PTSD. You got that from a military psychiatrist, yes?"

I nod. Slightly.

"Ok," she says, "I'm gonna go ahead and say that I do agree with that. But I'm gonna add something… I think you've probably been living with it since long before you were in the military."

Well, that gets my attention. I look up.

She finds my eyes. "I think you've been battling post-traumatic stress since you were a child. Because I think you've been dealing with trauma since you were a child."

I bite my bottom lip a little. Isn't fifty minutes up yet?

"And..." Nope. Still some time to go. "And I think you might look for reasons or situations that help keep you in a state of trauma. Not because you want to, but because it's familiar. Because you need to have something to fight against."

I feel like punching something right now, that's for sure. I feel like walking out of here, finding the first drunk group of frat boys I can find—all giving each other shit and joking with each other in careless and hurtful ways—and ripping off their arms and beating them to death with them. Not to teach them a lesson. Just because it'd feel good.

"But, hey, just my opinion. I have three degrees and have seen hundreds of patients, but let's be honest... nobody really knows what's going on inside anybody else. Maybe you're fine and it's the rest of the world that has PTSD. Could go either way."

She smiles again. It doesn't make me want to punch things any less, but it definitely makes me not want to punch her.

"Do you have any plans for Halloween?" she asks. "Are you seeing the girl?"

"Fuck. No. I wanted to ask her to a carnival at the firehouse that they do for charity, but I didn't get a chance."

"Why don't you call her and ask her? I think it would be good to start replacing this particular association you have with one that's more positive."

"I can't call her," I say. "I don't have her number. Or her name. Or like a real clear understanding that she's an actual human being and not just a fantasy that I created."

Now it's the doctor's turn to bite her lip. "Well," she says. "Um. That feels like it's worth talking about, but we're out of time."

"Oh," I say. Just a few minutes ago I was praying for this to be over and now that it is, I'm kind of sad. Which is surprising. Or else it's not at all. She reads my face. It's not hard to see, I imagine.

"Or," she starts, "I don't actually have anyone right away. If you want to talk some more… we can."

She tilts her head. It occurs to me all of a sudden that… I'm paying her. That 'talk some more' means pay her for more of her time. And that, on some level, this is what my relationship with Scarlett is about too. Paying for the illusion of something I want. Something I need. In Scarlett's case, it was about paying her for the illusion of desire. No, not desire. Salvation. I was trying to buy salvation. Right here, with the doctor, it's about paying for the illusion of what it would be like to have someone who gets me. Who understands me. Who cares at all. Paying for a surrogate mother.

And realizing this is just about the most sorrowful, most desperate thing I can imagine. So…

"Tyler?" she asks. "Would you like to talk some more?"

"Yeah," I say. "I would."

CHAPTER TWELVE

MADDIE

My mother calls on Monday.

I let it go to voicemail and then I stare at that little voicemail notification all day, telling myself I should just delete it and not listen. But she's just trying to be helpful and so it sits there like just another little red flag in my life.

I'm still trying to come to terms with last weekend at Pete's. Not only the way Logan practically kidnapped me from the alley, or the way Ford kicked his friend's ass and took his gun. But also what came afterward.

I've been trying to forget about it… but I can't. It was… hot.

God, I'm so disgusting.

But I can't deny it. This guy—whatever his real name is—just… does something to me. Makes me irrational. Turns me into a dirty little slut.

I know he's bad for me. I see all the ways this can go wrong. And I know I'm just as bad for him. I mean, shit. All I gotta do is look at the fucking calendar to understand why I'm acting this way.

I press the voicemail icon on my phone just as an excuse to stop thinking about him, and wince as my mother's voice blares through the speaker.

"Madison," she says in her calm Mom voice. "I have something really important to ask you. Can you please call me back? Thank you, darling."

The call ends.

My life ends too as I get lost in the reasons she's so insistent on talking to me this week.

But only for an instant. Because I decide I'd rather think about Madison's Slutty Adventures at Pete's than *that.*

So I masturbate to the memory of what he did. The way he felt. The way he made me feel. My back is scratched from being fucked up against the brick wall and there's a bruise on my left thigh from where his fingers pressed into my muscles as he ate me out. I lie in bed and close my eyes and pretend we know each other. That it was a prearranged fantasy date. I was just pretending to be a stripper. He was just pretending to be a stranger. That he's the love of my life and this is just our special way of keeping things fresh.

I come to that thought.

Annie doesn't come home Monday night and even though Caroline and Diane tell me not to worry, she's just on a job, I stay up until dawn waiting on her and get no sleep.

She walks in on Tuesday afternoon looking like… well a whore who's been on a call for eighteen hours.

"Don't ask," she says, dropping her heels on the foyer floor.

So I don't. Because I'm wallowing in my own mountain of self-pity right now and don't even have time for hers.

My father calls on Wednesday. He's not a message leaver, so he just calls and calls and calls all day long.

Sometimes I wish I worked during the week. Pete's is open all the time, so I *could* work during the week. But it's slow, so is it worth it? I mean, if Pete's becomes my full-time job, what does that say about me?

I'm desperate?

Yes. That's exactly what it says.

Wednesday night I break down and answer my father's call. "Hey Dad. What's up?"

"We've been calling you all week, Mads."

I roll my eyes at the nickname. "Please don't call me that."

"How are you?" he asks, ignoring my response. I can hear my mother talking in the background and then my father covers his phone with his hand or something, because her voice gets all muffled and distorted.

"Fine," I say automatically.

My mother grabs the phone from my dad. "Madison," she says. "I'd like you to come visit for the holidays. What do you say? Can I send you a ticket? I'll get you Global First Class." She sings that last part. Like it's a special treat.

It is. I don't go anywhere these days. And even when I did, I never went first class.

"They have beds in that class, Madison. And they serve you champagne as soon you sit down. It's lovely. Come stay with us for a little while. We miss you. Let me buy you a ticket."

"No," I say. "I can't, Mom. Really. I'm so busy with this new business, I just can't leave it right now. If I do, I'll lose all the momentum I've built up over the last few months."

Bullshit. I cannot believe how stupid I am for wasting twelve thousand dollars on a fucking drone. *You would've been better off buying stripper outfits with that money*, my little devil says.

Or paying Carlos back, the angel counters.

"Did you at least call Plu?"

"Who?"

"Dr. Brown."

"Oh, *her*," I say, unable to hide my disgust. Plumeria Brown is the daughter of my dad's old associate from his Vegas casino days. I knew her—sorta—all growing up. She's only a few years older, but the fact that she's now some kind of licensed therapist is just a big ol' slap in my face as far as I'm concerned.

"I think you'd really enjoy catching up with her."

"Would I?" I laugh. "Why do you think that?"

"Well," my mother says. "The two of you are close in age. You must have a few things in common. I think she'd be a good listener."

"You don't talk to people you know when you see a therapist, *Mother*." I snarl out the word 'mother.' "It kinda defeats the purpose."

"Well, she definitely understands the issues—"

"No one understands the issues," I snap back. "And I'm tired of you pushing this shit on me. Can you just stop? Please? Just let me deal with it the way I always do. I've gotten through enough anniversaries now. And those cards you send, they don't help. So just stop."

Silence on the other end of the phone.

I exhale. "Mom?"

She inhales. "OK, Maddie. If that's what you think is best then… then I'll stop caring. OK? How's that? I'll just throw up my hands and stop caring. Is that what you want? Do you want us to forget about you? Pretend we don't have a daughter?"

"I just..." I feel the water welling up in my eyes. Swallow hard. Then say, "I'm just not ready."

"It's been seven years, Madison. You *are* ready."

The tears fall down my cheeks, but I don't cry. Not sobs, anyway.

"You need to get out. Meet people. Move on, Maddie."

"I have," I say.

"No," my mother counters. "You start things and never finish them. Jumping from one crazy plan to another like you're desperate to fill up your life. You hide in your work, pretending to be busy—"

"I am busy," I say.

"And you don't date."

"I am dating," I say. Just wanting to stop her pity.

"You are?" my mother says. The surprise in her voice makes me stifle a laugh. "What's his... is it a *him*?"

Then I do laugh. "Yes, it's a him."

"What's his name?"

"Ford," I say, picturing the face that goes with that fake name.

"Ford. What's his last name?

Shit. "Chevy," I say, because that other car name flies right out of my head and I'm desperate to pull this off.

My mother tsks her tongue. "You don't need to lie to me, Maddie."

"OK, I don't know his last name," I say, exasperated. "But he really is called Ford. And I've only seen him a couple of times"—which isn't a lie, either—"so I didn't want to tell you, but you seem to think I'm some spinster hiding away in the attic just waiting to grow old and I'm not. I'm living, Mom. I'm fine. Everything is fine."

She thinks about this for several long, silent seconds. Probably trying to picture my life. If she knew I was stripping at Pete's she'd hang up the phone and fly home immediately, so I know that's not what she's picturing.

She's picturing some average guy, probably. Maybe tall. Maybe dark hair. Maybe that Ford guy, in fact. He's kinda my type. All manly and shit. I always did go for that type.

So I just fill it in for her. I tell her what he looks like. His handsome face. And his beard. Which makes me actually smile when I say it out loud. And I tell her about his scars. I'm not sure why, maybe to divert her sympathy from me to him.

"He was a soldier?" she asks.

"Yes…" I say, assuming, since he said I didn't want to know and I never got confirmation, but I have a feeling. Not sure why it matters, since it's all just part of a lie, but it does for some reason.

"Is he… normal?" she asks.

"What does that—?"

"Just… you know those soldiers sometimes come back with… damage."

"OK, this is over now," I say. My tears are gone and I'm fed up and tired.

"Will you call Plu?" my mother asks.

I hesitate. "I'm not calling Plu."

"Please, Madison," my mother begs. "Please. For me. Just one time. One talk. That's all I'm asking for."

"And you'll leave me alone?" I ask.

"I promise. If you go for one visit with Plu, I'll stop nagging about it."

"Fine." I sigh into the phone. "I'll call her."

"I've already set up an appointment. It's for tomorrow at noon."

"Jesus, Mom—"

"One time, Maddie. Then you're free of my worry. I've done my best and I'll move on too."

I give up. Fuck it. "One. Time," I say. "That's it. And you never bring it up again. You never send another sympathy card to prepare me for the anniversary. You never call me about it. And you don't make Dad call either. Because I don't need help, OK? I'm *fine*." My pride might very well be the thing that kills me.

"You've got yourself a deal, Madison," my mother says.

"Good," I say.

"I love you," she says, a soft whisper.

"I love you too," I sigh back, meaning it.

"And we all miss him. But he's gone."

The tears are back. They fall and fall and fall down my cheeks in rivers that might never end.

"Goodbye," I say, then end the call and throw myself on the bed face first so I can cry into my pillow.

"You can call me Plu. Or you can call me Dr. Brown."

I'm in Plumeria's office at noon the following day, just like I promised my mother I would be.

"It's funny, right?" I say, looking around her office. It's nice. She's in some kind of co-op with other counselors. Like roommates, I think. They all share a main reception area filled with high-end leather chairs and coffee tables with stacks of current glossy magazines.

I'm in her private space facing a window that's got a nice view of the mountains and a whole parking lot filled with mature palm trees that blow in the desert wind.

"What's funny?" Plu asks.

"Your name, ya know. You used to be Plumeria. So exotic and shit. But now you're Dr. Brown. Which is about as boring as it gets."

Plu smiles at me. Then writes something down on her pad of paper. She's fucking gorgeous. Always has been. Long dark hair. Almost black. Olive-colored skin with large hazel eyes. She looks like some kind of desert princess and the view outside her office makes me think of an oasis.

Which is good, right? That's what you want to think of when you come see a therapist.

"I know your mother made the appointment," Plu continues with a new more business-y line of questioning. "And I don't usually allow this. But since we're old friends, I made an exception. So tell me, Madison, what do you want to talk about today?"

I sigh. I want to scream at her that I don't want to talk about anything. But I'm the one who came. And she took the appointment. It's not her fault I'm here, it's mine.

"Your brother?" she prods.

I don't meet her gaze. Just continue staring out at the oasis. Pretending I'm the desert princess, not her.

"It's been seven years now, right?"

I nod.

"And it's still hard for you?"

I nod again.

"I know you were close," she continues. And then she laughs so abruptly, it startles me. "Remember that time when he got drunk at your parents' anniversary party?" she asks, tilting her head a little like she's trying to recall every detail, but it's eluding her.

I nod again. It seems to be the only response I'm capable of.

"He was so funny the way he did all those old dances with you that night. God, I miss him."

My throat is tight. It feels like there's a boulder stuck in there and I can't swallow.

"But I think my favorite memory of him was in ninth grade when he got stuck up in that tree, trying to save that nest of baby birds. Do you remember that? You were, what? Eight? Nine?"

Jesus, this woman is bad at her job.

"He had a kind heart, didn't he?" Plumeria goes on.

"He did." I force myself to speak, even though my throat feels like it might close up.

"He always raised the most money no matter what the fundraiser was for. Foster kids, feeding the homeless, Toys for Tots."

"Yep! He was the best," I say, forbidding myself to cry.

"And then he was gone," Plumeria says. She looks at me and her smile fades. "It's hard when people die young, Madison. It's not hard for him, because he's gone. But it's hard for you. And all the people he left behind, right?"

I just stare at her for a few seconds. How the fuck she ever got a license to do this is beyond me. "I'm not here to talk about him."

"Good," she says. "Let's talk about you. What are you doing these days?"

I sigh. Shrug, so I can pull myself together. "Just keeping busy I guess."

"Do you work?" she asks.

I laugh. If Perfect Plumeria Brown thinks I'm gonna open up to her about my current situation, she needs to take a few more psych classes.

"Well, what do you do?"

"I run a business," I say. "I do aerial photography for real-estate agents."

"Oh, how interesting. Tell me about that."

"Well… it's new. I just started it."

"OK," she says. "So what did you do after college? You finished, right?"

"Yes," I say, with more venom than I should. "Majored in business. And I've had lots of businesses since then."

"What kind?" she asks.

"Well." I sigh, not sure I really want to admit all my failures. But I'm looking at the clock, which says I have twenty more minutes left of this nightmare. So I either come up with shit to say or make a scene walking out. So I start telling her. It's safe, anyway. No feelings at all attached to those failed ventures. Plu just nods and smiles. Like she approves of what I've been doing. And when I'm done she just sits there. Still fucking smiling.

"That's all of them," I say.

She looks down at her pad of paper and writes something down. I crane my neck a little to see what it is, but she's got her pad tilted up so I can't see. When she brings her attention back to me she says, "Why do you think you have trouble committing?"

I laugh. "I never said I have trouble committing. I don't even know where you got that idea."

She taps her pen to her pad, five times. Like she made bullet points on there, listing all my failures, and she's enunciating each one. "You seem to have lost an awful lot, Madison."

"Look, the wedding business was going well until Carlos' stupid daughter got pregnant with another man's child. That's not my fault. And the pet bakery was great for a while. But it was just a trend, OK? I didn't realize it had no staying power. People make mistakes. So I've made some mistakes. But I'm only twenty-five fucking years old. Stop judging me."

"I'm not judging you, Madison. I'm just thinking… you've let yourself lose a lot."

"*Let* myself… Jesus fucking Christ. I don't go into these things wanting to fail, for fuck's sake."

"Of course not," Plu says. "You want to win. Everyone wants to win. You just don't seem to be able to get the job done for some reason. It's my job to help you figure out why."

"I know why," I say.

"Why?" she asks. And this suddenly feels like a trick. Like she's been letting me blab on about business but now she's back here, to the place I don't want to be.

A little timer goes off. Just a small ding near her desk. So I stand up and say, "Well, it's been fun, Plu. Thanks for the chat."

I don't even wait to shake her hand or listen to her goodbyes. I go for the door and ten seconds later I'm back in the safety of my car.

Alone.

It takes me ten minutes to start it up. And then another five to wipe that whole therapy session back there from my memory.

Ford, I decide. I'm gonna think about Ford. I really need that guy's real name if I'm gonna use him as my escape fantasy. But I'll probably never see him again. I did blow him off last weekend.

And then I laugh. *Blow him.*

I think I'll call him Lumberjack in my fantasy from now on.

So I do. I picture me and Lumberjack fucking outside in the alley like we did last weekend. In fact, I think I'll pretend this is a weekly thing we do. You know, to keep the relationship fresh.

I like that. It's enough for me. Fantasy men come with no expectations at all. No commitment. No risk of failure. Lumberjack man is a win if ever there was one.

And I could use a win.

I could really, *really* use a win.

CHAPTER THIRTEEN

Kids can be so cute. Especially on Halloween. Probably because they're all hopped up on sugar. Watching little Spidermans (Spidermen?) chase ghosts and shit and pretend to catch them in webs is hilarious. Watching their parents try to maintain control over them is even funnier. I'm kind of enjoying seeing them tear all over the firehouse/haunted house/carnival situation, wreaking havoc, until two things strike me.

One—I wonder what the hell happens if an actual call comes in. The engine is decked out like a hearse. Which can't be the kind of thing you want to see charging toward you if your house is on fire. And…

Two—These kids remind me of me, and Evan, and Scotty at that age.

And just as I'm about to drop down heavy into a deep pit of memory, Dean comes over to me. He's wearing a long, black, leather overcoat on top of a black turtleneck with gold chains and leather pants with these funky-looking platform shoes.

"Well, hello there. And you are…?

"Shaft, baby! 'I'm a bad mother—'"

"'Shut yo' mouth,'" I say.

Dean seems pleased that I'm *just* cool enough to know the lyrics to the *Shaft* theme song and he slaps me some skin. (I'm hip as shit. Everybody says so.)

"That's it, my brother," he says. "Um, what exactly are you supposed to be?"

I glance down at myself. I'm wearing my usual boots, my usual jeans, BUT I'm wearing a plaid, flannel shirt instead of my usual t-shirt.

"Dude… You can't tell?" I ask.

"I dunno, man. You look kinda like this rich motherfucker I know named Tyler, but that cat never wears a shirt with buttons. Too much effort, he says." Dean smiles a magnetic smile. "Nah, for real, man, whatchou supposed to be?"

"I'm Paul Bunyan."

"Paul Bunyan the lumberjack?" he asks.

"The same. Just a bad, axe-swinging motherfucker. Can you dig it?"

"You know I can," he says, slaps me more skin (Seriously. I'm hip as all giddy-up), and then heads over to stop a couple of little witches from fucking with Gladys the French Bulldog, who is wearing a tiny beret and a Picasso shirt.

"Yo," he shouts. "She can't have chocolate. She's a dog, baby!"

I look around. I see Bear and Rod dressed like Penn and Teller, which would be kind of an oblique costume choice most other places, but this is Vegas. The irony is that Rod's playing Teller, the one who doesn't talk, and if there's one guy on the planet who cannot shut the fuck up, it's Rod.

Alex, true to his love of cooking, is dressed like Guy Fieri. Blond-tipped wig (I hope it's a wig) and everything.

He's got two little rug-rats hanging on his arms, one on each, and he's doing bicep curls with them. Damn, man. If I live to be fifty, I hope I stay in good enough shape to do shit like that. If.

Even new guy Brandon is here. Which surprises me. Being new to the company and being as quiet and creepy as he is, I figured he'd spend Halloween at home sharpening his knife collection or whatever. But then again, Evan did tell me that story about him saving those kittens, so nothing should be surprising about this guy. Not even that fact that he's dressed like David Bowie circa the Major Tom era. Body paint, face paint, copper-colored hair, the whole nine. I'm getting more and more curious about him, so I approach him as he's ladling some punch into a red plastic cup. I feel like there's a lot more to know about this fella and I aims to find out what it is. (When I go into investigation mode I like to talk to myself like an old-timey detective from the movies.)

I saunter up, casually, grabbing a cup for myself. "How's it going, man?" I ask, super-pleasant. (I'm pleasant as fuck when I wanna be. Everybody says so.)

Brandon just stares at me. For a long time. Like a really long time. He stops ladling and just… stares at me. And then, after what feels like a month, he says, "Good."

And then he turns and walks away. OK. Nice. Feels like we're really taking our relationship to the next level. (To be continued, Brandon. To be continued. I've got your number, pal.)

And over there is Baby-Face Jeff. In a full-on Captain America costume. Because of course he is. Of course he is. Because he really is just like Scotty. It's so obvious. He's got something he's trying to prove to someone. And it breaks my heart to watch him. Even though he's laughing and having fun and playing with the kids—or maybe owing to the fact that he is—it breaks my tiny, knotted heart.

And I'm trying. I really am. Everyone's having fun and acting silly and I'm trying to just be here and be present like Dr. Eldridge encouraged me to be, and not think about Scotty, or Scarlett, or THE DREAM, or my mom, or my dad, or—

"Trick or treat," a tiny voice interrupts my self-struggle.

I look down and standing just below waist height I see a tiny dude dressed like Charlie Chaplin from *The Tramp*. Little bowler hat and everything.

"OK. Um. Trick," I hit back at him.

He stares at me with a confused look that makes his stick-on mustache crinkle.

I try to explain, "See, you say trick OR treat, and then I either give you a treat or you give me a trick. So I'm curious to see what the trick is. You got one?"

His little face scrunches tighter. "No. It's just a thing you say. Can I have some candy now?"

I laugh. I like this kid. "I don't have any on me, man. But there's a bunch of candy on that table over there." I point at a giant pile of individually wrapped candy bars and stuff on a nearby table. Jesus. Feels like they could've gone out and gotten some better options for growing bodies. But if it was just a bunch of apples and shit, no one would show up. The whole point of having this thing is to provide parents who want it a safer alternative than door-to-door trick-or-treating. Because, you know, the world is a shitty place and evil people do evil shit all the time. And all the proceeds from the carnival go to the boys and girls' club so that kids also have a safe place to go hang out after school if their parents aren't home or can't afford nannies or whatever. Because, again, evil and shitty are we.

Chaplin's tugging on my shirt tail now, saying something else. I must have drifted away again for a sec. "Sorry. What, man?" I ask.

"I said, are you a fireman?" He says. He rubs a runny nose with the back of his sleeve and knocks his mustache askew. This little fucker's so goddamn adorable I just wanna eat his stupid face. Not literally. That'd be fucked up.

"No, dude. I'm not a fireman," I say.

"What do you do?" he asks.

I don't really have a good answer for this. At least not one appropriate to share with a child. The honest answer, of course, is 'drugs, booze, and from time to time I fuck strippers in alleys and stuff.' But I'm not sure that the truth would go over well in this instance. So I start fumfering, "Um. I, uh. Y'know, I kind of—"

"He's a superhero." Evan's voice comes from behind me.

Evan comes strolling over now. He's dressed in a tuxedo. Because this year he's decided to be Jay Gatsby. Which I don't think is totally fair because he's already basically Jay Gatsby all the time anyway and also because I think it's just an excuse to wear a tuxedo. You know how sorority girls use Halloween as an excuse to dress like whores and get away with it? That's Evan and the tuxedo. He'd probably wear the shit everyday he's not at work if he could. It's too bad he didn't live in Vegas in the 60s. Guy missed his time. Anyway. He comes sauntering over with a curious little smile on his face.

Baby Chaplin does not seem satisfied. "He's not a superhero," he says.

"Sure he is," says Evan. "You don't recognize him?"

Kid eyes me closely. "I don't know a superhero with a beard."

"That's because he's in disguise," Evan whispers. And hell, at this point, I'm just as curious to find out who I am as Chaplin is.

Evan leans down low so that he's on Chaplin's level. I lean down too.

Evan whispers even more secretively, "He's the Dark Knight."

Chaplin's brows knit tightly together. He steps back. I stand up. Try to look superheroic-ish. "Yeah," I say. "You know. Like in the movie? When the Dark Knight comes back from exile and he's all dirty and homeless-looking? That's me, kid." I wink at Evan, who shakes his head a little and smiles.

Chaplin takes me in for a good, long beat. Then he says, "I didn't see that movie."

"No?" I say. "Well, then you don't know that it's not true!"

I strike a pose. Evan puts his arm on my shoulder. I wish I had a picture of this moment, quite frankly.

Chaplin looks us both up and down and then finally exhales. "You guys are weird." And he heads off to see Captain America, who is handing out the candy. (I decide not to contemplate too deeply the implications of Captain America serving as essentially a high-fructose drug-dealer.)

"Kid's not wrong," Evan says. "You are weird."

"No. He's not wrong," I say, unable to mask my forlorn tone.

Evan takes note. "You doing OK?"

I nod.

"I'm really glad you came, man. I think it's important."

I nod again.

"What's going on with that girl, by the way? The Pole Artisan." (Thanks, Evan.) "I was only half-joking. You shoulda asked her to come with."

"I did."

"You did? When? You didn't tell me that."

"Last week," I say. "I beat up these two guys who were chasing her with a gun and then we fucked in an alley and I asked her then, but she kinda said no."

"Oh. OK." Evan pauses. "Dude—"

"Man, I don't wanna talk about it. OK?" I cut him off.

"Yeah, OK. That's fine. Hey, we're gonna put Bear in the dunk tank, you feel like you wanna—?"

I cut him off again. "No, man. I think I'm just gonna go."

"Really? No, dude. Just, you know, hang here for a while longer."

"Nah, bro," I manage back. Suddenly I have hit a huge fucking wall. Or it has hit me. Hard to tell which. "I think I just need to go home."

"You want me to come with you? Or you wanna come over? Robert's just there alone handing out his homemade granola bars. We can watch him and laugh at the kids' reactions."

"That actually sounds kind of hilarious, but no. No, I'm good. I just wanna go to bed."

He eyes me skeptically.

"Seriously, dude," I say. "I'm OK. Really. I'll be fine. 'Joy cometh with the morning,' right?"

"What? What is that?" he asks.

"Not sure. Think it's from the Bible… I've told you about Nadir?"

"Which one's Nadir?"

"The Farsi translator. The genius one? The engineering degree? The guy who helped me create the specs for the bomb-defusing robot."

"Oh. Yeah. Yeah, I remember," Evan says, stoically.

"Yeah. I ever tell you what Nadir had planned to do with his share of the money when we sold the thing?"

Evan shakes his head no.

"He was gonna to use it to build schools for girls, and build fresh-water centers, and rebuild bombed buildings and shit. And every time he would talk about it I would be like, 'Dude, just take whatever we get for this thing and get the fuck out of here. Move to… Switzerland… wherever, and just fucking, y'know, roll. Like a pimp.'"

I take a second, remembering. Then start again.

"And he would always laugh and say, 'Oh, Tyler. I cannot. It is all of our responsibility to make our corner of this great, wide earth just a little better.' And then when I would say, 'Dude, look around. Bro, it ain't gonna get better any time soon,' he would just smile and say, 'Perhaps. Perhaps not. But how will I know if I do not wake up each day and try? Joy cometh with the morning.'"

Evan lets out a breath.

"So shit, man. Who knows? Maybe tomorrow's the morning that finally cometh with the fucking joy. Or something. I dunno. I'm saying I just wanna go to bed and I'll call you in the AM. Cool?"

Black eyes look into my black soul.

"Yeah, dude. That's cool. Just get home safe. OK?"

"Aw, man. Ain't nothing gonna happen to me. The Dark Knight don't die."

I wink at him. He nods back. Then he takes me by the shoulders and says, "Tyler? You're one of the best people I've ever known."

I'm a little stunned by this. Check that. A lot stunned. "Uh, you work with guys who risk their lives for other people like every day," I say.

"I know," he says. "So trust that I know what I'm talking about."

Then he pulls me in, gives me a hug, a kiss on the cheek, and pulls back and says, "I'll talk to you tomorrow. K? Peace, bro."

He winks and we slap palms.

And then he turns and heads back toward the brightly lit frivolity inside the firehouse.

And I turn the other way and start off.

But I'm not heading home. I'm not. I lied. I'm sorry, Evan. But if I go home I'll just think about all the things I don't wanna be thinking about. Because I don't how not to. Except that's not true. I do know how not to. I know that there's one guaranteed way I can stop thinking things I don't want to think.

I can forget myself inside someone else.

I can find someone. Any random, equally lonely and desperate someone. Another empty vessel who needs to be filled. She can fill me with diversion and I can fill her with me. And that won't fix anything. And I know that. But it will be something. It'll make the thoughts and sounds and tumult stop for the time that it does. And then maybe, just maybe, I can hope against hope that joy just, just, just might come with the morning.

It may. It may not. But for now, the darkness rules. And so off I go to embrace it. A Dark fucking Knight making his way alone out into a dark fucking night.

CHAPTER FOURTEEN

Last night at work felt like a welcome relief. Which scares me. Freaks me out. When did Pete's turn into a sanctuary from my real life?

But it was a good night, as far as Friday night stripping goes. And I made a little over a thousand dollars in lap dances.

I think it's because I'm getting the hang of this stuff. The whole fantasy thing. I think it's because I've kinda succumbed to my own fantasy life.

Lumberjack didn't show up last night. Not that I expected him to after the way I walked off last weekend. But… I had hoped he might.

I get in the shower to get ready for work and make the water hot. So hot the room fills with steam and when I get out and wipe the mirror clean, my skin is flushed red.

I look at my face, my eyes, my hair that looks almost black when it's wet, and imagine what it felt like when my brother died.

"Just make it through tonight, Scarlett," I tell the stranger in the mirror.

Which isn't even rational because tomorrow won't be the end of anything. It's a new beginning, actually. Day one of the countdown to the next anniversary, that's all.

But I can't think about tomorrow when I still have to get through now. Get ready. Go to work. Take my clothes off like I'm making toast, collect my money, pay my debts, go home, scald myself in the shower, look in the mirror… and wonder what's the fucking point?

"What *is* the fucking point?"

You go on, Scarlett, the little angel says. *One foot in front of the other.*

You could always give up, Maddie, the devil offers. Just like that. *You could always give up.*

If I knew what giving up actually meant… maybe I could. What *is* the definition of giving up?

That's my problem. I don't know. I'm the mountain climber scaling Everest. I only know how to do one thing. Inch my way up towards that elusive peak.

"You should come with us," Annie says, as I walk out into the living room. She's bustling around the kitchen whipping up something quick for dinner before she and the other girls get ready for their Halloween job. It's not one client, it's like… a whole party.

Normally I'd feel revulsion at the offer. I mean, how many men will they sleep with tonight? Four? Ten? More?

But I think I'm numb to this world now. I'm not even shocked. A year ago I'd be putting all kinds of labels on them. Slut. Whore. Desperate. Sad.

Not anymore. Tonight is the moment when all the things I've done come crashing into some kind of incoherent mess. Like rain falling for so long it gathers into a puddle, then a trickle down a hill until it collects into a pond that becomes a lake and then an ocean.

I am an ocean of… of what?

Of nothingness, I think.

"Maddie?"

"Hmm?" I say, dragging my thoughts out of my own despair and back to Annie.

"You wanna come with us? It's classy."

I raise an eyebrow at her. "Classy?"

"I know." Annie sighs. "But it is. It's at a private club just off the strip."

"I already have a date like that lined up, thanks."

"No," Annie says. "You're going to work at a shitty strip bar. This is a *club*, Maddie. High-end people with money to burn tonight. All you gotta do is show up in a costume and I'll tell Kimberly—"

"Jesus fuck, Annie," I say. "I'm not whoring for Kimberly."

She scowls at me, offended. "Whatever. Go wallow in your pity then. Fuck if I care." She grabs her sandwich and leaves to eat in her room.

"She's just trying to help," Diane says behind me. I didn't even know she was there. She sits on the sofa. "You don't remember me from freshman year, do you?"

I try to think back to any memory of Diane before junior year economics class. I can't place her, but in my defense, I was a wreck.

"I was sitting right behind you in freshman English when you got the message."

That day comes back to me like an unwelcome hallucinogenic flashback. The banging of the doors at the top of the auditorium-like classroom. The tentative footsteps on the stairs as they came towards me. I was taking a test, totally lost in my persuasive essay on the merits of ethics in scientific research.

The messenger had long blonde hair. It brushed against my arm as she leaned in to whisper in my ear. She was my roommate. Kate, her name was. And she said, "You need to call home."

That's it. That's all she said.

The whole class stopped to look at me. The professor—some young adjunct faculty woman whose name I couldn't tell you now if I had a million dollars riding on it—said, "Is there a problem?"

And Kate said, "Yes," in this soft, sad voice. "Yes," she repeated. "There's a problem and Maddie has to leave and call home."

"You lost so much weight that year," Diane says, pulling me into the present. "Just… like overnight. You left that day. Looking a little shell-shocked. And then you came back two weeks later and you were a wraith. That's the word I thought in my head when you sat in front of me the next time I saw you. A wraith."

I just stare at Diane. Unable to process anything but the memory of what came next.

"You might not think we give a shit, Madison. But we do." Diane sighs. Kinda loud. And then she shrugs, like she did her best and that's all she's got for me. "So go to work tonight. Or show up with us tonight. Or drink yourself stupid and fuck a guy for free. Whatever it takes to get to tomorrow, right? I get it."

I nod, feeling like I'm back in Plu's office the other day. Incapable of anything other than a nod.

"But if you want to be around friends tonight, then we'll be at Cabaret Royale. I'll put your name on the guest list."

She leaves as quietly as she appeared.

I force myself to get up and get ready for work. I'm going in early, I decide. Fuck it. If this is my job now, might as well do it right. I pack up several outfits. The pink one, the blue one, and the white one.

We're supposed to wear costumes, but before this moment I was old Maddie. And I didn't pick one up. Maybe I thought I'd get out of this day. Maybe I thought I could stop it from coming. Maybe I thought I'd give up before it got here.

I kinda think these same things every year. Halloween always comes, but there's a first time for everything.

I still have the damn angel wings and halo, so I stuff those into my bag as well. They're looking a little ratty and I really need new ones if I'm going to keep this whole girl-next-door persona going at Pete's.

But I don't think I need a new angel costume. I'm tired of pretending I'm good. I think tomorrow I'm gonna go buy a little devil outfit instead. Embrace the woman I really am. Dark, and slutty, and dirty.

I go outside, get in my car, drive to work like I'm making toast, and when I get there I park. Get out. Grab my bag and square my shoulders as I go inside.

Raven's mouth almost drops open when I show up an hour early. "Well, well, well," she says. "Look who's motivated tonight."

I don't say a word. Just drag myself back to the dressing room and start putting on my wig and the white negligee. One last time, for old times' sake.

There are a fuckton of other girls in here who normally work during the week because they have kids, or men, or whatever. I don't recognize a single face or the name to put to it. So I grab one of the vanities as a girl gets up to go out on the floor, and settle down to put my makeup on.

"What's going on?" Raven asks behind me.

I meet her eyes in the mirror but only for a second.

To my surprise she pulls up a chair and scoots over to me. "Scarlett?" she prods.

"What?"

"What are you doing?"

"Getting ready for work. Why else would I be here?"

"You're not on the schedule," she says.

"*What?*"

"It's Halloween, honey," one of the no-names says. "Holiday shifts go by seniority. And you're the new girl."

"Are you serious?" I ask Raven.

"You might want to start paying attention. I post the schedule every Friday morning, ya know."

"But I always work Saturdays. I just assumed…"

"Do you need the money?" she asks. And to my surprise, there's no bitter rivalry in her tone. "The stage fee tonight is double."

Double. Shit. That's almost eight hundred dollars.

"You don't look too good," Raven says. "Are you sick?"

"No," I say, gently patting the dark circles under my eyes.

"I mean… I can give you a slot if you need it and think you can make your money back," Raven says. "But… but you sure don't look like you're up to this."

For a few moments I just sit there and stare at the stranger in the mirror. I feel… lost all of a sudden. I've been working here almost four months now and every weekend I've had somewhere to go. Pete's was never my first choice, but it was… somewhere to go. Somewhere I could forget about my life and just… make some fucking toast.

I turn to look Raven in the eyes instead of her reflection. "Where would I go?"

She smiles and lets out a small laugh. "I dunno. On a date? To a party?" She shrugs. "Drinks with friends?"

I turn back to the mirror. Unable to move.

"Look," she says, a hand resting tentatively on my shoulder. "You can work the floor if you want. Hang out a little and just serve drinks. That way you only have to pay on your tips. But if I were you, Scarlett, I'd take the night off. Take a good hard look at what's happening in your life right now."

I just stare at her reflective eyes.

"I don't know what's going on or what you were doing out there, but I saw the empty car with the headlights in the alley last week and I didn't bother you about it after you came back inside because… well, I've been in some shit myself at times. And I saw Logan chase you out of here."

I look at her, surprised.

"Yeah. I know him," she says. "Not really well, but I sort of know who he is. I know who he works for anyway. So…" She shrugs again. "Whatever you've got going on, you probably need a plan."

"I don't think I have one," I admit. "Nothing is working."

"Stay here then," she says, standing up. "Serve drinks. Waste some time and figure it out. I'll have the guys keep an eye out for Logan and if he comes in, we'll let you know."

I stare at myself in the mirror. Because I am that girl staring back whether I like it or not. "OK," I say. "That's what I'll do." Because I cannot be alone tonight. I can't. Not tonight. Not Halloween.

"Good," she says. "But we don't need you tonight. So if you can't take it, just slip out. No one will even notice you're gone."

It shouldn't bother me that I'm not needed at Pete's tonight, but it does. It bothers me a lot that no one would miss me if I just… went away.

I don't know how long I sit there at the dressing table doing nothing. Long enough to be yelled at by several girls who come in and want me to move so they can get ready. But I barely hear them. I'm lost. I'm falling down and there's no one here to catch me.

Raven snaps at a few of them, telling them to leave me alone. And I suddenly feel indebted to her in a very big way.

Eventually she comes over, slings my pack over my shoulder, stands me up, and points towards the door. "Go," she says. "Just go home."

I nod. And I leave.

But I don't go home. My car drives itself. Or so it seems. I end up looking for Cabaret Royale. To find the girls. My name is on the guest list.

But after a while I realize, I have no idea where it is. I've lived here in this city my whole life. I've seen that sign a million times, but nothing makes sense right now. I text Annie, then Diane, but neither of them answer me.

I don't really know what to do. The only thing I do know is that I can't go home tonight. I cannot be alone tonight.

So I park on a side street, pull out my angel wings and my halo, put them on, and get out of the car and just stand there in the middle of the street, staring into headlights.

The angel says, *Move, Maddie! Get out of the fucking road!*

But I don't move. I just wonder why she's calling me Maddie instead of Scarlett.

CHAPTER FIFTEEN

I'm so pissed. I want to drive fast. I want to open this motherfucker up and just rip through the desert night headed nowhere. But I can't. Because it's Vegas on Halloween and everybody and their saggy-panty granny is out on the fucking road.

"This is BULLSHIT!" I declare to absolutely no one.

It is though. If I was really the Dark Knight I wouldn't have to stand for it. I'd have the Batmobile and like rocket boosters or whatever. Crap. I shoulda asked if they could outfit this thing with rocket boosters. You know they can. I saw some crazy shit in the military. They can do all kinds of things.

FUCK!

I need to get out of this nonsense. I need to leave. Leave Vegas and all this behind. I don't know what I was thinking coming back. I thought somehow it would make things feel better. Familiar. But maybe that's the problem. That's what Dr. Eldridge said. I seek the chaos because it feels familiar. And the problem with that is there's no shortage of chaos to be found in this world. So how's somebody supposed to not to seek it out?

COCKSUCKER!

I need to fight or fuck. Like right now. I can actually feel the temperature inside my body changing. The fire inside me is burning out of control.

Scotty.

SON-OF-A-BITCH!

I maneuver my way off this gridlocked bullshit of a main road by driving up onto the sidewalk (maybe the cops'll come after me and we can get into a high-speed chase, that'd be something). I look left. I look right. No cops. Damn.

I snake around some more cars and onto a side street that's a little more open. But now, suddenly, I hear car horns blaring. Not the "woohoo, it's party time!" kind, but more the "hey, get the fuck out of the way!" kind. And now, squinting up ahead, I see that some asshole is standing in the middle of the road.

Jesus. CHRIST! FUCKING PEOPLE! Everybody in this world is an asshole. And I'm not excluding myself from that indictment. Hell, I'm the biggest asshole of them all. But fuck everyone else, because… they're not me.

As I get closer I can see it's not a guy asshole. It's a girl asshole. Who are the worst kind of assholes. Because you can't punch a girl for being an asshole. Well… I suppose you maybe could, but it's really, really uncool and the kind of thing I tend to frown on. In fact, one of my favorite things to do is punch assholes who've laid their hands on women in a less than civil way. Even if the woman was being an asshole. Yeah. Fuck those assholes. Fuck those women-hurting assholes right in their assholes. Fucking assholes.

As I'm having this elevated discourse with myself…

The woman asshole who's standing in the middle of the road comes into clearer view.

Are. You. Fucking. Kidding. Me?

She's not an asshole. She's Scarlett. She's my angel. In the middle of the road. Like an asshole. Cars weaving around her, people yelling. What the hell is she doing?

More importantly, what is she doing HERE? And suddenly it occurs to me that I've never seen her away from the strip club. But here she is now. In full angel regalia.

In the middle of the road.

And I start to think… *is* she a real angel? Maybe she is. Maybe we think of angels as chaste and pure and shit because that's what all the myths tell us, but maybe they're just crazy little fuck machines. And that's what makes them angelic. Holy shit! I've just discovered a secret about Heaven! Angels exist to fuck good into the world!

OK. So that last car just almost hit her. This is not cool. She's not even moving. I guess that it's OK because… she's got divine protection? Or something? But I don't like the way this thing looks like it's playing out. So. I do something that makes complete sense and is one hundred percent the right thing to do.

I spin my car hard left, fishtailing it right, and block the oncoming traffic from possibly running my paragon of sexiness over. I jump out and shout to her over the roof.

"Scarlett?"

"Ford?"

Some asshole is now laying on his horn at me.

"Hey! Asshole! What the fuck are you doing? Get the fuck outta the road!" the asshole shouts.

"Me? I'm the asshole? Fuck YOU, asshole!" I can't believe this dickhead. (Who I just decided is not an asshole, but a dickhead. Fuckin' dickhead.)

Dickhead now decides it's a smooth move to get out of his Camaro and step to me. He's big. And he's dressed like a Viking. Great. Now I gotta fight a fucking Viking. But then I find myself very excited at the possibility that I might get to fight AND fuck tonight! My angel! She's like a good-luck charm.

"Ford?" Scarlett says again as she gets closer. "What are you—Look out!"

And at that, I turn just in time to see Dickhead's fist the moment before it makes contact with my jaw and rings my bell. Pretty damn hard.

So… two things about me:

One—This guy is most definitely a dickhead because I would never, ever, in a million years take a sucker shot at someone. No way. There's nothing worse in my book than rolling up on someone unaware. You look a man in the eye before you try to tune him up.

And two—I can take a fuckin' punch.

I twist my neck to crack it after the unexpected shock to the system it just took, and then I turn my head back to look at Dickhead in his dickhead eyes.

"Um… Get back in your car now, please," I say in as polite a tone as I can muster.

Dickhead stares me down like he thinks he's gonna try again. There's a moment where I consider grabbing the gun that's still in my glove box and really giving the old boy a Halloween scare, but that feels too easy. Plus, and I have to be honest about this, I want Scarlett to think I'm cool. I mean I AM super fuckin' cool. Everybody says so. But I want her to THINK I am.

"Pretty please," I say. "Or you and I can decide to learn a lot about each other real fuckin' fast here in the middle of this goddamn road. Your call, chief." (I assume it annoys other people as much as it annoys me, so I decide to drop it on him.)

Dickhead looks at me. Then he looks over my shoulder at Scarlett. I hazard a glance back at her. She's got a smug look on her face that I'm choosing to interpret as pride because she knows she's rolling in the company of awesomeness.

Then Dickhead backs up, points his finger at me (ugh, so fuckin' cheesy), gets in his bitchin' Camaro, bumping his Viking horns on the door frame as he tries to sit down (classic), and throws it in reverse. He's sort of boxed in, but, eh, fuck him.

"Hey," Scarlett says.

I turn to her. She's standing by the hood on the passenger side.

"What are you doing here?" she asks.

"Me? I'm just driving down the fuckin' street. What are you doing here?"

"Standing in the fuckin' street."

"Yeah. I caught that. Why?"

"I dunno. Because. Because I'm having a real bad night."

Her eyes go soft and sad. I wonder why she's having a bad night. I wonder if it's as bad as the bad night I'm having. I wonder if I can help. So I ask.

"Is there anything I can do?"

She shakes her head a little. Then she pauses and says, "I dunno. Maybe?"

"OK. I mean, yeah. Name it."

She takes a breath and I could be wrong, it could just be the way the evening lights are hitting her, but she looks a little like she wants to start crying. Then she asks...

"Will you fuck me?"

There are times in your life when you forget how to breathe. This is one.

I nod. "Fuck, yeah, I will."

I hit the button to unlock her door and she slides into the passenger seat. Her white dress has some dirt on it and her crooked halo and tattered wings make her look like she was kicked out of eternity and got lost in the muck trying to find her way home.

I slide into the driver's seat and close the door. I reach over and touch her chin. Turn her head to face me. "Um," I begin. "Are you OK?"

She smiles the tiniest of smiles. "No. I'm not."

I nod a bit. "Yeah. Me either."

And now my tongue is in her mouth. I've got my hands behind her head and her hands are reaching for my cock. We are urgent, angry, and needy. She is a fallen angel and I am sin itself.

I rip myself away and ask, "Is your place close?"

"Not really," she says.

"Cool. Mine is."

I slam on the accelerator, straighten the car out, and start hooking back around to the Strip as fast as I can without killing us both in the process.

Fuck! I shoulda got the rocket boosters.

CHAPTER SIXTEEN

MADDIE

There is a right way to do everything.

Like get through Halloween, for instance. I've done it six times before tonight, so I should know better than to get in this car, grab this guy's cock, and let him take me back to his place. I should know better because for me, Halloween has nothing to do with feigned fright over stupid costumes. It's got everything to do with the very real horror of how my brother died.

Since then, Halloween has required the distraction of strangers. Many strangers—preferably in the mood to do things they'd rather forget tomorrow. And alcohol. Copious amounts of alcohol.

But the key word here is strangers.

Not a guy I've already been with. Not *this* guy, who seems to show up every goddamned time I need saving.

I am, however, a pragmatist.

My options are pretty limited at this point. Most of the cars in the road just wanted to run me over and shout nasty names at me. None but this one came with an offer of solitude with a stranger.

Almost-stranger. But that's all I've got, so it's gonna have to do. Besides, I don't even know his real name. So that sorta counts.

Like I said, pragmatist.

Ford is swinging the car around corners in a desperate attempt to get back onto the Strip, so I go sideways a little, pushing up against the passenger door, and my hand slips off his cock.

He looks down at the hard bulge in his pants where my hand was, then glances up at me and says, "Put it back."

It's not even a request, so I just do as I'm told and grab him again and close my eyes as we hook around another corner, wheels screeching, enjoying the ride. Reliving the way he fucked me in the alley last weekend. Fantasizing how he'll fuck me tonight.

We stop at a red light, his leg bouncing in anticipation, or maybe irritation that we're no longer moving. But then the car in front of us turns right and he slams on the accelerator and we sail across three lanes, oncoming cars blaring their horns when we cut them off, and then slide into an underground garage entrance which brings us back up to street level, where he brakes in front of a frightened valet in fancy valet garb.

He's out of the car shoving bills into the valet's hand, and two seconds later he's pulling my door open and grabbing my hand.

"Come," he says, pulling me out of the seat.

Everything about right now is urgent and happens in fast-forward. His hand on my ass as we pass through the front doors. His quick steps as he leads me over to the elevator. The flash of his key card to open the doors. Stepping inside. Another key card flash as he pushes the button for the penthouse. Then walking me backwards, his hard body pressed to mine as I hit the back wall and the doors close.

Our lips press into each other. Tongues twisting inside mouths. Fast breathing and rapid heartbeats.

I grab his cock again just as his fingertips find my pussy. He bites my lip, his other hand sliding up to my throat, fingers pressing against my windpipe.

I swallow hard and feel his smile.

"Do you like that?" he growls.

I close my eyes because the answer is yes. But I say, "Shut up and fuck me."

His fingers find their way inside my panties and then inside me. I slump against the back wall of the elevator and enjoy it, acutely aware that somewhere, someone is probably watching us on a security camera, but not caring.

I am wet and I just want more.

"Scarlett," he whispers as he takes his urgent kisses to my neck, his hand still pressing into my throat. "If you don't tell me what you like, I'm gonna do whatever I want."

I open my eyes to stare into his, just as the elevator doors ding our arrival at the penthouse, and say, "I want someone to sin with me tonight. That's all I need."

He smiles the smile of a demon on his home turf. "I might take you to hell and back, angel."

The doors open to the lights of Sin City itself, flashing red, and orange, and yellow around the outline of his face.

I place both hands firmly on his chest and push him, making him step backwards as we enter his apartment. "So what are you waiting for?"

CHAPTER SEVENTEEN

TYLER

I stumble in through the door, grabbing her around the waist and pulling her along with me as I kiss and bite, licking along her long, arching neck.

"You just move in?" she asks. She is, I'm assuming, making a commentary on the… Spartan… way I have the apartment furnished. But I'm not real keen on having a conversation about home decorating just now.

"Shut up," I say, as I reach behind her to push the door closed, pulling my hand back to her as quickly as I can so that I don't have to be apart from her body any longer than necessary. I lift up the back of her little dress thing, slap both hands on her ass, nearly coming in my pants when she squeals, and pull her to me tightly as I keep walking her backwards into the main room.

The vampire in me is out again in full force, biting her bottom lip as I kiss her, almost pulling her along with my teeth just as much as I am with the rest of my body. She rips her mouth free from mine and I draw a little blood as she goes. She pauses for a nanosecond to touch her lip. She smiles when she sees the red on her fingertip, places her finger in her mouth, sucks the blood off and grabs my dick, hard, hammering us backwards into the glass of the windows.

She's the one who's biting now. Biting my neck. Biting my chin. She bites my cheek.

"Ah! Fuck!" I exclaim. Not in discomfort. Not in pain. In joy. In exultation. In affirmation. In relief. Because we are fire. We are combustion. We are the raging inferno of purifying flame that will singe away all our pain and leave us barren and ready to begin again. In the punishing passion that we share, we can torture away whatever nightmares plague us and both wake born anew.

We are each other's suicide.

She smiles and slaps my cheek where she just bit me, and I smile back. She grabs my shirt with both hands and rips it open. Buttons pop and fly off, skittering across the floor.

"This is like my only button-down shirt," I note.

"Shut the fuck up," she says with a shake of her head. Her head that I am now seeing the top of as she begins licking my scars. She's tracing each line. Each crevice. Each mutilated and broken ridge of my marred flesh. The whole time she's reaching inside the zipper of my jeans to work my cock with her strong, delicate fingers.

She's still wearing the wings and the halo, and if the view from here is the last one I ever see, I'll feel like a lucky son-of-a-bitch for the first time in my life.

She's tracing the one, long scar—the one that runs vertically down my stomach to just right above my cock—with her tongue. When she gets to where the button of my jeans is still snapped shut, she wraps her mouth around it and—and I swear to fuck, I don't know how; I've never seen a woman do this before—pops it open. David Copperfield isn't the only magician on the Strip tonight.

She pulls down my pants (or rips down is more accurate) to my ankles, glances up at me with those green, green eyes, and then wraps her gorgeous mouth around my cock. My head throws itself back, slamming against the glass, and I am reminded that we are exposed to the city below in the glaring light of my apartment as it bounces off the steel and wood and glass, leaving us vulnerable to gawking eyes if they so choose to notice us, and I get even harder. I recognize now that I *want* people to see. I *want* them to be made uncomfortable at the sight of my happiness. Because fuck them all.

She's twisting her head and neck at the same time she slides her mouth back and forth on my hard cock, causing it to bend and throb and tense and ache. I want to fuck her so bad I can't understand it. I reach down to touch her head so that I can help her. Not that she needs it. But I want to guide her as she swallows the whole of my shaft. I want to fist her hair and demand she do what I want even though she already wants it herself.

And as I extend my hand, I remember that she's still wearing a wig. And I realize that I've never seen her hair. I've never seen who is really underneath the halo. And the suspense has me hyperventilating. So I first pull the halo off, tossing it to the side, as she continues to stroke me with her tongue.

"Fuck, angel, please. Slow down. I don't want to come before I've split you open."

I can feel her smile spread around my tip as she pulls back slightly to tickle the edge of my dick with her tongue. Holy. Fucking. Shit.

And now I grab the wig the same way she grabbed at my shirt, but I don't rip it away. I slide it carefully off the back of her head so I don't hurt her.

And… I see red.

A bottled sea of red roiling on top of her head as the artifice is slowly stripped away. And suddenly all I can see is the wash of flaming red bobbing back and forth while she drives me insane.

I was right.

It is her.

She really is MY angel.

From MY DREAM.

Oh, my God.

It's her.

She's real.

MADDIE

My fingernails dig into the flesh of his legs and he goes still. For a moment I think this is it. He's gonna fist my hair, push my head into his groin until his balls are pressing against my chin, and come down my throat.

And even though I've convinced myself that I'm not the kind of girl who does that for men I don't know, I am. For him. Just him. Only him. All the time. Whenever he wants. Whatever he wants. I want to be his dirty little slut.

When I realize none of that is happening I tip my head up and stare at his wide eyes. Pull back and let his cock fall from my mouth. "What?"

His fingers go to my hair and he starts opening the clips that kept it tucked up inside my wig. Long strands of fire-red tresses fall against my cheeks. And then the whole thing comes apart as he slides the hair band off and it turns into an unruly mess of flames that falls down my shoulders like a river of lava.

"It's you," he says.

"Yeah," I say back. "It's me. The devil in disguise."

I grab his cock, squeezing hard but pumping slow as I kiss his tip and swipe my tongue around his head until he squints his eyes. Like he wants to close them so badly and go back to the desperate sex we were about to have.

But he can't.

He bends down instead, his back sliding against the window, both hands firmly on my cheeks until he's boxing me in with his knees, and we're eye to eye, and his intense gaze feels like he's staring into my filthy fucking soul, and he says, "I know you."

And for a moment, I wanna say, *You know absolutely nothing about me*. But then I realize he knows the only thing that matters. Tonight… I'm his. So I say, "Wanna know me better?"

He nods his head. Whispers, "Yeah. Tell me."

Which makes me laugh. "OK," I say, playing along. "I want you to stand back up and let me suck your cock. I want your hands fisting my hair as you push yourself deeper down my throat." My words are spilling out. Like I can't stop. Like I need to get all this out and tell him what I want. Make him understand how bad things are and what I need to make it better. "I want you to fill me up until I choke on it. And then I want you to come down my throat and feel satisfied and yet unsatisfied at the same time. Like you can't ever get enough. Because after that, I want—"

"What?" he says, blinking at me. Like he's confused. Which is kinda cute. That I can render a guy like him speechless with dirty talk.

"Just fuck my face, *Ford*."

"My name's not Ford," he says.

"I know," I say back. "And I'm not Scarlett. Doesn't matter. What matters is that I've got your cock in my hand when it really needs to be in my mouth."

His palms are still pressed against my cheeks when he leans in and kisses me. But it's not hard and desperate the way it was before. It's…

"I'm not gonna do it," he whispers into my mouth.

"What? Not gonna do what?"

He kisses me again and this time it's definitely not urgent. It's soft. Tender, almost. The way a man kisses his wife. Like… like he *loves me* or something.

I pull back because now I'm the one who's confused.

"I'm not gonna hurt you," he says, shaking his head to enunciate his declaration. "I'm not gonna let it all blow up. I'm gonna fix it, Scarlett. I swear. I'm gonna do it right this time. I'm gonna save you, and me, and it's all gonna be OK."

"What are you talking about?" I ask because… because it feels like… he *knows* me. And he can't know me. He has no idea what's happening to me tonight. How much I need him. How much I need *this* just to get through to tomorrow. To stop the countdown to catastrophe and begin fresh again.

"Tomorrow," he says, eyes sad and watery, still holding my face carefully in his hands. "When we wake up. It's gonna be OK. I promise."

Now it's my turn to blink back at him. "How do you know that?"

"Because I'm not gonna fuck it all up this time. I'm gonna do it right."

I know we're not talking about the same thing. I get it. But I don't care. Because he's telling me everything I need to hear tonight. He *is everything* I need tonight. Like… salvation. He's my fucking salvation.

He slowly begins to rise, his belt buckle jingling like a bell that rings in my head as his hands leave my face. I grab at them, desperate to keep the connection. But he just stands up and leans back against the glass. They slip away, leaving a rush of cold air where his skin was touching mine. Making me crave him in a way that makes no sense as I grab his thighs and dig my nails in, but since when does anything make sense anymore?

He smiles then. A smile as soft as his kiss was a few moments ago. "What are you waiting for?" he asks.

I'm struck dumb and silent. And like he knows this… like he knows I need his help… his fingers twine into my hair, twisting it slowly as he looks down at me. Gazes down at me like a god in the sky, bestowing grace and forgiveness on my sins. And he says, "Don't get shy. I need you as much as you need me."

He reaches for my hands, prying my fingers from their death grip on his thighs, and places them back around his cock. Like that's exactly where they need to be.

I squeeze him and watch, fascinated at the scene playing out before me, as his eyes close and he sighs. Like we've already reached the pinnacle of perfection together.

Both of his hands find their way to my fire-red hair and he guides my face towards him. I open my mouth and let him put himself inside me. My lips seal around his shaft, my tongue flat as he forces himself into my throat until he's so deep inside me, I gag. He holds me there just the way I told him to. Choking me with his cock. His hands firmly on the back of my head. Like he might never let me take another breath of air again.

"Look at me," he says.

I raise my eyes to his because I have no choice but to obey. He smiles as he begins to pull out. My hands grab at his legs, not wanting him to leave me empty. But just when I think his cock might slip out, he thrusts his hips forward, grabs the back of my neck, and pounds himself back into the heat of my throat.

I cough, saliva dripping out over my lips and onto my chin as he palms my throat to feel the bulge of himself deep inside me, and then does it all again.

Our eyes are locked together as I let him fuck my face just the way I asked him to. I'm gagging and choking and he's moaning and grunting until… he stops and all I hear is the sound of myself. Sucking in air through my nose.

I close my eyes when he comes. I swallow him, which sets him off again and he pumps his cock in and out of my mouth so fast, semen and saliva spill down the front of my little white negligee, staining it with our sins.

He lets go of my head, bending down so we're eye to eye. He kisses me softly, dropping to his knees and leaning forward until I have to give in and lie back.

I watch everything as he does this.

The grin on his face. Filled with satisfaction that isn't satisfied. The lust in his eyes that are begging me to beg him for more. And like we're reading each other's minds, I open my legs as he rips open my negligee and lowers his face to my stomach.

"Allow me," he says.

TYLER

Underneath the pure and white that I tear from her body, she's wearing a bra and panties that are both fire-engine red. As red as her hair. As red as the blood that remains tipped on her lips.

All that redness against her creamy white skin makes me think of a painting. Botticelli. She is the living incarnation of *The Birth of Venus*. But here on the floor of my apartment, she is still an incomplete work. I haven't yet laid my finishing touches on the canvas of her body. But I'm about to.

"You really are the fucking devil in disguise," I say. She smiles and licks her lips.

I pull my shirt off and toss it away, kicking off both boots and stripping my jeans from my legs. I nuzzle my face into the sweet, open space between her legs, allowing my nose to brush across her clit through the thin fabric that barely covers her. She whines in approval.

I pull back and stand up straight, scarred and erect, towering above her. I take note for a brief moment that usually after I come as hard as I just did, my dick loses a little of its enthusiasm. But looking at the fucking gift that's been delivered unto me is keeping me as hard as a goddamn fourteen-year-old. She wriggles on the grey wood floor, staring up at me, watching me stroke my cock while I stare back.

"What do you want?" she asks. "What do you want me to do?"

And I go insane.

I throw myself to the floor, the cold wood pushing against my hot, throbbing cock, and I yank off the cloth that covers her beautiful mound of bare skin. I bury my face there, driving my tongue inside her, reaching up with my hands to pry her thighs apart even further, keeping her spread as wide as I can. Making sure I keep the entrance to paradise open. The flicking of my tongue between the folds of her smoldering, wet pussy reminds me of a snake. And I realize I am. She is Eve, but I am not Adam. I am the serpent wrenching her out of Eden. And together, we are original sin.

I've got my face embedded so deeply into her sticky wetness that I can barely breathe. And suddenly I decide that I don't want to breathe. I want to be smothered inside her. So I place my palms on the floor beside her thighs, pull my knees underneath me, grab her by the hips and then, without ever allowing my mouth to drift from her impossibly perfect pussy, I stand, elevating her to the point where she can almost touch the ceiling—glancing at our reflection in the windows for a split second with the lights of Vegas twinkling on the other side, and being struck by how you can't tell where she ends and I begin—and then I lower us to the ground, legs thrust out in front of me, and her in a perfect split, sitting fully on my face. I yank her thighs down toward me further and she gasps.

"Shit! Your beard fuckin' tickles!" she squeals.

"You shaved, I didn't, get over it," I mumble out. I doubt she can even hear me that well with me eating her out like she is my last meal, but fuck it.

I keep sucking at her clit, biting a little too, and she begins to spasm, her stomach contracting and releasing as her body jerks involuntarily.

"Fuck, fuck, fuck, fuck you," she moans. God, I love it when she tells me to fuck myself. I do. And she's flailing her arms behind her now, reaching for my hard dick. But I need her to stop moving just a little so that I can keep going and also so that she doesn't crush my fucking head.

I grab both her wrists, pinning them behind her back, and then I reach behind her ass to steady her from rocking and heaving quite so much. And just to make sure I have a firm grip, I let my two middle fingers slide into her asshole.

She makes a sound that I can't identify. A guttural, desperate, animal sound. And I drive my fingers a little deeper as my tongue does its frantic dance in and around her glistening skin that's now dripping all over my beard. She's trying to pull her arms free, but I have her cuffed and she's not going anywhere I don't want her to. She is exactly where she's supposed to be.

As I bite and suck and lick and tease and finger and tighten my grip she begins mewing, begging me to let her free. But there's no fucking way. I keep going, harder, faster, and I can feel the pressure building inside her like a soda bottle all shaken up, with my thumb on the opening.

"No, no, no, no, no," she cries out. And I push deeper, tongue her faster, grip harder.

And then her thighs come crashing against both sides of my skull. She begins bouncing against my mouth, trying to get away, but I just hold on firmer, never stopping the unmerciful torment that my mouth is giving her. Since she can't get free like her body is demanding of her, she collapses forward in beautiful agony. And finally, I let her wrists go and allow her to fall to the floor, the gulping gasps of her breath making her pussy writhe and twist against my lips.

I gently remove my other hand from her ass, place both palms against her hips, and begin sliding her off my mouth and down. She giggles as the lips of her pussy graze along my beard, and she stops making any sounds when her thighs edge along the rippled flesh of my chest. I keep pushing her downward until my cock is resting against the entrance of her pussy and we are face to face. Red hair spilling around my eyes. And I am struck by how very much it feels like I know her. Like I have known her from well before now. Like I have known her since time immemorial.

I reach around and unfasten her firehouse-red bra which is that last bit of clothing that separates her bare skin from mine, lift her to the side, placing her on her knees, and I rise to my knees as well and I stare at her, wordlessly.

"What?" she asks.

I don't answer. Just keep staring.

"No. Seriously, what?"

"I dreamed of you," I tell her.

She arches up enough to make sure we can see each other clearly. "Yeah?"

I nod.

"What did you dream?"

I pause, trying to decide what's the appropriate information to share. Should I tell her that in my dream, she works in a Heaven that looks like an Apple Store? Should I tell her that I incinerate her and all that is around her? Should I tell her that she makes a really good cup of tea? None of these tidbits seem like information that will do either one of us any good to have spat out into the world, so instead I grab her around the waist, pull her to me, kiss her hard on her still-bleeding mouth, and say, "This…"

Then I lay her on her back, plank my body above hers, holding there for just long enough to see the gleam in her eye, and then I drive myself down and into her before the flames of our impending destruction can rise up and make me stop.

MADDIE

"Oh, shit!" I cry out.

He is not just entering me, or fucking me, or anything as common as that. He is penetrating me. In every sense of the word. I have never in my life—not once—cried during sex, but I can feel the tears starting to well up behind my eyes. And I have no earthly idea why.

He must be able to tell because he asks, "Am I hurting you?"

I shake my head, willing the tears not to fall. He withdraws from inside me.

"Where are you going?" I ask.

He stands up—he is an impressive sight. He looks like Michelangelo's *David*. But if David had fought his way through some kind of battle and emerged from it painted by the fury of the fight.

"Come here," he says as he reaches for my hand and draws me up to stand with him. Naked and exposed, we both look at each other in the warm light of this nearly empty apartment, with the frivolous concerns of the rest of the world carrying on beyond his massive windows, unaware that we are here. And I feel vulnerable.

I think he feels it too because now he takes me by the hand and leads me over to the kitchen area, which is a little darker, a little more hidden. When we land there, he picks me up around the waist and plops me onto his kitchen island. "Ah! It's cold," I let out.

"It'll warm up in a second," he says and winks. He opens a drawer and I glance down to note that inside there are only restaurant menus, some extra chopsticks still in their paper wrappers, and an assortment of condoms.

"We ordering in?" I ask. He ignores me and rips open the wrapper on one of the condoms.

"I want to be inside you when I come. Not that coming on your ass wasn't one of life's great joys, but, y'know, been there, done that." He winks again. Fuck, he's hot. Scraggly beard and all. Although I'm suddenly trying to imagine what it'd be like if he shaved. What the face that's hiding under that mess of hair might look like.

But instead, I follow up my previous question with, "And you keep them in the kitchen because…?"

"I keep 'em everywhere," he says, unrolling the latex and sliding it on his still-hard cock. "Never know when the delivery boy might be up for a little somethin'-somethin'."

I rub my foot up the inside of his thigh. "Mmm. It gets a girl so hot when guys talk about fucking delivery boys." He smiles. I get the sense that he gets off on it when I talk shit to him. Which is fine by me, because I love talking shit. So…

"Now fuck me like I'm the pizza guy," I say.

He laughs and pulls me close into him at the same time. He grabs two fistfuls of hair and I gasp. He kisses me hard, his tongue competing with mine. He slides it across my teeth and then he pulls it out and traces the contours of my lips. Then he nibbles at my chin. It's so fucking hot and sweet, my pussy starts throbbing remembering how it felt to have that same tongue inside of it just moments ago.

He eyes my legs. "What are you looking at?" I ask.

"You're tall," he says.

"Yeah."

"That's good," he says. "Here." He stands between my thighs, grips the outside of my hips, and slides me to the edge of the island where I'm sitting. "Stick your legs out," he demands.

I see what he wants now. So I do it. I extend my calves outward until the soles of my feet are on the edge of the counter behind him. And then I place my palms on the island under me and lift my ass so that I am suspended there, my pussy at the perfect height in midair for him to reach. He puts his hands under me for additional support, to aid me in fucking him like we're both dying for.

"Don't let me fall," I say.

"No chance," he says in return.

Hands on my ass, me strung across the chasm between the two surfaces on which I'm balancing, he stares hard into my eyes and draws himself inside, never breaking eye contact, staring through me, lifting and pressing himself deeper and deeper until I think there's no way I could possibly take any more of him in. And then… he pushes one last inch.

"Oh, my fuck," I gasp.

"Fuck, yeah," he groans out.

And I throw my head back, half laughing, half trying to catch my breath, as he begins the slow, methodical pulling and pushing of himself in and out. I begin rocking with my arms and legs to counter the way he's stroking the walls of my pussy. In and out. In and out. In. And out.

We begin picking up momentum, him pulling harder each time we close the space between us. In the wash of the blinking lights spilling through the windows from the outside, I can see the veins in his strong forearms tensing and bulging as he muscles his way inside me over and over. He stands on his toes and bends his knees slightly so that he can angle just right to hit my clit with his pelvis as he drives himself forward.

"Oh, fuck, fuck, fuck," I let out. Because this son of a bitch is going to make me come again. Again.

"You got that right," he moans out as he keeps pounding into me.

Every. Single. Push. He. Makes. Feels. Like. It's. Going. To. Make. Me—

"FUUUUUUUCK!" I scream. And I'm glad this is the only apartment on this floor, because there's no way someone wouldn't call the cops if they heard it.

I throw my head back completely, driving my body upwards as I do, forcing him to extend his legs straight up and stand on his tiptoes to keep me from pretty much ripping his dick off inside me as my walls tighten around his shaft. Which would be fine with me. I want to keep it all to myself. But I'm sure he wants to hang onto it too.

"Easy there, angel. Easy," he says, as he wraps his palms around my hips to force me back down to where I'm level with his waist. I lift my head back up to see his face. He's smiling. For the first time, I notice the little wrinkles around the corners of his eyes when he smiles. It makes some guys look old when they get those lines, but he looks more boyish somehow. Like a kid laughing at his favorite cartoon. Something about him is so—

"What?" he asks, and I realize I must have been staring too long.

"Nothing," I say, and I pull my legs away from the counter now, to wrap around him and draw him to me. I throw my arms around his neck and lift myself so that I'm staring down into his eyes, and still riding his cock.

"Turn around," I command.

"OK." He complies.

"Sit," I say. He lifts himself and places both of us on the island where I was sitting before.

"OK," he says. "And…?"

"And now I'm gonna ride you until you fucking come inside me."

"OK." He smiles.

I put my hands on his shoulders and start sliding back and forth on his lap, bending and massaging his dick with the grip of my pussy and thighs.

"Fuck," he exhales. "Y'know…" he starts.

"What?" I look at him and ask.

He gets another wry little smile and says, "You're much better at this than the pizza boy."

TYLER

Her body fits mine perfectly. And I don't just mean the way her legs are long and her torso hits me in the right place and all that usual bullshit. I mean even the way her breasts blend into the uneven rivers of memory on my chest. Somehow they just fill in the empty spaces and make it all whole.

And she wraps around my cock like she was built to live there. Maybe she was. I'm considering not letting her leave.

My legs are dangling over the edge of the island, but my toes can just touch the floor. So I'm allowing them to help me push up and into her as she glides back and forth, sliding my shaft along with her slow grind.

"Lie back," she tells me.

I do. I lower my back onto the countertop and stare up at her in all her fiery luminescence as she rides my dick, her shallow panting punctuated by the licking of her pouting lips. She is everything.

She leans back, hands just above my knees, and pushes herself up and then down, forward and then back, sometimes wiggling her hips in little circles, sometimes not. It feels like I'm being fucked, blown, massaged, tickled, drugged, and fed strawberry ice cream all at the same time.

"You gonna come for me?" she asks.

"I think I can make that happen," I barely moan out as I'm starting to lose the ability to make thoughts into words.

And now she begins to lift her body up and down, bouncing on my dick slightly as she goes back and forth. Stroking my shaft and bending it all at once, and I automatically start thrusting up to meet her on every return she makes toward me. And seamlessly, progressively, our thrusts get faster. She's punishing my cock and I'm trying as hard as I can to tear through the ceiling and launch us out into the night sky so we can touch the stars.

She's panting, she's moaning, she's squealing, and every sound that leaves her perfect, precious body just makes me fuck her that much harder.

Her red ringlets are bouncing up and down, her perfect, beautiful tits are bouncing with them. She has her hands on my chest now, giving me the sexiest CPR in history. I prop myself on my elbows so that I can get my hips up and dig into her as deeply as possible. Her eyes are closed as she bounces and wiggles and grinds.

I suddenly remember a Yogi I met when I was in India. He tried to tell me about Tantric sex but I kind of blew it off. I'm regretting that now. Big time. Because I don't want to come yet. I don't. I want to stay in this moment for as long as possible.

But unfortunately, I'm not a Tantric Yogi, I'm just a fucking dumb, broken, marred, undeserving, and—at the moment—very lucky SOB who's with a woman he's been dreaming about. Literally. And I can't hold out another second more.

"Fuck, angel, I'm gonna come," I manage to say.

"Yeah, yes, do it. Fill me up. Fucking fill me up. I need to be filled. Please."

And just like before, it's the 'please' that does me in. And with one last push, I unload inside her. My stomach tightens and I sit up straight, grabbing her behind the back and locking my mouth to hers. Her legs wrap tighter behind me, pulling us closer and closer together and pushing her hips down so that she can take as much of me in as is humanly possible.

I keep thrusting and I feel the inside of the condom filling with come. And I just keep coming. And as I shout out one last "Fuck," the final bit of sticky heat shoots out of me. I'm gasping for breath. So is she. We are both completely spent and drained and lost inside the other. I touch my forehead to hers and go to kiss her, kind of catching her on the nose by accident. She giggles.

I lean back, resting on my elbows, my legs dangling over the sides of my kitchen island (which is currently being put to the best use it's seen since I bought the place) and just… look at her. Her hair is a mess and it's beautiful. The cut on her lip where I bit her before has stopped bleeding, but the little nick remains. And it's beautiful. The creamy whiteness of her skin is blotched red from the workout she just had. And it's beautiful.

She's fucking beautiful.

She starts gnawing at her bottom lip, a gleam in her eye and a smile creeping up.

"What?" I ask.

She doesn't say anything. Just keeps smiling.

"What?" I laugh out a little bit.

She pulls her legs back so that she can bend over fully, she leans down close to my face so that our lips almost touch, she lets out a tiny breath, and she says…

"So. Did you come?"

CHAPTER EIGHTEEN

"You've got like twenty different kinds of whiskey, ten different kinds of beer, but no bottles of water..."

She's looking through my refrigerator and cabinets. I'm sitting on a stool at the island watching her. We're both still naked. She's so pretty.

"The fridge has a water thing in it—"

She grabs a glass and goes to press the water button.

"—but I can't get it to work. Think it's broken. I need to call a guy."

She stares at me, smiles and shakes her head.

"The sink works fine," I tell her.

"Gross. I'm not drinking tap water."

"You drank my come, but you won't drink tap water?"

"I don't know where the water's from. I got the come directly from the source." She opens the menu/condom drawer. "But I could be persuaded to boil some... I saw a couple of tea bags when you had the drawer open, and... aha." Indeed, she pulls out two tea bags. They must have been included with one of the Chinese food deliveries.

"You want a cup of tea?"

And suddenly, I'm having a very uncomfortable moment of déjà vu.

"Hey…" She waves her hand in front of my face. "Tea?" She holds up the bags.

"You sure you don't just want some whiskey? Beer?" I ask.

She laughs. "No. Normally I would. Usually I do. But I'm trying to… I think I'm gonna lay off drinking for a while. Fresh start. Tomorrow's gonna be a new day." She smiles. It melts me.

"Joy cometh with the morning," I mutter under my breath.

"What's that?"

"Hm? Oh. Nothing." Then I add, "But you're sure you don't want, like, just some plain old dirty tap water? Anything at all other than tea, maybe?"

She smiles again, but while making a tiny frown with her eyes. "Weirdo," she mumbles at me. She's right.

She fills up the electric kettle with water and hits the button to turn it on. "So what happened there?" she asks. She's referring to the charred toast briquette which I still haven't bothered to remove from the see-through toaster.

"Oh. Uh, toast. Is. Y'know. Tricky."

She turns to face me and eyes me with suspicion.

"What? It is," I say. "Plus, like everything in this apartment, it's all too fuckin' fancy to figure out. I think the settings on everything are metric or something."

She saunters across the narrow channel between the cabinets and the island where just a short time before she was suspended in the air, held aloft by my cock, and leans in across from me. She rests her elbows on the counter and I very cautiously place my forearms down and allow the tips of my fingers to touch hers. She doesn't pull away. Which makes me happy.

Then she takes a deep breath and says, "So… like, serious question?"

I tap my fingers on hers and nod, "Sure. OK."

"What do you do to afford this place?"

"The lumberjack game is crazy lucrative," I say.

"Seriously, dude. Are you, what? High-stakes poker player? Drug trafficker? Please don't be a fucking drug trafficker. I don't need that shit right now."

"No." I laugh. "I'm not… uh… I kind of helped invent a thing that we… or I… was able to sell to the government for a shitload of money, but like also I kind of was able to hold onto the patent so that I could sell it to private corporations for their own applications and shit and I also got to keep an ownership stake and royalties and blah, blah, blah, whatever, I made a bunch of cash."

She nods. "What is it?" she asks. "What'd you invent?"

"Just… me and this other guy, Nadir, we… do you know what EOD stands for?"

"Um… Excited Orgasmic Dicks?"

God, I think I love this girl.

"No." I laugh. "I mean, yes, but in this case… Explosive Ordnance Disposal. It's like a job in the military that's there to keep shit from blowing up on people."

"… OK."

"So, yeah, so it's a fucked-up, dangerous job, and me and this other guy invented this, like, Artificial Intelligence Augmentation—or, like, I kind of *thought* of it and then he figured out how to actually make it *work*—but this thing that could be applied to the robots they sometimes use to make 'em more, like, intuitive and reliable and whatever, and help eliminate the risk to, y'know, human people. Whatever. It's not actually all that exciting."

She's very, very quiet for a moment. I see her looking at my scars.

After a second, she asks, "Where's Nadir?"

I don't answer. Or I do. Just without actually saying anything.

"Yeah," she says. Then, "So why Vegas?"

"Why—? You mean why'd I move to Vegas?"

"Yeah."

I shrug. "Dunno. Tried other places. Lived in New York for a while. Kicked around. But I grew up here, so I figured I'd just come home. Plus, y'know, there's no corporate income tax in Nevada, so… Actually, I don't really understand that part, but my business manager told me it was a good thing."

She laughs. Kind of. Then she gets serious again.

"So you grew up here? In Vegas?"

"Yeah. Yeah, 'til I was eighteen and then I split."

She nods, again, *kind* of. Then she pulls her hands away from mine so that our fingers are no longer touching. Which makes me not happy. She stares off.

"What?" I ask. "What's up?"

"I—Nothing," she says. Then she asks, "Hey, how old are you?"

And suddenly I start to feel hot and a little panicky. "Oh, shit. Fuck me. How old are YOU?" I respond.

She half-laughs. "Relax, man. I'm twenty-five. I'm a big girl."

"OK. Cool. Sorry, I just—"

"No, I get it, but maybe you should have asked sooner."

"Well, hell, I dunno. I just figured you work in a strip club so you must be at least—"

"Yeah, no, I got it."

All of the sudden, it's awkward. I'm not completely sure why. But it's gotten quiet and it feels like it's hard to talk. I'm not sure what to say. But I try.

"So where are you from?" I come up with.

She eyes me, still with some reservation. "Vegas," she says, finally.

"No shit," I say. "Where'd you go to high school? I mean, we probably would've missed each other, but—"

"What did you mean, you dreamed about me?" she interrupts.

Things are very testy all of a sudden and I don't like it. I also wish that I hadn't told her that I dreamed about her. Because I cannot tell her what THE DREAM is all about. Best-case scenario, she thinks I'm crazy (I AM, of course, crazy, but I don't want HER to think that) and fucking takes off on me. Worst-case scenario, even just talking about THE DREAM brings it into reality somehow and it plays out in real life, here in my kitchen. I don't know the metaphysics of dream-to-reality science, but I don't need my whole world going up in flames. Especially not tonight. Not on this night of all nights. Not on this night where for the first time in years, I feel something other than shame, and misery, and regret. So I decide to see if I can get this train back on the tracks.

"I didn't mean anything. Hey, how long you been stripping?" I say. (Smooth, Tyler. Nice work.)

She squints. Like she's sizing me up. Like she's trying to figure something out.

"Not long," she says. "So where were you headed when you picked me up?"

I pause. Then, "I dunno. Just driving. I was maybe gonna get out of town. Fuckin' hate Halloween."

She shifts her neck back. Like she's pulling away. "Why?" she asks.

I don't understand why things are weird, but something inside me is telling me that too much truth right now would be a bad thing. I want to tell her the truth. I do. I want to tell her everything about me, but she's getting skittish and I know exactly what the air feels like before a bomb explodes, and that's how the air in this room feels right now, so I'm keenly aware that I should move ahead carefully.

"Just, you know," I start, "Halloween just feels like an excuse for idiots to play pretend that they're something they're not. Dudes get to act like superheroes even though they aren't and girls dress up like whores and prance around like it's funny or…" Shit. That seems to make her bristle a bit, so I add, "Present company excluded."

She still very much does not smile but we're in Vegas, so fuck it, I double down.

"I mean it! You look like… well, shit… you look like an angel. You're just… you're beautiful, and you're kind, and you're smart, and you're funny, and when I saw you standing in the road like that, you really did look like an angel fallen from Heaven. And, I dunno, I probably sound hokey, but whatever. I think you're amazing. And so, y'know, thank you. Because you helped me hate Halloween just a little bit less." I smile.

She sighs, bows her head, and peers up at me through her eyelids.

"Listen, it's true. And you know what? You can believe that or not if you want, because…" I put on what can only be described as a fucking terrible Rhett Butler impersonation and say, "Frankly, my dear, I don't give a damn."

She half-smiles, half-looks confused.

"It's from *Gone with the Wind.* 'Cause, y'know, 'cause you're Scarlett, and—"

"Yeah, I, I get it," she says.

She still seems annoyed. I shrug, "Sorry. I like movies."

I stare down at the floor. I feel like a little kid who got his hand caught in the cookie jar. I'm trying so hard not to fuck everything up but somehow, I'm failing. And I am immediately hyper-conscious that we are both still naked.

She takes a long breath and then slowly approaches the counter again.

"I'm sorry if I'm being weird. I just kinda hate Halloween too."

"Yeah? Why do you?"

She takes a long pause, studies my face, and then says, "Same reasons."

The bell on the kettle dings.

"Top shelf, bottom left cabinet," I say, meaning that's where she can find a mug.

She turns, pulls a mug from the shelf, places one of the tea bags in, and begins pouring the hot water. The steam rises up around her head, creating the illusion from behind of smoke coming off her fiery red mane. Then she places the kettle down and continues holding the mug. She doesn't turn around. Her shoulders lift as she takes in a deep breath, and then fall as she releases it. Then she asks…

"What's your name?"

My heart starts racing. Fast. Like real fast. Like holy fucking shit, I'm having a heart attack fast. Then I wonder if I am having a heart attack. Maybe I am. But they say that when you have a heart attack you're supposed to smell the smell of toast. And I don't. Smell toast. Or is that for a stroke? And does it matter? Because there's burnt toast still in the toaster, so couldn't it just be that I'm smelling that toast? Which I'm not. Smelling toast, that is. So I can't be having a heart attack. Unless that's not the smell. Fuck!

"Sorry. What?" I ask as calmly as I can.

"I said… what's your real name?"

I don't know why this is freaking me out. This is what I wanted. I've wanted to know her and to have her know me. I think. No. I know it. I know I have. I really, really, really like this angel. Shit, maybe I love this angel. I don't know if that's possible, but it's the feeling I feel. I think. Fuck. A. Duck. OK. She's asked a simple question and I should just give a simple answer. It'll be awesome. Now she'll know me and then I'll get to know her, and we can start building our perfect life together. Because that's how this is supposed to go. Because it has to. Because I've earned it.

Because I've earned it.

"… Um… Tyler," I say. "My name's Tyler Morgan."

— There's a famous moment in the movie *The Usual Suspects*. It's right at the very end. It's the moment where Detective Dave Kujan, played by Chazz Palminteri, discovers who the mysterious Keyser Söze is and that he's been talking with him, alone in a room, just the two of them, for the whole movie. He realizes suddenly that this entire time, he's been conversing with an entity of pure evil. An unrepentant, unforgiving, unconscionable myth of a demon whose only function here on earth is to hurt and punish and to serve his own base, selfish wants and desires. He has been communing with the devil himself.

And that moment of realization is symbolized by the coffee mug Detective Kujan has been holding, slipping, in slow motion, from his grip and falling to the floor where it shatters into pieces just as his understanding of reality and the world he occupies shatters along with it. —

That exact thing, to the letter, is what happens now, in my kitchen.

The mug goes crashing to the floor, spilling hot tea as it shatters around her feet. I jump up from my stool.

"What! What's wrong? What happened? Are you OK?"

She places both hands on the edge of the sink in front of her and her shoulders begin heaving and convulsing. I can tell she's hyperventilating. I jump up to come around and see if she's OK. She raises her right hand in the air, palm toward me, and shouts, "No!" I stop in my tracks.

"Don't!" she yells. "Don't you fucking come near me!"

I think I am having a fucking heart attack. For real.

"I—I—" I stammer, like an idiot. "I don't—What's wrong?"

I can sort of see, as I try to peek through the shroud of red hair that drapes her face, that tears have started streaming down her cheeks. She's attempting to get her breathing under control, gasping air and swallowing.

She wails, "Oh, God. Oh, my God. Oh, dear fucking Jesus God, WHY!!!???"

I'm seriously about to lose my shit. I've never felt like this in my life. Not even in combat.

"Please," I plead, "Please, please, please tell me what's wrong. Please…"

She takes two more short, sharp breaths, and then she turns to face me, eyes filled with tears, cheeks as fire-red as her flaming hair, and she screams right in my face…

"IT'S MADDIE! I'M FUCKING MADDIE CLAYTON, TYLER!"

—There's a reason I've watched a lot of movies. Escape. As a kid, after my mom died, I needed to get away sometimes, so I'd escape to the movies. Evan, Scotty, and I could sometimes sneak from one theatre to the next and spend all day there. And then when I was deployed, we all would watch movies a lot. Same reason. When you're not on patrol or on a mission, there's not always a fuck-ton to do so watching movies is a good way to escape your shitty situation and kill time. So now, all these years later, I still think of things kinda cinematically from time to time. And there's an effect they use in like horror movies and stuff, especially older ones, where they'll like move the camera backwards while pushing the lens forward and it makes it feel like the character on screen is being pushed and pulled at the same time or falling away and getting closer all at once. It's always that moment when someone's world has just been turned upside down… I can't see my face right now, but I know that's what's happening to me.—

"Oh, fuck!" I scream. "What the fuck?"

"Oh, God, oh, God, oh, God," she keeps saying. And the worst part about it is that I heard her say those same words a little while ago, but with a very different meaning.

"Oh, fuck," she goes on, "oh, fuck, oh, fuck, oh, fuck." And then she starts coughing. And then she leans over my beautiful, fancy, industrial-looking, stainless-steel sink… and she throws up.

Maddie Clayton. Maddie Clayton, the kid I last saw when she was thirteen years old and I was driving out of town. Maddie Clayton, the adorable, fresh-faced little over-achiever I used to marvel at because she was smarter everyone else, even then. Maddie Clayton, who always looked at me like I was the coolest guy on the block, and who you could just tell was gonna do great things one day. Maddie Clayton, WHOSE HAIR WAS LIKE MORE OF A REDDISH-BROWN! WASN'T IT?

Maddie Clayton. My dead best friend Scotty Clayton's baby sister.

Here.

With me.

Caught in an eruption of flame that consumes us both.

"What the **FUCK**?" I exclaim, over and over—and over—as I pace frantically but aimlessly, both hands running through my hair, trying to pull my brain from my skull.

Maddie has finished throwing up and is now sitting on my kitchen floor. I approach her. "Don't you fucking come near me!" she lets out. I stop. Again. I put my hands out in a gesture that says, 'I'm staying here, see?' as I lower myself to the floor in kind.

We both take a moment to try to figure out… fuck… anything. After what feels like a while, she goes first.

"When the fuck did you come back?"

"I… few months ago."

She nods her head and gives an air-snort-laugh kind of a thing.

I decide to keep talking. "I didn't know you were still here. Evan told me you guys moved to, like, Monaco or something a few years back."

She shakes her head. "Mom and Dad. I stayed."

"Fuck me. Evan said he hadn't talked to you in… and that he thought that… Shit. I didn't know."

She looks at the wall. She looks back. After a beat she says, "You've seen Evan?"

I nod. "Yeah. He's pretty much the only person I see. Him and my shrink. That's it."

"Fuck you," she says over a bitter laugh. And now all the things that I liked when they were exclaimed at me sound harshly different.

There's so much, I don't know where to start. I go with, "What the fuck are you doing working at a strip club?"

I wish I hadn't started there.

"Oh, Jesus, fuck you. Go fuck yourself," she responds. Which seems fair.

"Dammit," I say in return, "Maddie… I… look, there's clearly a lot to… but… listen, are you in like trouble or something? Those guys who were—?"

"No!" She stops me. "No. You do not get to ask me questions. You get that? You do NOT."

I nod. I'm stumped. I don't know what my next play is here. So I just wait. Finally…

"What happened to you?" she asks.

I look up. "What? Whatayou mean? All this shit?" I point up and down at my scars.

"No. I could fucking give a shit. I assume you must've almost gotten killed. Which would be a much better sentence if I could take the word 'almost' out of it."

Ouch.

"I mean… you know… one of the things I remember about you most was how goddamn rah-rah you were about loyalty. You remember that shit? How you and Scotty and Evan were the fuckin' Three Musketeers and how loyalty is the most important thing in the world and how… what was that shit you used to talk? All that hoorah, military bullshit about like, 'be whoever you are, just be there for me when I need you' or whatever it was?"

Hearing my own bullshit mantra thrown in my face like that hurts worse than any goddamn explosion could ever feel. I'd take getting blown up a hundred more times over what's happening to me right now.

"So," she continues. "So. What. Fucking. Happened?"

I have nothing to say.

"You were family. And you just… you were a ghost… in the wind. I sent you emails. I tried to call you on a damn sat phone. I wrote letters! Like actual fucking letters to a dude at war like it's 1942, and I never heard back from you. I don't know if you can even start to get your head around how fucked up that is, but it's pretty damn shitty. So it's a simple question. What happened to you?"

Here's what happened. I felt guilty. I felt like a piece of shit. I felt like it was all my fault and I was too ashamed to tell you all. I felt like I could've saved Scotty and I failed. I felt like I would have to answer questions and own up and be responsible. I felt like my life was over too and so I threw myself headlong into work, hoping I could make it a reality. I became reckless. I tried to get myself killed. And then instead I got even more people killed. That's what happened.

I'm sorry.

But, of course, I say none of that. Instead… I shrug.

She goes stock still for, I'm not exaggerating, ten full minutes. Then…

"I gotta get the fuck out of here." She stands. And—and I know this is fucked up, I do, but—she looks so sexy, naked, and angry, and spent, standing there in front of me.

I just want to grab her and fuck her and pretend none of this is real, and that what is real is that she's Scarlett and I'm Ford and we can live happily the fuck ever after.

But that shit ain't the truth. The truth is… I'm fucked.

"I need clothes," she says. "Gimme some goddamn clothes."

I nod slightly and stand up. "Bedroom," I say.

I walk into the bedroom. She stops outside the doorway. I reach into a dresser drawer and toss her the first t-shirt I find. A white *Reservoir Dogs* t-shirt. One of the ones with all the characters wearing their suits and walking and smoking.

"Really?" she says. I shrug yet again. "Fuck it. Give it to me." I toss her the shirt.

"Pants?" she asks.

"Um," I say, "Shit. I dunno if—" I start looking through drawers trying to find anything that might fit her. "Uh, I don't think… I might, um—" Suddenly I find a pair of women's yoga pants in my hand. "Oh. Here," I say and toss them to her.

"What the hell are you doing with these?" she rightly asks.

"I dunno. Not sure. Somebody musta left 'em, I guess."

She takes them and, with disgust, puts them on. Then she heads for the front door.

"Wait," I say, following. "You don't have shoes and you can't—Where are you going anyway?"

She turns, fiercely. "I'm gonna go see if my car is still there, which I'm sure it isn't because I left my bag in it and my keys inside, which is perfect because that means my house has probably now been robbed too, but you know, Tyler? Even with all this…" And then she points me up and down. "I mean even with ALL this, this isn't the worst Halloween I've ever had."

I know what she's going to say. Of course I do. The worst Halloween she had was seven years ago, when Scotty died.

"The worst Halloween I ever had was six years ago, the year after Scotty died."

Oh. Guess I didn't know.

"Because, and there's no way you'd know this, I guess, but…" She takes a breath. It's clear she doesn't want to say whatever it is she's thinking.

I tell her, "If you don't feel like—"

"Shut the fuck up," she says. I do. She stares at the floor, fills her lungs with oxygen, and begins.

"I don't know how I made it through that first year. I really don't. Partially because I was drunk and high for a lot of it. But I did. I muscled through. Even managed to pull a 2.5 GPA, which… I mean not flunking out was a miracle in and of itself."

"Why didn't you just take some time off? Don't they let you—?"

"I said shut. Up." I do. Again. She continues. "And I figured all I had to do was take the summer after that first year of school, pull my shit together, and then I could go back the next fall, kick ass, and show myself what I was made of. Because that's what Scotty would have done, right? That's who my brother was. He never quit. He never backed down no matter how hard something got. He never gave up."

She pauses, I'm assuming to give me a chance to say something stupid again, but I refrain. She resumes.

"I had no idea if you were aware of any of what was going on at the time because all my calls were unanswered and my emails and letters didn't get responses, but I kept writing them and making the calls and trying, because I felt like I was at least sharing with somebody. Somebody who could maybe understand. Somebody I—Whatever. You know how my parents are, so…"

I'm getting the sickening feeling that I know where this is going and I'm starting to feel very, very ashamed right now.

"So even though you never responded or tried at all—and I didn't know then if you were reading the letters and just choosing not to respond, which is shitty, or ignoring them altogether in the first place, which is worse—but even though I never heard back, it made me feel OK to at least *pretend* that there was someone out there helping me through. But. That illusion got dispelled for me on this day, six years ago. Because on that day, the one-year anniversary of my brother's death, I came home—I was living back at home—to be greeted with the news that Dad had accepted a new job and that my parents were moving to fucking MONACO. Which, I'm sure you'll understand, was quite a shock. And I think I was still a little in shock when I went to the mailbox to find that the last letter that I ever tried to send to you had come back to the house marked 'Return to Sender.' With a handwritten note on the back—in, I presume, your handwriting—that read, 'Please stop sending me letters.' This sound familiar at all?"

She's trying to look me in the eyes, but she can't because they're facing the floor, my chin buried into my chest.

"Yeah. And for whatever it's worth, I poured my guts out in that letter. Oh, man, I really did. I said all kinds of shit. Shit about how I was feeling then. How I had been feeling for the last year. How I felt about YOU. How I had felt about you for a long time. How—even though I was a kid when you left—I had kind of always thought I loved you—"

That snaps my attention back up.

"Oh, yeah. Oh, yeah. I said ALL that shit. And I meant it. I meant every word of it. I don't wanna brag, but as letters to soldiers at war go, man, it was right up there with the all-time greats. Shame you never got to read it."

And this is how the world ends. This. Is how the world. Ends.

"And so…" She keeps going. "So that was the night that I realized, 'Oh, shit. Wow. I am really and truly ALONE in the world.' And y'know what?"

She takes a long, long breath.

"I guess I kind of have to thank you. Because tonight…" She shakes her head. "Tonight could've been really, really awful, but THIS doesn't even compare to THAT. Oh, it sucks. I mean, sure, it sucks, because I thought maybe I'd met this weird guy who I had some kind of strange, inexplicable connection with and that maybe, *just maybe,* things might get be getting better for me or they may start turning around or becoming, like, y'know, *tolerable.* And that, gee, maybe I won't have to keep rumbling along all by myself, just bouncing off wall after wall until I become numb to the pain. But then it turns out that it wasn't a real, like, decent human man hiding behind that beard… but you."

Ouch. Again.

"And so yeah, this BLOWS, but it's nothing new. I didn't learn a single new thing. This just reinforces everything I've known since that night six years ago…"

She gets close. So close that I can smell myself on her, still. And just like before, it's fucked up, but my dick twitches a little. And she says, "I'm the only person in this fucking world I can count on."

She turns.

"So I will."

And before I can say a goddamn word, she has her hand on the doorknob.

"Maddie, please! Wait!"

And I don't know why, but she does. She pauses. Head down, hair covering her face, but she pauses and I take my Hail Mary shot.

"I'm sorry! I'm so, so, so, so, so, so very sorry. I was scared. OK? I was scared and I was destroyed, and… and… you talk about being alone? Yeah, I get it. I fuckin' get it. I feel that way too. Felt that way the whole time I was gone. And I never knew if the next day was gonna be my last, and I was so scared that if, y'know, something happened to me that you—and your mom and dad too, but mostly you—wouldn't be able to deal. And I did read your emails and your letters. I did. But they were hard. They were hard for me. Because I was over there and you were here and I hadn't seen you in so long, but I could hear in the writing and in the things you said that you had become this amazing, special, really cool woman and it hurt. It hurt my heart for you because I knew you were hurting and I… I know me, Maddie. I do. I know myself. There's no way that I wouldn't make you hurt worse. Because that shit is what I do. Best case: I die and you have to deal with that loss too. Worst case: I live, show up back in your life and fuck it up some other, terrible way, because that's what I'm known for. Ask anybody."

I take a breath so she can say… something, but she doesn't.

"So, I mean, look, this is obviously some bitter fucking irony here, because what's happening RIGHT NOW is the very thing I was trying to avoid, but… I've changed. Or… AM changing. Am trying to change. And I can make it right. I know I can. I swear. Please. Because everything that I have felt for you over these last couple of weeks have been real. Even though I didn't know it was you. And you didn't know it was me! And when you didn't know it was me, you felt it too! I know you did! So let's just be those people. Or… those versions of ourselves. Because—and it makes so much sense now!—because I think I may love you, Maddie. Like, I think I'm falling in love with you. YOU. Because, because of course we knew each other. Of course we did. That's why this feels like it does. Because we have known each other since our old lives, since before all this broken reality for both of us began. So we are connected. Pure. Real. On a cellular level. Somehow, this is what was supposed to happen. I did dream of you. I did. And in my dream you were so ethereal and kind and wonderful. Just like you are now. Just like the real you is now. And I'm SO sorry. And I'll never be able to say it enough, but we have connected and I think we need each other and better late than never and please just give it a chance. Please. Please… Because I do. I think I love you. I… think I love you, Maddie."

That's it. That's all my inside voice spilling out in an unedited torrent. I have laid myself bare in all ways, and I stand here naked and stripped in all ways, prostrating myself before her. Begging forgiveness for my sins. Asking for her grace.

She continues staring at the floor. Then, out of seemingly nowhere, she says, "Do you know how Scotty died?"

"I—" I do, but suddenly I find myself questioning. "I—I mean, I think… Yeah, I mean, he died trying to save that guy, the other hotshot guy who he pushed out of the way of the falling tree or whatever it was… right?"

A beat as she twists her head slowly back and forth in a tiny shake, before she sighs out and says, "Fuck, man. It's funny. Some people, y'know, like Scotty? They do all the right things, live with as much integrity as they can muster, try to stand for some kind of… I dunno… principle? Give of themselves to others, sacrifice, live a righteous life, and then at the end of it all they get handed the most horrible kind of fate imaginable. And then other people, shitty people, people with no true north, no guiding principle, no reason for you to believe anything they have to say, and who just kind of do what they want, when they want, how they want without thinking about how it's affecting other people, people they claim to have love for…" She sniffs a bitter little laugh. "Shit… they get to go to sleep tonight in this fucking penthouse."

She twists the doorknob, opens the door, steps into the doorframe, and—silhouetted by the shadow of the door on her face, trapped between the light from the hall and the flickering neon lights of Vegas shimmering through the windows onto her cheek—she turns her head enough for me to see her profile, sighs a small sad sigh, and almost inaudibly, she lets free her final, parting words.

"Why did it have to be you?"

And as the door falls softly shut, I close my eyes knowing…

There will be no joy. There will be no morning.

CHAPTER NINETEEN

MADDIE

For every action there is an equal and opposite reaction.

I know this is some kind of universal law I learned in seventh-grade science class, and why I know it—and have known it since the first time I read it in my middle-school textbook—is about as understandable as anything else that's happening to me at the moment. But it fits. It fits my life like a goddamned glove.

I clearly did something once, something terrible and ugly, and all this bad luck isn't bad luck at all. It's fate. It's destiny. Maybe I'm just an inexplicably evil person or have one of those dark souls. Or fuck it... maybe I'm just paying the price for original sin.

Who really gives a fuck?

I deserve this. It's the Third Law of Motion. I am a million examples of equal and opposite reactions. Every single thing that's happened to me has been nothing but a reaction to my actions.

Even Tyler Morgan.

So it turns out I was wrong. This whole time. There is no right way to do anything. Not make toast, or get to work, or get through life trying to be happy.

The elevator dings and opens. I walk out, stunned silent and on autopilot.

"Ma'am?" the doorman says as he opens the door for me. "Are you OK?"

The next thing I know I'm walking down Las Vegas Boulevard and I can only assume I never answered him. I look down at my feet because I have no shoes on and the sidewalk is cold, and notice somewhere between there and here, I cut myself. Looking over my shoulder I see a trail of red footprints behind me.

This is Vegas. Home of the weird and sad. So no one takes any notice of me at all. Life goes on all around me in a blur of motion that makes me feel like I'm just an extra in someone else's movie.

I head toward Pete's because I have nowhere else to go. I have no phone, I have no car, I have no money… I have nothing because I am no one. Going back to Pete's feels like returning to the scene of a crime. The crime I committed was allowing myself to believe that things might turn out OK. I'm not being morose or feeling bad for myself—I'm really not—I'm just confronting a bitter reality. If this is, in fact, reality.

It takes an hour to make my way back to Pete's. It's cold. Desert cold. Dry and dusty and barren. As I approach the alley behind the club, I think of what we did back here. And how good it felt. And thinking about how good it felt makes me feel bad now. I think of what he said to me—"You're going to kill me"—and I remember thinking that maybe we'd kill each other. Seems more like a premonition now than just a random thought.

Tyler Morgan. Shit. The potential for some chance at happiness ripped from my precarious grip by the inconceivable arrival of Tyler Morgan. Just one more example of all the equal and opposite reactions I deserve.

Why did it have to be him?

Because, the devil on my shoulder says, *there was no one else it could've been.*

The angel doesn't even show up to give her opposing opinion. Apparently she's done with me. I have finally fallen from her grace and there is no amount of penance that can cleanse my soul.

I shoulda moved to fucking Monaco.

There's a car idling in the alley. A Mercedes parked just outside the back door. Its headlights illuminate me in all my wasted glory. I lift my hand and squint to shield my eyes from the glare. Which doesn't help, but I do it anyway.

Then the rear driver's side door opens and a leg extends itself. A man gets out, leaving the door open. "Madison," he says in his somewhat thick Spanish accent.

"Carlos," I say back, not even scared. Just… no longer able to be shocked by the seemingly endless parade of ridiculous shit that's happening tonight, and ready to get this over with. Just take me to the desert and kill me. My situation would improve dramatically if this whole stupid nightmare called life was over.

"Would you come with me, please?" he asks.

"Dunno. Pretty busy just now," I say.

Then the driver's window lowers and there's Logan. Holding a gun. Pointed at me.

"Hey, you got a new gun. Good for you," I say to him. He doesn't seem amused.

Logan says, "Shut up and get in the fucking car."

I stare at him for a moment. Then I shrug and say, "Yeah, sure," and head over.

Just then, the back door to Pete's swings open and Raven appears, silhouetted by bright white light. Like she's pretending to be the angel who deserted me. I don't know how, or why, she decided to come out here at this exact moment, but there she is. Standing witness to my mistakes.

"Scarlett," she yells. "Come here." Her eyes dart to Carlos, then me, as she extends her arm and holds out her hand, beckoning me to her with flicking fingers.

"Madison," Carlos says. "Please." He again gestures for me to come to him.

Like the devil on my shoulder, he makes a lot more sense than Raven. Because if I go to her, they'll shoot me, or run me over, or hell, maybe just come back another day to finish me off.

If I go to her, there's a chance that this… all this that's happening tonight… will never end. And I just want it to be over. I don't want to climb this fucking mountain anymore. I'm so tired of pulling myself back up. I just want to fall now. I'm done.

I look to Raven, smile a sad but grateful smile—who would've thought she'd turn out to be on my side?—and then turn back to Carlos. I walk over, stand next to him, look him right in the eye, and say, "Happy Halloween."

And then I slide into the backseat and glance out the window to the dark corner where not so very long ago, a stranger that I once knew showed up and made feel happy and safe and warm.

Carlos gets in and slams the door shut.

And as we pull out of the alley and off into the desert night, I close my eyes, lean my head back onto the headrest, and whisper to myself, "Stop climbing now, Maddie."

CHAPTER TWENTY

TYLER

Drywall is easier to punch through than most people might realize.

I am making a series of companion holes to accompany the one I think I made before. At least this time I know it's me doing it. This is the only time I've ever wished I owned more shit. Because then I would have more shit to break.

I tear into the kitchen, pulling drawers out of cabinets, throwing silverware on the ground, ripping appliances from the wall. I grab up the toaster—the toaster with the charred bread inside—and I remember the thought I had that if I was burning alive in this apartment, that that's how I would look to the people on the street below. And I also remember that at the time it gave me great comfort, even if I didn't know why.

Now I do.

I throw the toaster down, race into the bedroom, rip the mattress off the frame, drag it into the main room, and toss it into the middle of the space. I topple the dresser and rip out all the clothes, gathering them into a pile on top of the mattress. I drag the dresser itself into the other room too and throw it on top of the pile.

Kindling.

Then I head to the kitchen, open the liquor cabinet, grab the bottle of Johnny Walker Blue, and pour it over the whole thing.

Accelerant.

Then… I go looking for a lighter.

Where the fuck is a lighter? Why do I not have a lighter? Jesus! I should never have quit smoking! Fuck!

Matches? Do I have matches? I tear through the kitchen cabinets now looking for matches. No matches. Son of a bitch!

And then I catch a glimpse of myself in the reflection in the windows. Naked, scarred, scared, frantic, insane. I have crossed over. I have crossed over to full-blown insanity. I am no longer in clear control of my actions.

If I ever was.

And then I think about MY DREAM.

Of course it was Maddie all along. Who else?

I'm so sad that I couldn't see it clearly before so that I could make it right, right from the start. But that's why THE DREAM keeps coming back to me. That's why it's recurring. That's why every time I dream it, it's just another opportunity to crack the code, solve the puzzle, repair the problem, make it right. It's fucking *Groundhog Day*.

All I have to do is find the way to fix it. To keep the world from ending. If I can solve the mystery of what I need to do and how I need to do it, then I can put everything straight. And then Maddie and I can try to start fresh. With each other. AS each other. Not as fucking Ford and Scarlett. As Tyler. And Maddie.

I can fix this, I know I can.

I believe it now. I think I didn't believe it before because none of it seemed real. But this is real. Maddie is real. Maddie is Maddie. Holy shit. I have fallen in love with Maddie. Little Maddie Clayton. I wonder what Scotty would think. He'd probably hate it. He'd probably be, "Dude, that's my sister!" But that's only because he wouldn't know that I've changed. Am changing. Have tried to change. If I could show Scotty how I have changed and what a good guy I am, I know instead he'd be like, "Dude! That's my sister! Yay!" I know he would. I don't even have to convince myself.

But I do have to make this right. I have to. I have to. I have to.

I have to do it for Scotty. I have to do it for Nadir. I have to do it for my mom. Fuck, I have to do it for Maddie. I WILL do it for Maddie. I WILL fix this. I CAN fix this. I am going to fix this. And then we WILL live happily the fuck ever after. I can feel it. I know it.

Fuck. I'm calming down. Everything's going to be OK. It will. God or whoever will forgive me and I am going to be able to make everything turn out OK.

I know it.

And in this moment of knowing—this calm, almost Buddhist state of knowing—I find peace.

And I breathe.

And I believe.

She has made me into peace.

And I know it.

Which is why I'm just as surprised as anyone when the fire alarm in the apartment goes off, terrifyingly loud.

And I look over to see that the burners on my fancy gas stove are all lit.

And then I look down at my hand.

And I see that I'm holding a menu from a Chinese restaurant.

And it's on fire.

And I have touched it to the bonfire I erected.

And as I stand here, naked, holding this makeshift torch, watching an escalating wall of flame burning out of control in front of me…

I am… confused.

But I'm not scared.

And I'm not sad.

If anything, I'm… hopeful.

Huh.

Look at that.

I'm hopeful.

Why did it have to be you? Her words ring in my ears along with the screeching of the alarm.

And I say aloud, as if she can hear me… because somehow, I know she can…

"Because. There's no one else it could have been."

And as the flames begin spreading and fanning out across the great, empty apartment, replacing my magnificent view of the skyline with a blistering mountain of violent orange and red…

I think of her.

And I smile.

END OF BOOK SHIT

Well, fuck, you guys. And so ... here we are.

One only gets to do their first EOBS as JA Huss's new writing partner once, and I'm not even sure where to start. So, I'll just start at the beginning:

What follows is an excised bit of an email I received from Julie's audiobook publisher, dated 6 September 2016.

"I've...got 2 different J.A. Huss titles that I thought of you for. Mr. Romantic is one book in a series by Huss, where each book follows a different couple, so we'll be casting a different pair on each.

Wasted Lust is the other...I've attached both scripts here.

Now, these titles do venture a bit into the erotic side of romance...Both also have male leads that are a bit on the bad boy side of things (yes, even Mr. Romantic - Huss tends to write complex, layered characters).

Take a look, and let me know what you think."

If you've not seen the videos Julie and I did, that's how it all began. And everything that was pitched to me was true.

After recording *Wasted Lust*, I discovered that Julie was following me on Twitter and I followed her back so that I could message her privately. (Up until very recently, I’ve been extremely social media averse. I only had a Twitter account because my manager suggested I get one in 2016 because of a job I was doing. It was literally the third time I had set up a Twitter account, after bailing two previous times over the years. Julie was one of the first people to follow me this time.)

This is what I sent to her via Twitter, dated 10 January 2017:

“Hi there! Since you managed to track me down on the webnet, you clearly know that I narrated two of your recent audio releases. So A) thanks for taking the time to find me! That is both gracious and thoughtful. And B) I want you to know that in narrating the last chapter of "Wasted Lust," I choked up. Seriously. Which is, to state it modestly, rare. The adult fiction genre has no dearth of writers, as you know. But the nuance, detail, and - dare I say - sophistication with which you write is, well, a fucking delight to interpret. Thanks for having let me be a part of your storytelling. Best of luck in all things. –J”

This is part of what she wrote back, two hours later:

“Dude. I <3 you so much...You rocked Wasted Lust...it's my favorite book, of all the books I've written, and I so wanted you for that project. I loved, loved, loved it. I've listened to it twice (but I skip the sex scenes!) lol. I just can't deal with those. And you did such a great job with Mr. Romantic. Nolan Delaney is the most f-up character ever and you did it perfect. :) Sorry for going all fan girl. You're probably like - OK, that's enough of her. But really, thank you...”

I have to say, as I sit here and I type this, that’s all less than a year ago and I can’t believe it’s been that brief a time since Julie and I first made person to person contact. I couldn't have imagined that from that tiny bit of mutual admiration, she and I would have wound up here.

Jumping ahead to speak about this book, *Sin With Me*, specifically ... Well, here's how it came to be:

After Julie and I finished working on the pilot script for THE COMPANY (in Hollywood, people reference TV shows in all caps – dunno why), and it went as well as it did, collaboratively, she made the now famous phone call when she asked me if I would be interested in writing novels together. It took about two seconds for me to say "yes," and we were left with trying to decide what we should write.

And then a curious thing happened: We wound up with like 10 ideas, all spilling out over the top of each other. Julie started talking about stories she'd had percolating for a while but never had the time to take on. I did the same. And then, I mentioned a TV show pilot concept that I had come up with probably nine years ago, that I loved, but that I never found the time to develop into a proper pitch. She said, "Well, pitch me on it now." So I did.

The working title of that show was "Blast Radius," and it was to center around a guy who was a bomb specialist/fire inspector who was *himself* a live bomb. A guy whose life was out of control and he just kind of set fire to everything he touched. (In my mind, he was always sort of Hugh Laurie from HOUSE, but a bomb guy.)

And that was it.

Julie loved the rough idea, and said, "Let's do this one first." Once we had this as our jumping off point, we spent some time on the phone developing the major players and the world and where the twists and turns would be, and it became quickly apparent that this was too big an idea for one book. Now, most of Julie's worlds are too big for one book, but we realized that not just this *world*, but this individual *story* was too big. There were so many tendrils, and they just kept sprawling, so we came to the conclusion that to tell this tale properly, we would need multiple books.

But. We also decided that we didn't want to wait and take months and months to release everything all spread out, so we concluded that we would do something INSANE and write them all, back to back to back to back, releasing them with just enough time in between for readers to get through one and be ready for the next.

This excited me because I LOVE a good cliffhanger. But I also HATE waiting for the cliffhanger to resolve. So, this seemed like the best way to address both of those concerns.

And then we decided ... let's set it in Vegas!

At first this was because we had the concept of *Sin With Me* as the title and Vegas *is* Sin City, and also because in my research, the Vegas bomb squad division of Fire and Rescue kept coming up as impressive and top tier. Also, both Julie and I know Vegas pretty well and seemed like we could do an authentic job of setting the story there.

And then 1 October 2017 happened and 58 people were murdered and 546 injured in Las Vegas in the worst mass shooting in US history.

And Julie and I discussed what would be appropriate. And what we decided is that it would be disingenuous and wrong not to tell the story we set out to tell. (You may notice that there is a tiny reference to the shooting in chapter 1 of this book, and then we just went back into telling the story we had conceived of.) Because ultimately the story we're striving to tell is one of redemption and love, and that feels like a way to pay homage as well.

(**Side note:** I was in NYC on 9/11. I lived there. I was actually *about* to go to the airport to catch a flight to LA that morning. I never made it to the airport, of course. Experiencing that event so close and firsthand was a defining moment in my life. I'm the kind of person who, when something like that happens, tends to run toward it as opposed to away from it. Not because I'm brave or noble. Not at all. But because I feel a sense of defiance and probably obligation. I used to say, in the weeks after 9/11, "Shit, if they'd let me go to fucking Ground Zero and set up a tent, I'd live there." I felt like I ... I dunno ... *owed it* to NYC to show it that it was still loved. And in some way, I think that's how I felt about this story and Las Vegas. And, as is evident in this book, I love firefighters. I admire and lionize them. They are, to my mind and as a cadre of society, some of the best of who we are.)

And then we dug into the details of this specific tale.

Now ... we have other books planned for the future that will explore all kinds of shit worth exploring. The darker sides of sexuality, or the funnier sides of sexuality, or the surreality of sexuality but for this, our first offering, we wanted to tell simply a tale of alchemy. The story of two people who crash into each other's lives and must to figure out HOW they work together, WHY they work together, and WHO they are to each other, while simultaneously battling personal demons both internal and external.

Not at all unlike the way a new writing partnership works. ☺

And although we created both of the central characters together, I'll talk about Tyler because my job was really to work with him in this book. (As we move forward in other books, we're talking about experimenting with all kinds of things – like I may write the woman's voice and Julie the man's, we may alternate, we may do a couple of other things with "voice" that change it up completely.)

I wrote in a blog post for Julie that everything I write is, like, 1/3 my imagination, 1/3 things I've seen/learned, and 1/3 my experiences/me. That is 100% true here. There's a lot about Tyler's sarcasm and sense of humor that is me. And there's a lot about him that's based on mates I've had and people I've known.

Right as we began discussing this book I got cast on the CBS show SEAL TEAM and I met the chief technical consultant, a former Navy SEAL and Delta Force operator called Tyler. I was incredibly impressed by the guy. Young. Forty years old and served his country with honor. (BTW, I feel about the military the way I feel about firefighters.)

Also, Tyler couldn't have been sweeter and more unassuming and just generally awesome. I didn't wind up getting to do as many episodes of the show as I would've liked, and so didn't get to spend as much time with Tyler as I would've liked, but I respect and admire our servicemen and women with an abiding devotion, so Tyler is named after this one great guy I knew for a minute.

Originally Tyler's last name in this series was "Bell." No particular reason, Julie and I just thought it sounded right and fit. And then, shortly after we sent out the media kits to promote this book, someone mentioned to Julie that "Tyler Bell" was already the name of a central character in another romance novel that came out not too terribly long ago. This was tough, because we had come to understand our guy as "Tyler Bell," but we also wanted to avoid the appearance of anything unsavory, so we thought for a couple of days, cycling through other surnames that we thought might fit and *feel* right. (Sometimes it's just a feeling.) We hit on "Tyler Morgan" and that *felt* right to us. And thus, Tyler Morgan is the man you are reading about. And also, we learn his middle name in book 2, and it all seems like it fell into place.

(I'm sharing this info largely because you may see some blurbs out in the world with his old name, since those media kits came out before we were aware of all this, and if so, that's why. Oh. There are also apparently a couple of other books titled *Sin With Me*. But we didn't know that beforehand and it just IS the name of this book, so that's how that goes. Like how Ne-Yo and Game both have albums called *R.E.D.*, or Jay-Z and The Beatles and Metallica all have *The Black Album*, or Sean Puff-Daddy/P-Diddy/Diddy Combs and The Wu-Tang Clan both have joints called *Forever.* I'm saying – Julie and I are like the Ne-Yo/Game/Jay-Z/Beatles/Metallica/Sean Combs/Wu-Tang Clan of Contemporary Romance. But y'all knew that shit.)

As far as the actual writing goes ... Julie likes to write in the early morning and I like to stay up writing all night. (Laura, my wife, gets up crazy early too. I'm pretty sure she and Julie text each other while I'm still asleep and make fun of me.) The nice thing about our schedules is that I get what Julie's written in the afternoon and then spend the evening crafting, pass it off and it's waiting for her to read and work on first thing in the AM. It's how we're able to keep ping-ponging back and forth and not lose our flow.

We stumbled on the device of writing the sexy scenes back-and-forth the way we are kind of as an experiment, and then we realized it was both fun to write that way and made the sex ... well ... sexier. So that may wind up being our trademark thing.

It leads to some very interesting phone conversations. Ones that, I have joked, would go over badly in most other work environments on the planet. One call that springs to mind involved me telling Julie about my having gotten down on the floor in my house at 1:00 in the morning and contorted my body in various ways to make sure that some of the things I was describing were physically possible. (They were. Thankfully, I work out with a trainer who keeps me nimble.) Fortunately, neither one of us are particularly shy or easily embarrassed. And also, we don't have an HR department to report to. Thank God.

Ok, lovelies...!

I think that's it for now. There's surely a lot more to say, but there'll be a lot more of these EOBSs to say it all in. Tyler and Maddie's journey is just starting. I'm beyond excited to share with you all where this odyssey leads. It takes twists and turns you can't expect, and just like the big revelation in chapter 18 of this book, there will be scenes that will BREAK MY HEART when I read them back. Because I'm an enormous fucking softy. I hope that they will work their way into your hearts as well. I love both of these characters very much.

Oh. And just because this is the kind of thing I think people can be curious about...

I listen to music when I'm writing. I'm always on the hunt for new beats, so as you read these things going forward, there may be seemingly no rhyme nor reason to what I'm hearing, but whatever I'm vibing on at a given moment is what propels my creative process. For some reason, I've been digging into a lot of Stoner Rock lately. Maybe because it's Autumn and The Harvest Moon makes me feel extra groovy. I dunno. But...

The artists and albums I listened to most while writing *Sin With Me*:

Heavy Eyes, Maera, and *He Dreams of Lions* by The Heavy Eyes (from Memphis)

Heavy Lips by Gorilla Pulp (from Italy)

Rituals and *Lost Ghosts* by Red Scalp (from Poland, but they say they love "space and Indians," meaning Native Americans. They then say, "We are space Indians!" Which is just adorable.)

And various stuff by *Asking Alexandria.* Because singers screaming at me always gets me AMPED!

The one song I listened to on repeat for like an hour while writing this EOBS:

You're Nobody 'Til Somebody Loves You by James Arthur off his eponymous 2014 debut album. (That there is some British, blue-eyed soul that is funky as fuck.)

All my love and gratitude always...

-JM
10 December 2017

TURN THE PAGE FOR JULIE'S EOBS

JULIE

You've probably heard the story of how Johnathan and I met on Twitter the day the audiobook released for Mr. Romantic. He's the voice of Nolan in that book (though the credit goes to his pseudonym, Tad Branson)

I was gonna tag him (Johnathan him) and say thank you, but then remembered he was Tad, so I just settled for following him. Later that evening he sent me a direct message saying hi, and he noticed I followed him, and some stuff about Wasted Lust (which he also narrated) and hey, how about that Mr. Romantic, huh?

If you've read Mr. Romantic, you know that's a joke. He was the filthy fantasy-rape guy. And he did some really fucked up shit. And when I asked my audiobook publisher to ask Johnathan McClain to narrate for me, I asked for him to be Mr. Mysterious because he was a funny kinda fucked up, not a holy-fucking-shit-this-guy-is-fucked-up kinda fucked up. But scheduling was a bitch for five narrators, and Johnathan/Tad was asked to do Mr. Romantic instead. And isn't that always how it goes? lol The guy I love the most gets the most fucked-up character I've ever written and I'm thinking, Johnathan McClain probably thinks I'm like… pretty fucked up in real life because I wrote this character and he had to SAY all that fucked up shit out loud! And I was… MORTIFIED!

Anyway, that night I flipped out and told my entire

fan group that I was fangirling over my favorite narrator because he messaged me on Twitter.

And that was about it for a little while. Until he got the narration gig for my book, Taking Turns (He's Quin in that series) and he sent me another message saying he liked a line I wrote and could we maybe chat in email.

I played it cool, you guys. I was like, "Sure. Here's me." And he's all, "Here's me." But privately I was all freaked out in the best way possible. And then after that we started emailing every now and then. Just little notes about whatever. The audiobooks, mostly. Until one day he got the job narrating James Fenici in my Company books. And then he wrote me this long email (God, I read that thing like 600 times before I wrote back) pitching an idea that we maybe turn The Company into a TV pilot or a movie or something, because he thought it was great.

And I wrote him back with my JA Motherfucking Huss Manifesto just to feel him out and see what he'd say because I'm a control freak with very strong opinions and he should know that, and he wrote back with his Johnathan Motherfucking McClain Manifesto probably for the same reason, and we realized – holy shit, this might actually work out because even though we are very different in so many ways, in all the ways that count we are exactly the same.

Eventually this turned into a phone friendship, and we wrote that script, and I was amazed every time he turned in words because of his talent. And we finished it after a few months and then one day we were writing more than a TV pilot. We were writing books.

Before we started writing I sorta had this moment where I was a little bit afraid. Not of bombing or his writing talent, for fuck's sake. He's so very talented with the words. But about writing the sex scenes together.

I just… didn't know what that was gonna be like, ya know? I'd never written with anyone and to be honest, I think writing sex scenes with a woman would be weird too, but he's not a woman, he's a man, and… yeah.

So we were talking on the phone and I'm having like a needy melt-down moment that I was not proud of, and he's telling me it's gonna be fine, and I'm nodding my head, but still pretty nervous about it, and he insisting that it's all very clinical and he's done plays on stage totally naked before and…

I decided to just go with it. He says it's gonna be fine, I'm gonna believe him.

He's very easy to believe, BTW. Like, Johnathan says something to me and I'm like OK. Because he's done things. And seen shit. And he knows EVERYONE and he's been places, and even though I'm kinda reclusive these days, I've done things, and I know people, and I've been places, and seen shit too. And I could tell that this was not bullshit.

So I believed him about the sex scenes.

And he was mostly right. lol There were a few times when I thought too hard about it and I was like…WTF am I doing? But he didn't pull any punches and I'd read his scenes and be like HOLY FUCK! And so I'd have to up my game a little to try and make him say, HOLY FUCK! And I don't know if he actually ever said that about any of my scenes, but…

Sex scenes stopped being something I hated and turned into something I almost looked forward to. You see, romance authors like me write so many sex scenes, it's hard to be original and even though the readers see the final product and it's all hot and sexy, writing them isn't very hot and sexy. It's agonizing. I mean, yeah, anyone can write a sex scene but very few can write a great sex scene and I don't like to write boring sex, so it's hard.

But then Johnathan comes along and he's got ideas I've never thought of before and I'm like FUCK YEAH! This scene is great. (Maybe I could get him to write all the sex scenes from now on? He said no to that, BTW) lol

And everything about writing was new again.

I'd missed that. I've written a lot of books over the past five years and when I'd get into a little slump I'd often think back to when I was writing my first science fiction series, (I Am Just Junco) and remember how exciting it was, and how much I loved the story and the world, and I'd feel nostalgic about it. I used to get completely LOST in that world. Just so wrapped up in those scenes, and those characters, and their sadness, and their fight. I used to write so fast just to get the story down so I could READ IT before I went to bed. I wrote that series for me and only me and I LOVED IT. Still do. Junco, man. She's amazing. I'd sometimes wish I could just write Junco all over again like it was the first time. Because I was IN LOVE WITH THAT STORY so much and it showed on the page, and some parts of me had gotten a little complacent over the years and maybe I wasn't challenging myself anymore.

Like maybe I'd never love another story the way I loved Junco. Maybe I'd never feel that way again.

And that was a sad, sobering thought every time I had it.

It's not true. I love Rook & Ronin series so much. Everything about it was just as real to me as Junco was. But they came second. You only get one first, ya know? You only get to experience the joy of putting your very first story down on paper one time.

Johnathan McClain changed all that. He turned my life upside down for the better in every way imaginable. And it's not the TV pilot, we haven't even sold it yet. And it's not the idea of knowing him, or that he's an actor, or how he can turn walking into a men's shoe store into a "thing" that ends with us drinking champagne with the salesmen, or that he's on my fucking TV, or anything like that.

I'm not impressed by things. Or presents. Or trips, or money, or events.

I'm impressed by PEOPLE.

Not what they look like, or what they do for a living, or what their net worth is. I'm impressed by what's inside them. Their thoughts, their art, their dreams, their fears.

So it's just... HIM that impresses me.

He feels like my friend from seven lifetimes ago and we almost got through this incarnation never bumping into each other and this whole thing is just… fate. Or something. Because it makes no sense at all and all the sense in the world at the same time.

But more importantly, writing this first book with Johnathan was like writing Junco again. Only different. It's not the same, but it is. It's our first book together and even though we wrote the script first, writing a script isn't at all like writing a book. So many things to discuss – like what will our cover look like? And what happens next? The script was basically just a reworking of a book I'd already written. Sin With Me was 100% new and every part of it was discussed and decided on together. So when we had our cover reveal and I saw that our book was live on Amazon, I was so excited!

When was the last time I got excited about a book

going live on Amazon? Like that butterflies-in-the-stomach kinda excitement that lets you know you're about to do something NEW.

I really don't know. Maybe it was… Ford's book. That was a long fucking time ago. I mean, it was only three years ago, but it was a LOT of books ago. Like 30 books ago.

And I have said publicly lots of times that I never set out to be a writer and if that astronaut job comes along I'm gonna take it and go to Mars and never come back and not feel sorry about any of it. I'm just outta here, right? Because that's who I am. I am a risk taker and I'm not afraid to go die out in the dark nothingness alone.

But… even that has changed. I think I'd ask Johnathan's opinion before taking the gig on Mars. And if he said, "Nah, you should stay here and write books and scripts with me forever," I'd have to tell NASA, "Sorry man. He just can't live without me."

But it would be a lie. Because I just can't imagine a life without him anymore. And this is our first book and we're gonna write a shitload more, and it's only gonna get better from here and it's all because of that one message he sent me on Twitter.

And I'm pretty fucking happy about that.

So…

Thank you, Johnathan.

You rocked my 2017 pretty fucking hard.

JA Huss
December 10, 2017

Turn the page for more…

Original Sin is a four-book series that releases three weeks apart starting March 6, 2018. So chances are good that next book is already on sale. Maddie and Tyler have a lot of shit to get over, but isn't that the fun part of finding someone old is new again? You knew each other once, and now you don't, but you still kinda do. And you can imagine them then, and see them now, and put all the pieces together in a way that fits.

That's Maddie and Tyler's story.
Get ready.
It's gonna get hot.

Johnathan and I would like to thank all of you for reading our first book together. We hope you enjoy it just as much as all the books I wrote alone. Actually, we hope you like this better. :)

And if you've got a minute, and you liked the world we created, and the story we told, and the characters we gave life to… then please consider leaving us a review online where you purchased the book.

We are not traditionally published – WE ARE INDIE.

And we rely on reviews and word-of-mouth buzz to get our books out there. So tell a friend about it if you have a chance. We'd really appreciate that.

Much love,

Julie & Johnathan
www.HussMcClain.com

About the *Authors*

Johnathan McClain's career as a writer and actor spans 25 years and covers the worlds of theatre, film, and television. At the age of 21, Johnathan moved to Chicago where he wrote and began performing his critically acclaimed one-man show, Like It Is. The Chicago Reader proclaimed, "If we're ever to return to a day when theatre matters, we'll need a few hundred more artists with McClain's vision and courage." On the heels of its critical and commercial success, the show subsequently moved to New York where Johnathan was compared favorably to solo performance visionaries such as Eric Bogosian, John Leguizamo, and Anna Deavere Smith.

Johnathan lived for many years in New York, and his work there includes appearing Off-Broadway in the original cast of Jonathan Tolins' The Last Sunday In June at The Century Center, as well as at Lincoln Center

Theatre and with the Lincoln Center Director's Lab. Around the country, he has been seen on stage at South Coast Repertory, The American Conservatory Theatre, Florida Stage, Paper Mill Playhouse, and the National Jewish Theatre. Los Angeles stage credits are numerous and include the LA Weekly Award nominated world premiere of Cold/Tender at The Theatre @ Boston Court and the LA Times' Critic's Choice production of The Glass Menagerie at The Colony Theatre for which Johnathan received a Garland Award for his portrayal of Jim O'Connor.

On television, he appeared in a notable turn as Megan Draper's LA agent, Alan Silver, on the final season of AMC's critically acclaimed drama Mad Men, and as the lead of the TV Land comedy series, Retired at 35, starring alongside Hollywood icons George Segal and Jessica Walter. He has also had Series Regular roles on The Bad Girl's Guide starring Jenny McCarthy and Jessica Simpson's sitcom pilot for ABC. His additional television work includes recurring roles on the CBS drama SEAL TEAM and Fox's long-running 24, as well as appearances on Grey's Anatomy, NCIS: Los Angeles, Trial and Error, The Exorcist, Major Crimes, The Glades, Scoundrels, Medium, CSI, Law & Order: SVU, Without a Trace, CSI: Miami, and Happy Family with John Larroquette and Christine Baranski, amongst others. On film, he appeared in the Academy Award nominated Far from Heaven and several independent features.

As an audiobook narrator, he has recorded almost 100 titles. Favorites include the Audie Award winning Illuminae by Amie Kaufman and Jay Kristoff and The Last Days of Night, by Academy Winning Screenwriter Graham Moore (who is also Johnathan's close friend and occasional collaborator). As well as multiple titles by his dear friend and writing partner, JA Huss, with whom he is hard at work making the world a little more romantic.

He lives in Los Angeles with his wife Laura.

JA Huss never wanted to be a writer and she still dreams of that elusive career as an astronaut. She originally went to school to become an equine veterinarian but soon figured out they keep horrible hours and decided to go to grad school instead. That Ph.D wasn't all it was cracked up to be (and she really sucked at the whole scientist thing), so she dropped out and got a M.S. in forensic toxicology just to get the whole thing over with as soon as possible.

After graduation she got a job with the state of Colorado as their one and only hog farm inspector and spent her days wandering the Eastern Plains shooting the shit with farmers.

After a few years of that, she got bored. And since she was a homeschool mom and actually does love science, she decided to write science textbooks and make online classes for other homeschool moms.

She wrote more than two hundred of those workbooks and was the number one publisher at the online homeschool store many times, but eventually she covered every science topic she could think of and ran out of shit to say.

So in 2012 she decided to write fiction instead. That year she released her first three books and started a career that would make her a New York Times bestseller and land her on the USA Today Bestseller's List eighteen times in the next three years.

Her books have sold millions of copies all over the world, the audio version of her semi-autobiographical book, Eighteen, was nominated for a Voice Arts Award and an Audie Award in 2016 and 2017 respectively, her audiobook, Mr. Perfect, was nominated for a Voice Arts Award in 2017, and her audiobook, Taking Turns, was nominated for an Audie Award in 2018.

Johnathan McClain is her first (and only) writing partner and even though they are worlds apart in just about every way imaginable, it works.

She lives on a ranch in Central Colorado with her family.

Made in the USA
San Bernardino, CA
21 June 2018